PRAISE FOR THE

Here are some of the over 100,000 five star reviews left for the Dead Cold Mystery series.

"Rex Stout and Michael Connelly have spawned a protege."

AMAZON REVIEW

"So begins one damned fine read."

AMAZON REVIEW

"Mystery that's more brain than brawn."

AMAZON REVIEW

"I read so many of this genre...and ever so often I strike gold!"

AMAZON REVIEW

"This book is filled with action, intrigue, espionage, and everything else lovers of a good thriller want."

AMAZON REVIEW

BLOOD IN BABYLON
A DEAD COLD MYSTERY

BLAKE BANNER

RIGHTHOUSE

Copyright © 2024 by Right House

All rights reserved.

The characters and events portrayed in this ebook are fictitious. Any similarity to real persons, living or dead, is coincidental and not intended by the author.

No part of this book may be reproduced in any form or by any electronic or mechanical means, including information storage and retrieval systems, without written permission from the author, except for the use of brief quotations in a book review.

ISBN-13: 978-1-63696-018-0

ISBN-10: 1-63696-018-9

Cover design by: Damonza

Printed in the United States of America

www.righthouse.com

www.instagram.com/righthousebooks

www.facebook.com/righthousebooks

twitter.com/righthousebooks

DEAD COLD MYSTERY SERIES
An Ace and a Pair (Book 1)
Two Bare Arms (Book 2)
Garden of the Damned (Book 3)
Let Us Prey (Book 4)
The Sins of the Father (Book 5)
Strange and Sinister Path (Book 6)
The Heart to Kill (Book 7)
Unnatural Murder (Book 8)
Fire from Heaven (Book 9)
To Kill Upon A Kiss (Book 10)
Murder Most Scottish (Book 11)
The Butcher of Whitechapel (Book 12)
Little Dead Riding Hood (Book 13)
Trick or Treat (Book 14)
Blood Into Wine (Book 15)
Jack In The Box (Book 16)
The Fall Moon (Book 17)
Blood In Babylon (Book 18)
Death In Dexter (Book 19)
Mustang Sally (Book 20)
A Christmas Killing (Book 21)
Mommy's Little Killer (Book 22)
Bleed Out (Book 23)

Dead and Buried (Book 24)
In Hot Blood (Book 25)
Fallen Angels (Book 26)
Knife Edge (Book 27)
Along Came A Spider (Book 28)
Cold Blood (Book 29)
Curtain Call (Book 30)

ONE

IT WAS AL'S BIRTHDAY. THAT GAVE HIM AN AIR OF importance as he made his way south down Virginia Avenue from the Hugh J. Grant Circle. It wasn't just any birthday either. Joy had told him that. He was sixty. Sixty was a big number. It was an important age. An age when a man should do important things. He'd been through several important ages: Harvard, Mexico, Brazil. Twenty had been real important, but he couldn't remember much about twenty. That was like another life. Forty had been important too. That was when he'd started to go wrong.

The sun slipped behind the trees and the rooftops, casting long winter shadows across the road. The temperature dropped and Al shuddered. It was getting dark, and he wanted to be home. He wanted to be safe.

Dr. Epstein and Joy had been nice to him. They were always nice to him. They'd made him feel special. They'd given him a cake and laughed with him. That had made him shy, but it had also made him stay too late, because he didn't want to leave. Now the darkness was closing in, and he did not like to be out in the street when the darkness closed in.

He hurried with big, jerky strides, holding his birthday card with his hand in his pocket, gulping breath through his mouth, because when he hurried, he couldn't breathe through his nose. He hurried past Newbold Avenue and tried not to look up at the towering apartment blocks on his left. They always made him feel like they were looming over him, like angry judges watching him. Joy and Dr. Epstein had told him it wasn't true, that apartment blocks could not watch you or judge you, but he knew, inside, that they could. So he kept going, with heavy, hurrying steps, gulping air through his mouth, even when he heard the shout. When he heard the shout, he ignored it and just kept on going.

"Hey! Freak! Weird ass! I'm talkin' to you!"

Al didn't look. He didn't need to look. He knew who it was. He quickened his lumbering pace. He felt a strong hand grip his heart, making it harder to breathe. He became conscious of the wheezing and gasping in his throat. He also became conscious of the running feet behind him: not sprinting, not a charge, just running to catch up. Instinct made him hunch his shoulders. He could see the green shop front of the upholstery store on the corner with Ellis Avenue. He was almost home.

"Hey! Freak! I'm talkin' to you, bro!"

The voice was much closer now, right behind him, and he could hear laughter across the road, high-pitched, screeching laughter, as though they were all being strangled by invisible wires. It was what they deserved. The thought brought on a sudden rush of fury, but he knew better than to confront them. He kept lumbering forward, tried to control the croaking in his throat, kept his eyes on the darkening blacktop in front of him.

A voice, at his elbow now. "Hey, man, why you make that noise when you walk?" More laughter from across the road. Now the speaker was smiling too. "What is that? You sick or something? Or you just singing yo'self a song while you walkin' along?"

The laughter was now like shrieks. Al prayed silently that they should become real shrieks of pain. He had reached the upholstery store and started across the road toward it. A hand plucked at his shoulder. "Hey! I'm talkin' to you! You don't disrespect me, you motherfockin' piece a' shit!"

Al broke into a stumbling run, grunting as he went. He heard his own voice saying, "No! No . . ."

The door of the upholstery shop opened. A small group of men and women emerged, talking. Two men and a woman stood at the door of the deli next door, going in. He almost collided with them. One of them half shouted, "Whoa! Look where you're going, pal!"

He ignored them, hurrying on, listening. The voice came again, more distant now. "Wait up, freak! I wanna talk to you!"

He kept going. His heart was pounding in his chest. His breathing was loud, like the roar of giant waves. He passed the apartment block, the gated alley behind it. He lumbered on, passed 1929, passed the house next door with its pretty wrought iron porch, and then he was at the gate of his own house.

Now he could hear feet, lots of them, running in earnest. His hands were shaking badly and he fumbled with the latch of the gate. His gasping breath turned to a whimper. He pushed through the gate and stumped up the four steps to his door. His whimpering turned to sobbing as his fingers, large and clumsy like sausages, struggled with his keys. Behind him, feet skidded to a halt: four, five, six pairs. He dared not look.

"Hey! Freak! I'm fuckin' talkin' to you! We got questions for you!"

The key slipped in. Behind him, the gate clanked open. He pushed in, wrenched the key from the lock, and slammed the door. But it did not close. Instead, there was a terrible scream of pain. He wrenched the door open and slammed it again, putting his full three hundred and ninety pounds behind it. Another scream, and again he pulled it open and slammed it. This time, it closed and locked.

He backed away, sobbing violently. Outside, he could hear screeching, shouts, furious voices, judgment, hatred: a great tidal wave of hatred washing over his house, and him. He turned and stumbled into his small kitchen area. There he grabbed for the phone and called Dr. Epstein. Joy answered and he cried out, an inarticulate noise of relief and love, and grief and fear.

"Al? Is that you, baby?"

He tried to say it was, but a primal grief deep in his gut would not let him shape the words out of the awful noises in his mouth.

"What in the *world* is wrong with you? Now you take a moment and breathe . . . that's right, you just take one good, big old breath and relax. Good, and another . . . Now first off, you tell me right now if you are okay."

His breath shook, but the tightness in his chest eased. "Yes . . ."

"So what has you so upset?"

"They were waiting for me."

"Who were, honey? You sure it wasn't somebody you imagined . . . ?"

"No." His voice was clear, educated, articulate, strangely at odds with his huge, graceless body. "No, it was that boy, and his gang. They wait for me. They call me a freak. He says he is going to cut me. And they make dark waves that come at me from the street."

"Now, honey . . ."

"I am *not* hallucinating. You can't see it. But it comes when they close in on me. It overwhelms the house. I don't know *how* they do it, but they do."

"Are they still there?"

"No, they've gone. But they might come back. They always come back. Joy, I think they followed me from Mexico. I saw them in Mexico, but they were farther away. But if they have found a way into my dreams, if they can get in during the night . . ."

"Okay, baby, now here is what I am going to do. I'm going to call the police and I'm going to have them swing by and make sure you're okay. Can you tell them what these boys look like?"

"I never look at them. You mustn't look at them. That's how

they followed me. But I know his name. I hear them call him Ned."

"Ned? You sure about that?"

"Yes, I'm sure about that."

"Okay, good. So you be sure to tell that to the officers when they come by. And Al? Remember, these are not evil forces, they are just stupid boys whose momma was too soft on them. If I take my belt to them, they gonna find out what good manners are *real* quick!"

That made him laugh, and she laughed too. They spoke a moment longer, till she was sure he was okay, and then they both hung up.

After that, he did the rounds of the house, keeping the lights off, peering through the darkened glass at the empty, lamplit streets outside. The windows had bars. He had insisted on that when Joy had got the house for him. Dr. Epstein had thought it was a good idea. He had said it was good to see him making important decisions like that.

The kitchen door out to the backyard was locked and had two heavy dead bolts. The windows here also had bars. He stood awhile, transfixed by the shadows cast across the floor by the lamps in the parking lot beyond his backyard. One of those lamps was behind a tree, and the shadows of the leaves tossed slightly in the pool of light on his floor.

He went to his living room and stood for a long while, staring out at the empty street. He still had his birthday card in his hand. When he was satisfied there was nobody there, he went and closed the drapes. Then, he lay on the sofa and covered himself with the blanket he always kept there and switched on the TV. He had it set up and ready. He was starting *Murder She Wrote* from episode one for the thirty-fourth time. As the music started to play, he hummed along, and as the dialogue started, he spoke it silently with the characters. His eyes closed, as though of their own volition, and he drifted into sleep.

Everything was safe. Jessica would take care of everything.

When the hammering on the door came, he didn't know how long he had been asleep. Episode two was almost finished. He walked stiffly into the hall and stood holding the living room doorjamb, staring at the door. It hammered again and his heart jumped and started pounding.

Then the voice. "It's me! Open up!"

He went to the door and unlocked it. He smiled. "Hi, I was watching TV... Come on in."

He led the way into the living room, pointed at the TV, and smiled. "I like Jessica. She makes everything okay." He turned to smile at his visitor but frowned instead at the large, silver blade of the kitchen knife. It entered swiftly and with precision, slipping between the fourth and fifth ribs on his left side, slicing through his lung and his heart in one smooth thrust.

His body briefly went into spasm. His consciousness endured for a few seconds, enough for him to be aware of the strangeness of the feeling, and to reach back for the sofa. But as the blood drained from his brain, darkness enfolded him and he crashed to the floor.

―――

I FOUND Dehan doing a dangerous mixture of yoga and tae kwon do in the backyard. She smiled at me, winked, and delivered a devastating side kick to an invisible foe who, judging by the height of the kick, must have been seven feet tall. I withdrew to the kitchen and made coffee.

She came in just after the coffee had started to gurgle and the rich, dark aroma had wafted out to the backyard and hooked her by the nose. She was panting, flushed, and perspiring slightly, dabbing her face with a towel. I sighed and wondered, not for the first or last time, what I had done in a previous life to earn such good kama.[1]

―――

1. *Kama* in the original Pali, *karma* in Sanskrit. Stone is of course aware of this.

She stopped dabbing her face and stared at me. "What?"

I shrugged with my eyebrows and shook my head.

She continued wiping. "I know, I look a wreck, but I want that third dan, and that's hard work."

"You want coffee?"

"Is the Pope a Catholic? What's wrong? You look troubled."

"I'm in a kitchen with a beautiful woman who is flushed and breathing heavily. Naturally, I look troubled."

She smiled and fluttered her eyelashes. "Okay, smart-ass, you got your brownie points. Now pour me some coffee and tell me what's really on your mind."

I poured. She sat at the kitchen table, and I rested my ass against the sink. I sipped and said, "Aloysius Chester, otherwise known as Al."

She nodded. "What about him?"

"I just wrote the prologue."

She grinned. "That's amazing. Can I read it?"

I shook my head. "Not yet. And I'm not sure I'm going to write it."

She frowned with her cup halfway to her lips and set it down again. "Why not? You said it was perfect."

"I thought it was."

"You stood right there and told me it was insoluble, so you could build a whole set of fictional circumstances around it. Perfect for your first attempt at writing . . ."

"I know. I know what I said, and that was what I thought."

"So . . . ?"

"I think it should be our next case."

"You just told me you know what you said. What you said was that it was insoluble. That means 'can't be solved.'"

I raised an eyebrow at her. "Stop being a smart-ass and listen to me. Just reading the case file, reading the reports, trying to imagine what it was like—for *him* . . ." I trailed off. "It's hard to explain, Dehan, but hell! Bottom line is, whether I write the book or reinvestigate the case, I'm going to be doing the same damned legwork! And I just feel this guy deserves justice. Let's look into it. What's the worst that can happen?"

She shrugged and made a face to go with it. "We get our first unsolved cold case."

I pulled out the chair and sat at the table, leaning forward on my elbows. "Who came to the door that night? Can you imagine how he felt? He must have been terrified. Why would he open the door? If it was the kids who'd been harassing him, he would not have opened the door."

"Are you sure he did? The forensics were inconclusive. Somebody might have picked the lock."

I grunted. It was one of the many—too many—unanswered questions shrouding the case. "You've seen the crime scene photos . . ."

"Many times."

"He didn't *look* as though he'd . . ." I hesitated, not liking the vagueness of what I was about to say. "There are questions I want to ask about those photos."

She nodded. "Sure, I get that. Me too. There are a couple of things that don't make a whole lot of sense. But it was twelve years ago, and those questions are not questions anybody can answer anymore. Sometimes the truth just . . ." She made little explosions with her fingertips. "Fades away. Even when the trail was still warm, they were hard to answer. Now . . ." She shook her head.

I sighed, sipped, and watched her. "What can I say? I have a feeling, Dehan. Something in my gut just says there is *something* there, something in what happened that night. Something," I repeated, "maybe, in the photos, that we can use. I don't know how else to say it. Al *deserves* that we should make the effort. Poor guy, you know?"

She smiled, not unkindly. "That is sentimental reasoning, Stone, and has no place in police work."

"I know." I nodded. "But at the end of the day, it's why we do what we do." I sat back. "Well, what do you say?"

She spread her hands. "Frankly, personally, I think it's a waste of valuable police resources on a case that is probably never going to be solved. Having said that, you know I'll back you up, whatever you decide to do."

"See? That's why I married you. That and the whole . . ." I gestured at her with my open palm. "The whole flushed cheeks, heavy breathing, slightly perspiring thing you have going on there. It really works for you."

She leaned back and gave me the kind of smile that should be against the law but, thankfully, isn't. "Does it work for *you*?"

"Kind of does."

She stood and winked at me. "Well, I'm going to take a nice, looong, hot shower. You can be gathering up your case notes, and maybe prepare a salad for lunch."

She took her big grin upstairs with her. I sat a moment, staring after her. Then I rose, opened the fridge, and stood staring at the lettuce and the tomatoes, till I heard the hiss of water from the shower. Then I closed the fridge and went upstairs.

TWO

The shadows were growing long across the lawn. There was a slight breeze, and thin wisps of smoke, with an occasional, lazy trail of sparks, drifted over the grass to be lost among the rosebushes. Rosebushes my mother had planted, I had neglected, and Dehan had brought back to life.

She stepped out from the kitchen onto the patio, holding plates, cutlery, salt, and pepper. Her hair was still wet from her second shower, hanging long down her back, making damp marks on her summer dress. I watched her, feeling the heat of the barbeque on my back.

She set down the load, grabbed a bottle of wine by the neck, and stabbed the cork with a corkscrew. As she began to twist, she said, "The guy was crazy, right?"

I nodded. "But don't let the thought police hear you saying things like that. He was diagnosed with schizophrenia and also paranoia."

The pop of the cork echoed in the early evening. She set the bottle down and pointed at it with the corkscrew. "Now you have to let it breathe for at least an hour."

"No kidding. Where do you learn that stuff, Dehan?"

"Some guy who was coming on to me. I forget his name. So he had a psychiatrist who he was seeing for his meds and stuff..."

"Indeed, Dr. Epstein."

She leaned down, pulled two bottles of beer from a bucket of ice, and cracked them both, then handed me one and sat. I took a pull and continued.

"His practice was, and still is, at 1910 Benedict Avenue, just off the Hugh J. Grant Circle. A short walk from Al's place. In fact, he had just been to see Epstein the night he was killed. According to Epstein's statement, Al was not great at keeping up with his meds, but he always made a point of turning up on his birthday, November twenty-third, because they always made a fuss of him and brought him in a cake."

"Cute. That's nice. I should go crazy so people would do nice things for me."

I ignored her and went on. "It seems he stayed a bit late that day. Apparently, he would just sit in the waiting room, or chat with the staff. By all accounts, he was a pleasant kind of guy, polite, well educated, so they didn't mind him hanging around."

Dehan was frowning. "Seriously?"

"I know. It sounds odd to me too, but that is what we have at the moment. So he hung around and then left, intending to go home. What happened next isn't one hundred percent clear. It was pieced together from eyewitness accounts. He crossed the Hugh J. Grant Circle, as he would have to to get home, saw a couple of people who knew him and greeted him. Then he made his way down Virginia Avenue, toward his place on Ellis. It's not a long walk—two hundred yards from the Circle to Ellis, and another fifty to his house."

She was frowning at me over the rim of her glass as she sipped. "Is that relevant? You seem to be stressing it like you think it's relevant."

"I don't know yet. The thing is, as he is walking those two hundred and fifty yards or so, some kids start hassling him. As I said, this is put together from accounts of people who saw or heard things as he walked past. Remember, he had been in the neighborhood for a long time, and he was known as a kind of local character. According to what they were able to piece together in the original investigation, this gang..."

I hesitated and Dehan said, "You don't mean like a real gang, like the Chupacabras..."

"No, not at all. It was just a gang of kids, sixteen to eighteen, who used to hang around and make a lot of noise. But there was one of them, Ned, who, according to local gossip, kind of had it in for Al, used to call him the Freak, and anytime he saw him he'd give him a hard time, shout abuse, call him names..."

She leaned back in her chair. "Is there any record of physical violence?"

"Yes and no. Ned was always getting into fights, was known to carry a knife, and he was certainly on the radar. There is no record of his ever having physically attacked Al..."

"That doesn't mean it never happened."

"No, it doesn't, but neither do we have any record of Al suffering from any kind of injury that might have been inflicted in a fight. So if there ever was a physical confrontation, it didn't lead to much."

"Okay, so that evening, these assholes start giving him a hard time. What happens next?"

"He panics. He was seen by several people passing the upholstery shop and the deli on the corner of Ellis and Virginia, and all of them reported him as being in a very agitated state. Apparently Ned was right behind him, seemed angry and aggressive, and Ned's pals were holding back, but laughing. The witnesses watched Ned and his friends follow him to his house and go into his front yard. There was a slam, like a door slamming, a lot of screaming, and the kids left. The people at the deli said it looked like Ned had hurt his hand. They thought about calling the cops but felt the whole thing had blown over."

"So presumably, Ned then became the prime suspect and was easily traced because he has a bruised, swollen hand."

I smiled, removed the tinfoil from the two T-bone steaks I had beside the barbeque, and sprinkled them with Maldon sea salt. Then I dropped them onto the iron grill over the burning coals. Flames leapt three feet high around them, licking at the herb-seasoned oil I had soaked them in.

I swigged my beer and went on. "Unfortunately, it is not quite that simple. Al telephones the surgery. Judging by the time of the call, it must have been almost as soon as he got in. The call was taken by one Joy Jones, Dr. Epstein's receptionist, assistant, and general factotum—his words, not mine. According to her testimony at the time, he was practically incoherent. She managed to calm him down and he told her, more or less, what the detectives at the time managed to piece together, and I have just told you. Except that he added in a fair old dose of paranoia about tidal waves of darkness engulfing him and his house, and evil beings who had followed him from Mexico. She told him she'd call the precinct and ask for somebody to pass by and make sure he was okay."

Dehan frowned. "And did she?"

I flipped the steaks. "No, she didn't. In her statement, she said she thought about calling the cops, but decided against it. She knew that Al imagined things. She also knew there was a bunch of kids who used to call him names, but she was pretty sure they were not dangerous. She didn't feel it was right to waste police time, so she left it at that. Martinez, that was the investigating detective at the time, said she was devastated when she discovered what had happened."

"So what did happen?"

I took the scorched steaks and put them onto our plates. Dehan poured the wine, and we sat and ate in relative silence for a while, broken only by Dehan making small noises of visceral pleasure. When she had got halfway through her steak, she sat back with her wine and smiled. "Man, love a good steak."

I nodded and returned the smile. "What happened? That's the million-dollar question. Here's what we know. He didn't cook. He didn't make himself any food at all. He didn't turn on any lights. He closed the drapes in the living room and put on a DVD from a box set of *Murder She Wrote*."

"I love that show."

"Who doesn't? He obviously did. According to Dr. Epstein, he had watched the entire series more than thirty times."

"Wow, that's intense." She started cutting into her steak again.

I continued. "He wasn't found for three days. Joy Jones got worried when she didn't hear from him and he wouldn't answer his phone. She doesn't live far from his house, so on the way home from work, she went to see him. There was no reply when she knocked, and, when she questioned the neighbors, nobody had seen him since his birthday. So she called the cops."

She stuffed the last piece of steak in her mouth and spoke around it as she chewed. "They found him on the living room floor, with a stab wound to his heart."

I drained my glass, refilled hers and then mine. "That misses all of what Holmes would call the most interesting features, my dear Dehan. First of all, the place had been trashed, turned upside down, though nothing was broken. Second, he was, as you say, killed by a single stab wound to the heart, but the blade of the knife was exceptionally long and broad, consistent, according to the ME, with the blade of a large kitchen knife. He was lying on the living room floor, beside his sofa, with the TV still playing Jessica Fletcher on repeat, over and over."

"That's kind of creepy to think about."

"There were shots fired."

"What?"

"Three shots. Nobody heard them. That is not surprising in itself: residents of the Bronx have a peculiar deafness where gunfire is concerned. However, the nine-millimeter rounds traveled from the living room through to the open-plan kitchen and shattered various items: the kettle, a stack of plates, and a radio sitting by the sink. The radio had a clock, so the lab was able to establish at what time the power was cut off."

"So we have time of death . . ."

"Ten thirty on Friday night, the twenty-third of November, 2007."

"Good. So what happened?"

"The first thing Martinez did was haul Ned in for questioning. He had a very badly bruised right hand with two broken fingers. At first, he said he got his fingers caught in a car door. That's what it says on his medical report from the ER department. But later, he admitted that it was Al who had slammed his front door on his fingers when they were, and I quote, 'messin' with him and just trying to scare the old guy a bit.' They didn't mean no harm."

"So they charged him?"

"No, he came up with an alibi. He was with his friends all that weekend, nursing his hand, and he didn't go out. His friends were willing to testify that they were with him every hour of every day from Friday lunchtime to Monday morning."

"So the son of a bitch got a false alibi."

"Perhaps; either way, they were unable to shake it or make anything stick. Forensic evidence was very thin on the ground. There was not a trace of DNA evidence, not a single thing to link him to the scene of the crime *at the time* of the murder. They had to let him go."

She sat forward with her elbows on the table. The light from the flames in the barbeque bathed her face and danced in her eyes.

"Well," she said, "there is no mystery to this case, Stone. Making the evidence stick may be a problem, but you and I both know exactly what happened. Ned was having some fun tormenting this poor guy. Maybe he got pissed because he didn't like the way Al answered him, or maybe he got mad because Al ignored him. Whichever. You know—you don't disrespect a bro from the hood, know what I'm sayin'? You feel me, dude?"

"I feel you, man."

"Assholes like that don't need an excuse. They smell your weakness and they go after you. So things get out of hand and they try to force their way into his house. He slams the door. The guy was big and heavy..."

"Six three and almost four hundred pounds."

She grinned. "So when he says, 'I'm gonna close the door here,' he closes the door. Only this time, he closes it on Ned's fingers. Ned goes away to nurse his hand but comes back a few hours later with a nine-millimeter, picks the lock, and goes in planning to shoot Al dead. Al freaks out and panics. So Ned has four hundred pounds of panicking crazy to contend with. He panics too and fires. The shots go wide. Maybe Al snatches the gun or knocks it out of his hand." She shrugged and spread her hands. "So Ned stabs him."

I took a deep breath and swirled the wine around in my glass. I took a sip and sighed.

"That is pretty much word for word what Martinez concluded."

She nodded and snorted. "But you have some pain in the ass Sherlock Holmes observations which make it impossible, my dear Watson."

I shrugged. "Not impossible, but they are, as he would say, features of interest. For a start, when questioned, Ned was asked if he had a knife. He admitted that he had a switchblade. It was a barely legal folding knife with a five-inch blade. More than enough to kill a man with."

"So...?"

"Well, the blade was much smaller than the one that was used to kill Al. So, make the movie in your head. What happened? He went home from the hospital, sore as hell. He packed a nine-millimeter pistol, which we assume he had, though it was never found, and, even though he had a lethal knife, which he carried everywhere with him, he also went and took his mother's huge, cumbersome kitchen knife, just for good measure?"

Dehan grunted. "Maybe he used one of Al's knives."

"Wait, we're not there yet. Assuming still that he took the kitchen knife with him for some reason—that knife has, at the least, an eight-inch blade, maybe three or four inches wide at the base, plus it has a four- or five-inch handle. If he already has a gun and a knife, why does he burden himself also with this very large knife that he doesn't need? Where does he carry it?"

"And what for?"

"Exactly: What for? And when the gun is knocked from his hand, does he wrestle this short sword from his jacket pocket?"

"Point taken. So now can you answer my question? Did he use Al's own kitchen knife?"

"No. The one knife he had that might have fit the wound had only his fingerprints on it, and those had not been smudged by latex gloves or anything of the sort. Plus, there was no trace of Al's blood on the knife, not even in the grooves by the handle. To have been cleaned that thoroughly . . ."

"The prints would have gone too. Okay."

"There is another point, which is quite important."

"What?"

"Have you ever had a broken hand?"

"No . . ."

I laughed. "It hurts. A lot. The last thing you want to do with a broken hand is fire a gun. If he's shooting left-handed, then that might account for the shots going wide. But the knife wound to the chest did not go wide. That was precision engineering, powerfully executed, dear Dehan. That blade was placed and thrust without a second's hesitation. And with considerable force. That was not done with a broken hand, or left-handed."

"Son of a gun."

I nodded. "No, I don't like Ned for this. I have a feeling somebody else went to visit Al that night."

"But what motive could anyone possibly have to kill him? The guy was harmless."

I made a protracted "hmmm" noise. "I don't know if he was harmless." I shrugged. "He may well have been. But there was a rumor, which most people paid little or no attention to, that said he'd had a pretty wild, shady life and kept a vast sum of money in his house, in a paper bag or a carton or some equally stupid container."

"Oh . . . and the place had been ransacked."

"Yup, and when you look at the photographs . . ." I sighed. "I don't know, it looks to me like a search that somebody has tried to disguise as a fight or a struggle."

She laughed. "How the hell can you tell that?"

I hesitated. "Nothing is broken. That struck me as odd. When two people thrash around fighting, they break things, but not necessarily when they are searching. And every time I look at the pictures, it strikes me as more odd. Why is nothing broken?" I shrugged. "And naturally, no trace of the money was ever found."

"You think he really had a stash of money?"

"I shouldn't think so for one moment. But it may well be that somebody in Ned's gang thought it was worth exploring the possibility."

"Did they pull in the other kids?"

"They asked them questions, but they were all each other's alibi. So the case stalled."

She gazed at me for a while. Then she spoke suddenly and emphatically, nodding her head. "No, that is a really interesting case. It has, like you said, interesting features. But, Stone, how the *hell* do you plan to crack it? Where do you begin? It *is* insoluble."

"I know," I said, and smiled. "That's why I want to solve it."

THREE

Next morning, we dropped in on Dr. Epstein's practice on the way to the precinct. We approached through heavy morning traffic via the Metropolitan Oval and peeled off into Benedict Avenue, where I managed to find a space for my ancient, burgundy Jag, right outside his block. By the time I'd climbed out and slammed the door, Dehan was already on the sidewalk, doing little jumps on her toes. It wasn't cold, but there was enough chill in the morning air to bring out pink flushes on her cheeks. That made me smile. She ignored it and said, "So, you want to tell me what it is you hope to find out here?"

We entered the lobby. There was a thick, dark green carpet, there were wood-paneled walls, brass lamps, and a mahogany desk for a porter. But there was no porter, the lampshades were flyblown, and the thick green carpets were worn thin from years of being trodden on by increasingly cheap shoes. I pressed the button to call the elevator and shoved my hands in my pockets.

"I hope to find out," I said, "what it is I hope to find out."

"Have you been reading annoying books on Zen philosophy again?"

I closed my eyes. "I *am* annoying Zen philosophy, Dehan. You godda be de watter, Ritoo Glasshopper."

The elevator doors slid open and we stepped in. I pressed the button, and as the doors closed, I said, "Let me explain: somewhere in this apparently insoluble case, there is one small, loose end, but we don't know what it is yet." We began to climb. "So if we are busy looking for fingerprints, but the loose end is a handkerchief with blood on it, we may never find it, because we are looking in the wrong place for the wrong thing."

"So?"

"We must look nowhere—and *everywhere!*"

She smiled with hooded eyes. "I bet you used to watch all those shows and movies, didn't you?"

The elevator stopped and the doors slid open. "What shows and movies?"

She followed me out to the landing. "You know, Bruce Lee, kung fu, *Karate Kid* . . ."

I spied Dr. Epstein's brass plaque and headed for it, speaking over my shoulder. "Never heard of them. It seems to me, however, young Dehan, that you are quite familiar with *all* of them! Here we are . . ."

I tapped lightly on the door and stepped through to a comfortable reception area while Dehan muttered something behind me. The walls were plain cream with half a dozen unobtrusive prints hanging. There were chairs and a couple of small sofas that had been new not so long ago, but weren't anymore, and there was a coffee table with lots of magazines on it. Opposite the door, and slightly to my right, there was an old oak desk, and behind it there was an attractive woman in her late thirties or early forties. She had large, humorous eyes and a mouth with generous lips and very white teeth that found it hard not to smile. When she spoke, her accent said she had once been from Barbados, but she was now from the Bronx.

"Good morning, what can I do for you?"

We showed her our badges. "I'm Detective Stone, this is Detective Dehan, of the NYPD . . ."

She was already shaking her head and laughing. "Oh, I know

you're cops, darling!" She laughed and flapped her hand at me. "You got that written *all* over you! But tell me what I can do to help you."

I smiled. "We'd like to see Dr. Epstein."

She glanced at her watch. "He's got his nine thirty in twenty minutes." She eyed me with a hint of mischief. "Procrastination, but he is always late!" She screamed with laughter and flapped her hand. I heard Dehan snort behind me. She picked up the internal phone and pressed a button, still chuckling. "Procrastination . . . always late. I swear it's true . . . Dr. Epstein. I got two beautiful detectives from the NYPD here to see you . . ." She paused, watching us and nodding, then said, "Twenty minutes, but you know he's *always* late . . . okay."

She pointed to a mahogany door across the room and said, "That door. He's noisy, but he's a good man."

"Thanks for the heads-up."

She winked at Dehan, and I went and knocked on the door.

"Come!"

I opened the door and we stepped in.

Dr. Epstein was on his feet, rising from his large oak desk, gesturing at us with a huge hand. "I told her to send you in. Why do you need to knock? If she tells you to come in, it's like *I* told you to come in! Sit down. What do you want?"

He was a big man, though not tall. He had a white shirt with thin brown stripes and a burgundy tie. His hands were large and hairy. He had a large, gold wedding band, and the nails of his right hand were long. Those on his left were short. He used gold cuff links.

The office was comfortable, more like your favorite uncle's study than a place of work. It was elegantly shabby, well used, and smelled of pipe tobacco. The bookcases, the oak desk, and the sideboard were all genuine antiques, and the books on the shelves were an eclectic mix of leather-bound tomes and well-thumbed paperbacks, filed according to the nearest available empty space system.

I assimilated this in the time it took him to swing his arm from pointing to the door to pointing to the ancient leather armchairs across from his desk.

"Sit down," he said again. "You'll be more comfortable sitting down than talking on your feet." He dropped into his own huge leather chair and we sat. "When you stand too long, all the blood drains from your brain to your feet, makes it harder to think. That's a joke, but it's also true. So what do you want?"

I let him finish, smiled, and waited in case he was going to start again. After he didn't, I showed him my badge and said, "You were Aloysius Chester's psychiatrist, back in 2007, when he was murdered?"

You read about people's faces darkening. Epstein's actually did. He frowned, and his tan seemed to take on a deeper hue.

"I was. I saw him the very day they say he was killed, in fact. It was his birthday . . ." He waved his hand vaguely toward reception. "We did a little thing for him." His eyes shifted from Dehan to me. He looked like he wasn't sure whether to be mad or not. "He liked the attention, the affection. It made his load a little lighter." His face darkened further, into a scowl. "He was a kind, loving person trapped in a damaged body, and a damaged brain."

I drew breath to ask my next question, but he barked suddenly at Dehan, "I hope you're not one of those people who spout trite little Facebook wisdom bites, like, 'Everything happens for a reason'!"

I saw her repress a smile and raise an eyebrow. "Excuse me?"

He waved a dismissive hand at her. "A pet beef of mine. You know them? Those people who greet every damned tragedy in life with that trite little phrase, 'Everything happens for a reason.'" He looked at me, hunched his shoulders, and narrowed his eyes into incredulity. "*What?*"

I was about to tell him I hadn't spoken, but he said it again. "*What? Excuse me?* I mean, what does it *mean?* Everything happens for a reason! Yeah, your husband got killed and the *reason* was, he stepped in front of a goddamn car! Children in developing countries die of malnutrition. The *reason* is human beings are sick and corrupt! Six million Jews were exterminated in German death camps. The *reason* was that the Germans elected Hitler to power! These are the *reasons* bad things happen, not because of some goddamned benign, all-knowing Universe!"

Dehan smiled. "We're cops, Dr. Epstein, not philosophers. We just want to ask you . . ."

"It's like those people—I want to shoot them—somebody says . . ." He sat forward and rearranged his ass. "Somebody says, 'Hey, did you hear? John's got terminal cancer.' And some asshole always says, 'Oh my God! His *poor* wife!'" His face collapsed into an exaggerated gape. He showed it to Dehan, then to me. "Excuse me? What? No! *John* has cancer, not his goddamn wife! Poor *John*! Am I right? Am I right or am I wrong about that? I mean, it's *John* who has cancer, right? So poor John!" He flopped back in his chair. "I can't stand that. Compassion is for the person who is dying, right?"

Dehan tried again. "Dr. Epstein, we really just wanted to . . ."

"Dehan? You're Jewish, right? I can see it in your eyes. You're always asking questions that can never be answered. We don't have a cross, right? We're Jews. But if we had one, that would be it. The eternal questions. Godda love the stereotypes."

"Dr. Epstein?"

He turned to face me.

"We are taking another look at Al's case. We have the full report, obviously . . ."

"Obviously."

"But it would be really helpful . . ."

"You wanna hear it from the horse's mouth. Of course you do. What do you wanna know? What happened that last day? How he looked? Did he seem worried about anything? Preoccupied . . . ? Who'd know, if not his shrink?"

I sat back in my chair. "Yes, all of that, and anything else you can think of."

He dilated his nostrils and took a long, deep, noisy breath.

"What can I think of . . . ?" His eyes became abstracted. "He was a beautiful person. Kind, humane, compassionate." His eyes locked onto mine for a second. "Brilliantly intelligent. Highly, *highly* intelligent. A seeker for truth. But . . ." He tossed his right hand, like he was throwing away something that had once had promise but had since been found wanting. "Like so many young people of his generation, he thought the way to wisdom was to burn your candle at both ends." He paused and smiled at Dehan, studying her face. "My candle burns at both ends;" he quoted, "It will not last the night; but ah, my foes, and oh, my friends—it gives a lovely light."

I sighed loudly and made no effort to hide it. "If we could get down to concrete . . ."

"Facts! It is a fact that Aloysius Chester was a brilliant student. Wellington College prep school, in England, Marymount High School, New York, Harvard Medical School. He had a glittering career all lined up at the top of his profession as a heart surgeon. But unlike his family, the man had a heart. He had a soul! He *cared* and asked *those* questions . . ." He eyed Dehan. "He wasn't a Jew, but we haven't got the monopoly on searching questions, right?"

"Right."

I asked, "What are *those* questions he kept asking?"

"Why? Who? How? He asked how a lot, but mainly, why?"

I sighed again. "Dr. Epstein, we really haven't got time . . ."

"You think I'm being facetious, but I'm not. He really did ask those questions. And it was the asking of those questions that shaped his life. Now, he was twenty years old when he was at Harvard. I'm talking about the late sixties. And we all know what was going on—*and what was going down*—at every campus in the U.S.A. during the late sixties. And there . . ." He gestured with his open hand at the middle of the floor. "Right there, was Tim Leary telling us all it was okay! Am I right?"

"So you're telling us that . . ."

"And big, powerful brains like William Burroughs, Allen

Ginsberg—you know?—telling us this is good! This is spiritual evolution. And these were no intellectual slouches! Not like Jack Kerouac, who was, if you will forgive me, intellectually lazy *at best*. So there we were, at the dawn of a new age, being offered the fruit of the tree of knowledge. I was a bit younger than him. He was there right at the start, and who could blame him?"

Dehan said, "For being there at the start?" And frowned.

"No, for experimenting with LSD and mind-altering drugs. He was pretty wild, unafraid. And, you know, at that time, we were all reading Carlos Castaneda, *as well* as Ginsberg and Leary and the Beatles. Everywhere you turned, there was this message, 'Get high! Turn on! Blow your mind...'"

He went quiet, staring at nothing, seeing his memories.

"I met him once, you know that? Castaneda. Interesting guy, mild-mannered, polite, very academic. It was all true, what he wrote about. He told me."

"Al...?"

"Yeah, so he dropped out of college, went to Mexico, met a shaman, just like Castaneda. He did the whole peyote mescalito thing. His family were horrified. They disowned him. He didn't care! He didn't give a goddamn. He was on a mission, brother!"

He threw his head back and roared out laughing, intoning in a booming voice, "*He was on a mission, brother!*" Then he subsided into chuckles. "A mission to find the Truth, with a capital *T*. From Mexico, he went to Brazil, in search of a shaman who could teach him to use ayahuasca." He sighed noisily through hairy nostrils and shook his head. "It wasn't enough. He never found the Truth. The *Truth* is never *out there*, is it? So, he came back, deeply disillusioned with Latin America, believing now that we in the West were closer to the answer. This was Our Time, he thought. We were searching, in our collective unconscious, for the ultimate illumination. And for this reason, we had created LSD. He used it immoderately, recklessly, and it drove him into a doddering, ineffectual, *infantile* psychosis. He was made *stupid* by his own, wild search for Truth."

I leaned forward and raised a hand. "Let me just take this one step at a time, please, Dr. Epstein. You are telling me that Al's schizophrenia was caused by his abuse of hallucinogenic drugs?"

"I thought I had made that clear."

"And that he, Al, came from a privileged background . . ."

"I was also under the impression that I had made *that* clear."

I struggled for a moment, trying to see the implications of this new information. Dehan scratched her throat with her index finger, narrowing her eyes.

"You said his family disowned him, and please, don't say you'd made that clear."

"Oh yes, the Chesters are one of the great families of New York. They are so privileged that nobody has heard of them. Anonymity is the true mark of class . . ."

I smiled. "Like the British royal family."

"Exactly, vulgar German upstarts. The Chesters were among the first settlers in New York, long before the War of Independence. Since then, they have produced a string of eminent medical practitioners, particularly surgeons. Every generation has produced at least one eminence. It was widely thought that Aloysius would be that eminence in this generation. But his soul burned too bright."

There was an edge of impatience to Dehan's voice when she said, "So they disowned him."

He shook his head. "Not at first. His mother had died when he was young. I have no doubt this affected his attitude to life—and women. She was, perhaps, the answer he was forever seeking, but was doomed never to find. Be that as it may, he was raised most of his life either at boarding schools or, on the rare occasions that he was at home, by nannies. He had very little contact with his father. But while he was in Brazil, his father died. He did not return for the funeral, but he did return shortly after that for some kind of Harvard reunion. His brothers and his sister met with him and gave him an ultimatum: toe the line and take up your position as head of the family, or we will disown you."

I couldn't help giving a small laugh. "What does that mean? What would be the consequences of being disowned?"

He viewed me a moment, then nodded a few times. "You mock, and perhaps in some cases you would be right to. To be disowned by the Chester siblings would mean social ostracism. His clan, his class, his social peers would all disown him. They would all turn their backs on him. He would be cast adrift, and his old school tie would be of no use to him whatsoever. That can —and did, for Aloysius—have very serious consequences, professionally and financially. The well of privilege suddenly dried up!"

I nodded, aware that he was telling me something that was important, though I wasn't exactly sure why. "But this case was different in some way?"

"Oh yes, very. Because when Aloysius got back from Brazil, it soon became apparent that he had suffered serious neurological damage. So not only did they disown him, but then they had him diagnosed as suffering from paranoid schizophrenia. He effectively lost control of all his wealth overnight. His shares in the family company were put in trust . . ."

I frowned. "In trust?"

He snorted. "In *trust* . . . ! Meaning that his brothers and his sister administered his shares in the company, *and the proceeds from those shares*, and I was appointed by the court to be his guardian. It was up to me to oversee his care, watch over him if you like, and also to make sure his siblings did not abuse the trust too outrageously."

Dehan asked, "What is the family company?"

"Their father, Isembard Chester, invented a small, visually insignificant, yet medically essential valve which is used in every cardiology department in the world. He founded the company, Chester Cardio-Valves, and now they all live like kings on the proceeds. They were always rich, now they became insanely rich. And Aloysius had inherited twenty-five percent of the shares in that company. When he was diagnosed as suffering from paranoid schizophrenia, the siblings requested a court order to enable them to administer his share of the company. Then they disowned him."

I said, "So he lived on an allowance from the family?"

He shook his head. "The company paid him a director's salary every year. It was far less than the other three received, because they claimed he had no input into the firm. His shares were worth millions—a king's ransom! But he was not allowed access to it because they claimed he was a danger to himself—a statement you could hardly argue with."

"And once he died?"

He shrugged. "That was where my involvement ended. Everything reverted back to the estate. He had no heirs, nor could he make out a will, because he was not of sound mind. So his brothers and his sister got everything."

Dehan's eyebrows shot up, but she didn't say anything. I stared at Epstein a moment. "You talk about him and his family as though you knew them..."

He spread his hands, flopped his head on one side. "He was in my care for a long time. I liked him. He was a couple of years ahead of me at Harvard. He didn't know me, but I saw him around and I admired him. I admired his relentless *search*! It was fortuitous that later in life he would be put into my care."

His internal phone rang, and he snatched it up. "Yes!"

He listened a moment, then hung up without saying anything. To me, he said, "My patient is here. Joy might be able to tell you more. She was more directly involved with Al on a day-to-day basis. Talk to her."

I pointed toward reception. "Is that Joy?"

"Not anymore. She opened up and let you in this morning, bless her. But now she's at the church. Mondays she volunteers to combat the encroaching darkness of Babylon. Right now you'll see her daughter, Mary. Dim, IQ of about ninety-eight point five, but willing. She'll tell you how to get to the church. Now, go, please."

FOUR

Mary was pretty and smiled as easily as her mother. Her skin was a little paler than Joy's, but she had her mother's big eyes and generous lips. I put her in her early twenties and figured that Epstein's assessment of her was probably not a fair one. I pegged her as more submissive than dim.

"You want to see Mom? She's at the church. Monday is always a busy day there. They have the soup kitchen, legal advice, medical advice, and any other charity they may be running at the time!" She laughed like she'd said something funny and rolled her eyes. "Mom's been going for years, so they can't do without her. Indispensable Joy! That's what the pastor calls her."

Dehan gave a sweet smile. "That's nice. Where is the church, Mary?"

"Okay." She put her hands together like she was praying and gave a little bob on her knees. "You're going to turn right out of the building, and at the end of Benedict Avenue, you're going to make a left onto Metropolitan Avenue." Here she paused to give a little giggle and another bob. "Go down Metropolitan Avenue and *cross* the circus, but kind of turn right?" She made a contorted gesture with her hand to indicate a car turning right. "Onto White Plains Road? And it's like a block down, on the corner with Gleason. It's called the Church of the Sacred Apocalypse." She grinned sheepishly at Dehan. "Apocalypse means revelation. That's because the Book of Revelation is all about the Apocalypse."

I patted her shoulder in a fatherly fashion. "Thank you, Mary, you have been extremely helpful. You have a peaceful day."

Her cheeks flushed pink, and she gave me a breathless, "Thank you!"

We stepped out of Epstein's practice and sought the elevators. Once we had stepped into the car and started to descend, Dehan looked at me with narrowed eyes and shook her head. "Is it just me, or is everybody insane today?"

"I can't remember who said it, but somebody said that normality was just a psychosis we all agree upon. Dr. Epstein struck me as a very sane man, actually."

She eyed me a moment. "He did, huh?"

I nodded. "Mm-hm."

"Well, I gotta tell you, buddy, I don't know if that says more about him or about you."

The doors slid open, and we crossed the seedy old lobby out into the fresh, early summer morning. I unlocked the Jag, and we climbed into the warm leather and walnut interior and slammed the doors. We both sat in silence for a while, staring through the windshield.

Dehan spoke first: "So we have another motive. A considerably more powerful one than a semi-mythical box of cash."

I nodded and said, "Define it for me."

"Whatever his share of the company was worth—millions of dollars—plus the fact that their brother was bringing continued shame down on the family. That's two motives in one."

I thought about that for a moment, then turned the key in the ignition. The big old cat growled and I pulled away.

"We'll have to go and talk to them. Their names are in the file. I'm surprised none of this came up in the original investigation."

"Maybe it did, and Martinez decided it was a dead end."

I made a noise that meant I wasn't convinced, then added, "Anyway, let's see what the Indispensable Joy can tell us. Something tells me she holds things together."

"Somebody better. It's beginning to feel like the Mad Hatter's Tea Party 'round here."

The Church of the Sacred Apocalypse was precisely where Mary had said it would be, and after only a couple of minutes, I pulled into the parking lot and killed the engine. It was an oddly sinister building to look at, in yellowish brick with sharp gables and narrow windows. There were not many cars in the parking lot, but as we approached the main entrance on White Plains, we became aware of a desultory stream of people approaching in ones, twos, and threes from all directions, like a congregation of zombies. They gravitated toward the broad forecourt of the temple, then climbed its thirteen steps to the large, arched red doors, which now stood open.

We followed them up and stepped into the cavernous half-light of the great nave. For a moment, all I could see in the gloom, having come from the glare outside, was the thin, luminous forms, in violent reds and deep blues and yellows, of the stained glass windows at the far end of the temple. Then my eyes adjusted, and Dehan took my arm and pointed.

"Over there."

I could now make out a door that stood open down the aisle on the right-hand side, and a scraggly line of people who were making their way through that door. We followed.

What we found on the other side was a large hall with wooden floors and a high ceiling. Twenty or thirty benches stood in long rows across the room, populated by hunched men and women bent with serious concentration over bowls and plates of food. At the far end, a long table was set out with hot food: soup, baked potatoes, pizza, and hamburgers. There was a line forming, from the door, around the room and up to that table, where Joy and a couple of other women were dispensing the food to the hungry, the destitute, and the marginalized: those specimens society cannot use to generate revenue, so it uses them to generate charity instead.

She saw us approaching, smiled, and waved. She had a quick word with one of the women helping by her side and came around to greet us. The smile was still there. "I thought I might see you in here. You ain't comin' for the food, are you? I hope not! Or maybe you *brought* some food!"

Dehan was observing her with a curious smile. I made a noise that might have been a laugh or a snort. "None of the above, I'm afraid. We just hoped we could ask you some questions about Al."

"Al? Aloysius?" She shook her head. "That poor man. He didn't have a mean bone in his body, but he had strayed so far from the righteous path . . ." She sighed and smiled at us both in turn. "But you don't want to hear that kind of thing, do you? You have a *job* to do, and you'd like the facts. Come on into the little lounge over here, and I'll tell you what I can."

I saw Dehan's eyebrows rise up toward her hairline. "Hallelujah."

Joy laughed and playfully slapped her arm. "Did old Dr. E give you a hard time? He can *talk*! Sweet Jesus!" She laughed out loud and crossed herself. "Can that man talk!"

We weaved our way through the tables toward a door in the far wall, which had a red plaque on it that said, *Private*. As we arrived, Joy pulled a key from her pocket and unlocked it. Glancing at Dehan, she said, "May the Lord forgive us, but sometimes we just need to get away from . . ."

She pushed the door open and ushered us in. It was a featureless room, twenty feet square, with a small kitchen and a couple of nests of chairs scattered around a couple of coffee tables. Joy stepped in after us and closed and locked the door behind her. She stood a moment. "Well, away from all the suffering and the unhappiness. I know we should shoulder it with the strength of Jesus in our hearts, but sometimes we are weak and we just need to get away and have a cup of tea!" She laughed, but it sounded strained.

I smiled at her. "I'm sure, Joy."

"But listen to me going on about my woes and you are here to ask me some important questions. Sit, sit. Can I make you some coffee? We have some lemonade . . ."

I shook my head. "No, thank you, Joy. We just have a couple of simple questions and we'll let you get on."

We all three sat around a low, round table. Joy sat forward, with her elbows on her knees, and unconsciously we imitated her pose. Dehan spoke first.

"Dr. Epstein said that you had more contact with Al than he had . . ."

She sighed and rolled her eyes. "That is not *exactly* accurate. Dr. Epstein was his psychiatrist, and they had known each other for a *very* long time. Dr. Epstein had a lot of respect for Aloysius. Al had been a very intelligent man at one time, I am sure Dr. E told you all about that."

"Yes, he did."

"Poor Al strayed a long way from the path, and there really was no way for him to be cured, not with modern science, anyway. So we prayed—Dr. Epstein didn't pray! He claims he is a godless atheist!" She threw her head back and laughed. "But Mary and me, and our brothers and sisters at the church, we all prayed. Often, I would ask the congregation to pray for poor Al, to find a way back."

Dehan raised an eyebrow. "So *did* you spend more time with him?"

She shook her head. "No, the doctor had his sessions on a regular basis, and they would have long talks sometimes. They were like old friends. But I would help Al out with small, practical things. I helped him to get his house. We had to go and see a lawyer to persuade the trust . . ." She hesitated.

I nodded. "We know about the trust."

"His brothers, Maximilian and Justinian, and his sister, Annunziata, they didn't want to release the money from the trust to allow him to have a place to live. They said he should go to a residence or a shelter. So we hired a lawyer and put pressure on them—I think Dr. Epstein threatened to go to the press and make a scandal, so in the end, they agreed to buy the house so that he could live in it for the duration of his life."

I rubbed my chin with my palm. "You took care of that for him? That must have been tough, a lot of work."

"The Lord helps us get through."

"Al must have been very grateful."

She smiled with what looked like genuine affection, and her eyes became abstracted. "He was always very grateful. In as much as he could understand what was happening, he was grateful to us for the help we gave him, but what he was truly grateful for was the friendship and the love that we gave him. He was a lost soul, clinging to us with his fingertips. I only hope the Lord took him to His bosom when he died. I am sure he did. I want to believe that."

Dehan cleared her throat. "Joy, I know you're busy, but do you think you could talk us through what happened that night, the night of his birthday?"

She took a very deep breath and gazed away at the wall. "Well, let me see. It was twelve years ago, so I might be a little hazy on the details, but I seem to remember he came in about two or three o'clock in the afternoon. He was not great at keeping up with his medication, and sometimes we had to chase him up. But he would always make a point of turning up on his birthday, as though he had *no idea* what day it was, and always with the pretext of collecting his medication!" She leaned back in the chair, laughing with real pleasure.

"Well, of course Mary and I would *always* make a cake for him and surprise him with it, and he *always* looked so pleased! I remember he used actually to laugh, and then cry, like a gigantic baby. Poor, sweet Aloysius."

I sat back and crossed my legs. "So on that day he stayed late?"

She raised her eyebrows and drew breath, like she was about to say something, but changed her mind. Then she let the breath out in a sigh. "You know, Dr. Epstein comes across as this big, noisy, angry man, but really it is a front. He has a *huge* heart, and his practice thrives *because* he is so compassionate. Half of his patients treat his practice as a drop-in! I am not exaggerating. And you know what he says? He tells me, 'Joy, what people need in this world is love, not therapy. Love.' And he calls himself an atheist!" She chuckled, shaking her head. "I am not sure if he is a hippie in disguise or just a saint. But he never kicks anybody out. He insists that his office must be quiet, and a peaceful place for his clients to go and speak to him, but aside from that, there are no rules except love and be kind."

I glanced at Dehan to see if she had a question. She was frowning and listening hard. I said, "So what happened?"

"He stayed. He was feeling so happy, and everyone who came or left said 'Happy birthday, Al!' to him, so he sat there. Sometimes I would chat to him, mostly he just sat quietly."

Dehan asked, "So at what time did he leave?"

Joy thought for a bit, giving her head little shakes. "I honestly can't remember. It was November twenty-third . . ."

I nodded. "Friday, November twenty-third."

She echoed my nod. "And it was dusk outside when he left, so . . ." She shrugged. "Four thirty?"

"Okay. So, how long after he left did he call?"

"Not long. Not long at all. Do please remember it was twelve years ago, and with the best will in the world . . ." She trailed off, staring up at the ceiling. "Not more than twenty minutes, probably more like fifteen."

Dehan said, "So basically he got in and went straight to the phone to call you."

"From the distress in his voice, I would say that is probably right."

Dehan's frown deepened. "If he was that distressed, why didn't you call the cops, take some action . . . ?"

For a moment, Joy seemed to fold in on herself. She retained her smile, but the happiness had gone from it, her shoulders seemed to slump forward, and she sagged. She stared at the floor, then looked back at Dehan. "It's a question that has tormented me every day since he was killed. And to you, looking in from the outside, it's a question that makes perfect sense. But honestly, Detective Dehan, ask any professional in this line of work and they will tell you the same thing."

She paused, reading Dehan's face. Dehan's face said that Dehan still didn't get it. So Joy explained it. "Do you know how many panicking phone calls we get in a week? Do you know how many of them turn out to be fantasies? More to the point, Detective Dehan, if Mrs. H called me and said she had a gang of youths trying to break in, I would call the police instantly, because Mrs. H suffers from OCD, but she is not delusional. But if Mr. B called, I could not make such a simple judgment, because Mr. B is paranoid and a schizophrenic who is constantly hearing voices that warn him that people are coming for him."

"Had Al made that kind of call before?"

"Many times." She sighed. "And of course it was complicated by the fact that there was a gang of kids . . ." She hesitated. "They were not a 'gang' in the sense we understand the word in the Bronx!" She gave a small laugh. "They were just five or six young teenagers who had nothing better to do than hang around the streets making a noise. They often used to taunt Aloysius because he . . ." She spread her hands. "He stood out in a crowd! He was huge, and his breathing was heavy and labored, and he was very blond with very blue eyes . . . They noticed him, and this one boy used to taunt him, call him a freak. We talked to the local police about it, and they said they'd keep an eye on the boys, but the fact was they had no record of serious violence or breaking and entering . . ."

I said, "But Ned did try to break into his house. He got his fingers broken doing it."

She nodded. "I know. Good for Al. But nobody could have seen that coming, and believe me, the precinct would not thank us for reporting every panicky call we receive. Your boys are stretched to breaking point as it is. This . . ." For a moment, there was real distress in her eyes. "This is Babylon! So hard sometimes to know what is best to do."

I nodded. "It was a difficult call. I wouldn't like to have to make it."

"I told him I would call the police and ask them to pass by and make sure he was okay. With one thing and another, I simply forgot. I had half made up my mind to pass by his house on my way home to make sure he was okay. As it was, by the time I left, I had to rush to get to the church. So I told myself I'd drop in on the way home. But again, it was late, and, may the Lord forgive me, Mary and I had been looking forward to watching a film. I can't even remember what it was ∴ . but I had made a cake and we had promised each other we would watch it together. I remember I got home at ten fifteen or ten twenty-five or thereabouts, just as it was starting. Mary was making a big fuss." The smile faded from her face. "If I hadn't been so selfish, who knows? Maybe Al would still be with us today."

Dehan sat forward with her elbows on her knees. "Or you wouldn't. Don't think of it that way, Joy. You're not responsible for his death, whoever killed him is. You are responsible for giving him a lot of happiness while he lived."

Tears flooded Joy's eyes. She nodded. "Thank you, dear."

I smiled and stood. "I think we're about done for now, Joy. Thanks for your help."

"I'm afraid I haven't been able to add anything to what I told your detective before."

"Fresh eyes, fresh ears . . . Who knows?"

I winked and she smiled. "Yes, who knows . . . ?"

FIVE

"Take a walk with me."

I said it staring up at the clear blue June sky above the Church of the Sacred Apocalypse. Dehan was standing with her hand on the car door, waiting for me to open it. "Okay..."

I beckoned her toward Gleason Avenue. "Walk and talk."

She bounced a couple of strides to catch up with me, then fell into step. "Walk and talk, huh? Okay, well, first impressions: Epstein and Joy are out of their minds, but oddly grounded and sane. Above all, they are good people—capital *G* good, for real, and I think Al was damned lucky to have them." I drew breath and she raised a finger. "I'm rambling, sorting chaff from seed. You said walk and talk, I'm walking and I'm talking. I'm rambling."

"That's good. That's funny. Rambling. I like it."

"Shut up. So, Ned. Local patrol uniforms thought he was basically harmless because at—what was he? Eighteen?—he still hadn't got into serious trouble. But that's like saying a girl can't get pregnant because she's a virgin."

"What?"

She nodded and shrugged, spreading her hands in a Mexican kind of way. "Well, you're a virgin until you're not, right? And then you get pregnant! It's the same with crime. You're innocent until you commit a crime. Then you're guilty!"

"Wow . . ."

"The fact is that he got his fingers broken trying to break into Al's house. We both know he wasn't going in to wish him a happy birthday. You said there was a rumor going around that he had a shady, wild past and fortune hidden somewhere in his house. Well, we just found out the wild, shady past was more than a rumor. Maybe the money was too. Maybe Ned found that out. So it's a slam dunk that Ned was after that money."

"He had a broken hand."

She waved an impatient hand at me. "This is the Bwanx, white boy! These are tough kids. I grew up in this kind of neighborhood. They're hard-ass." I sighed and she went on loudly, "*However*, I take your point that it's hard to stab somebody with precision if you have a broken hand. But he might not have come back alone. In fact, he almost certainly did not. He came back with a pal or two. One had a gun, the other had a knife with a big blade."

We had reached the corner of Virginia Avenue and Ellis. It was leafy and shaded. On the far side, there was a five-story apartment block. It had once been red brick, but the bricks had weathered to a dull reddish gray. At the corner, the steel shutters were down over what had once been the deli. The premises were for let. Next door to them, the green upholstery store was still there. I pointed down Ellis.

"It's the second house after the apartment block."

We strolled the fifty yards to the house. The front yard was overgrown with weeds. The drapes were closed, and through the glass, you could see they had become bleached by the sun. The upstairs window looked pretty much the same. There was a low iron gate that gave access to a driveway and a garage at the back. It was closed with a dead bolt and a padlock. I vaulted it and walked down the drive to the back of the house. It was the same as the front. Everything was closed: door, windows, drapes.

As I walked back up the path toward the gate, I saw Dehan climbing the steps to the house next door, and as I drew a little closer, I saw that she was talking to a woman of about fifty in jeans and a sweatshirt, standing on the porch. I vaulted the gate again and joined them, pulling my badge from my jacket pocket.

"Detective John Stone, we're from the local precinct. Do you happen to know who lives next door?"

The woman shook her head, absently wiping her hands with a tea towel.

"No, I was just telling your partner, there ain't nobody lived there for ten, maybe twelve years."

Dehan asked, "Were you here back then, ma'am?"

"We been here over twenty-five years."

I cut in. "Since Al Chester lived here? Nobody moved in after he died?"

"Nobody. It was real sad. House standin' empty like that, with nobody in it, to make it a home."

Dehan asked her, "Did you know Al much?"

The woman smiled. "Well, we was a bit scared of him to begin with, and we didn't thank Joy for movin' him in at first, but when you got to know him, he was as sweet and gentle as you could wish."

Dehan frowned. "She moved him in?"

"I say that, but what I mean is, she helped him to buy the place, organized things for him, like. She told me she wanted him near the church, so he would have folk lookin' out for him. Didn't help him much in the end, though, did it?"

"Did you witness any of the events of that night?"

"People told me about it, but I was out at work at the time, otherwise I would have called the police. Then later that night, well, I was at the church, helpin' out."

I nodded. A bird had started singing in the plane tree behind me. "So you saw Joy there?"

"Yeah, oh yeah! We're both regulars."

Dehan frowned. "You can be sure of that after twelve years? That she was there?"

The woman laughed. "Well, when something like that happens, it kind of fixes everything in your mind, don'it? And him getting killed like that, right next door to my house. Poor soul, and it was his birthday too."

I smiled. "I guess it's never the right day to get stabbed in the heart. So Joy was there and you spoke to her?"

She returned the smile a little uncertainly. "Of course, I didn't mean . . . Yes, I spoke to Joy, for sure. She was all flustered 'cause she'd promised her daughter, Mary, they was gonna watch a movie together."

"You have a remarkable memory."

Another nervous laugh. "Like I said . . ."

"So do you remember at what time Joy left?"

She frowned. "Joy ain't a . . . ?"

Dehan laughed. "Not at all! We just need to get the whole sequence of events clear, so we know who was where and when."

"Sure, well, I guess she left a little after ten. I know she kept sayin' her movie was at ten thirty, and she don't live far from the church."

"Thank you, Mrs. . . . ?"

"Forester, Aileen Forester."

We made our way down the steps, heard the door close behind us, and strolled back, through the midday sunshine, toward the church parking lot where we had left the car. After a minute, Dehan said, suddenly, "Walk and talk. So Ned had motive, means, and opportunity."

"Arguably, but I wouldn't mind being the defense attorney on that case."

"Don't interrupt me when you're thinking."

"Cute."

"Now, who else had motive? Maximilian, Justinian, and Annunziata Chester. I don't know what that company is worth, but if their valve is in every cardiology department in the world, the company is worth hundreds of millions of dollars, and twenty-five percent of that is one hell of a motive."

"It is indeed, especially when it's in the hands of somebody who is bringing shame on a family that is sensitive about its reputation."

"But not just that, Stone. If he'd been sane, or normal, at least, he could have contributed handsomely to the family stock, enhanced their reputation, and contributed positively to the company. Instead, he runs the risk of damaging the family brand beyond repair. So, yeah, we agree. The Chester siblings have a hell of an incentive to get rid of their brother. But what else do we know about them? Did they have opportunity? Did they have the means? I want to know why Martinez never pursued that angle."

I thrust my hands into my pockets and sucked my teeth. "Maybe he'd made up his mind it was Ned. Maybe he spoke to the siblings and they convinced him they were in the clear. There is virtually no reference to them in the report."

I unlocked the car and climbed in behind the wheel. Dehan got in beside me and slammed the door. Then I sat tapping the walnut steering wheel with the key. Dehan watched me for a moment.

"You going to play me a tune or are we going somewhere?"

"I might break into song, with 'Rivers of Babylon.'"

"Boney M.? Seriously?"

"When we get to the station, let's find out exactly who owns the house. Let's find out where the Chester siblings are and drop in to see them. We also need to trace Ned. I want to find out if his fingers still hurt when he looks in the mirror."

"Ouch."

"Yeah."

I cruised slowly back up to the circus and then came down White Plains; all the way, I was forming a map of the area in my mind, positioning the few players we had so far where they had been at the time Al was stabbed, ten thirty on the Friday night.

When we got to the station house on Story and Fteley, Dehan

went to dig up what she could on Ned, and I went to do some background research on the Chester family of eminent surgeons.

For an eminent family, they tended to keep a pretty low profile, but there was enough available from both official and unofficial sources to put together some kind of a picture.

Max Chester was the "patriarch" of the family. That was a position that, had he not become psychotic, Aloysius would have occupied, being the eldest son. Max was the next in line. He had been married to the same woman for almost thirty years and had two children, a boy and a girl. He was the CEO of Chester Cardio-Valves Ltd, as well as a practicing heart surgeon. He lived in New York, in a large apartment in Manhattan.

Justinian Chester, the youngest of the three brothers, was also a surgeon, though his specialization was neurosurgery. He was also married and also had two children. However, in the last five years, he had retired from practice and now devoted his time to research, and his family. He lived in Queens, in a large mansion beside the John Golden Park, by Little Neck Bay. He was listed as one of three directors of CCV Ltd.

The third director was his sister, Annunziata Chester. She was a neurologist, but not a neurosurgeon. She specialized, like her brother, in research, but of a different type. Where Justinian researched and developed equipment for the company, Annunziata researched the functioning of the brain, how we store information as memory, and the impact of degenerative diseases like Alzheimer's and dementia. She, unsurprisingly, was also married, though I could find no reference to children. She divided her time between her vineyards in Northern California and her apartment on Riverside Drive.

I picked up the telephone and called Chester Cardio-Valves Ltd.

"CCV Limited, how may I direct your call?"

"This is Detective John Stone of the NYPD. Put me through to your CEO, Maximilian Chester."

There was a tiny hesitation. "Hold the line, please."

I held the line for three minutes and was about to hang up and get my jacket when the voice came back and said, "Thank you for holding, putting you through."

His voice was quiet and oddly devoid of emotion or feeling. He said simply, "Who is this?"

"Mr. Chester?"

"Yes, this is he. To whom am I speaking, please?"

"Detective John Stone, of the NYPD."

"Why are you calling me?"

"It's about your brother, Mr. Chester."

"Justinian? What has he to do with the police?"

"No, your brother Aloysius, Mr. Chester. The one who was murdered."

There was a very long silence. I was about to ask if he was still there when he spoke abruptly.

"I have nothing to add to the statement I made at the time of his death, Detective Stone. We had disowned Aloysius as far as it was possible for us to do so, and I really have no interest in reviving this business. He shamed our family, and none of us wants anything to do with him or his *legacy*!" He said the word like it made him sick and he wanted to spit it out of his mouth.

"Nevertheless, Mr. Chester, you may have information relating to an ongoing homicide investigation. All we want is to have a short conversation with you and ask you a few simple questions. I hope you'll cooperate with us."

He sighed. "Of course I'll cooperate with the police. But I have a business trip this afternoon and I shan't be back until tomorrow. I'll have my secretary call you as soon as I get back."

"Thank you, Mr. Chester."

He hung up, and I sat looking at the phone. Dehan loomed over me with a paper cup of coffee in each hand. I took one, sipped, and grimaced. She sat.

"I didn't have time to go down to the deli. Be happy with what you've got."

"Our emergence from the caves was predicated on the exact antithesis of that very advice."

"Ned."

"Yes."

"While you were scratching your ass and talking to your rich friends in Queens, I found Martinez and asked him how come he didn't look at Al's brothers and sisters as suspects. He says obviously he did, but they all had alibis and there was not a shred of evidence to connect them to the crime. DA said it was a nonstarter and to focus on Ned."

I shrugged. "Makes sense, I guess. What about Ned?"

"Okay, get this. He's still in the 'hood. He lives at 1942 Chatterton Avenue, his workshop is at the back of his house, at 1957 Bruckner Boulevard."

I raised an eyebrow. "His workshop? What kind of workshop?"

She leaned back and crossed her ankles on the corner of the desk. "Ned was the only suspect Martinez ever had. As far as he was concerned, there could be no other suspect because Ned had done it."

I grunted.

She raised a finger. "The problem was that there was nothing —literally nothing—to tie Ned, or anybody else for that matter, to the scene of the crime."

"I'm aware of that, Dehan. Tell me about the workshop."

"Be patient, Sensei, I'm getting to that. So, about a year after Al died, once the investigation had gone cold, some anonymous relative of Ned's ups and dies too, leaving Ned some money in trust, on the condition that he get some qualifications and makes something of himself."

"Are you kidding me?"

"No, sir. I am tellin' you God's own truth. So, Ned went to community college, learned how to fix cars, and set himself up in a garage: Ned's Auto Repair and Hot Rod Workshop. Seems to be doing well too, 'cause he bought the premises and the house at the back of it an' all."

"Son of a gun . . ."

"You ain't wrong, compadre. That's what he gone done."

I spread my hands. "So we get a court order and we follow the money. Either he's telling the truth and it's a bizarre coincidence, or he's lying and he set it up himself."

"Gotta be a cinch."

"So why didn't Martinez follow this up?"

"He didn't know. The case went cold. Let's face it, Stone. This *is* Babylon, like the woman said. If a fat, old schizophrenic gets mugged and dies, it doesn't take long for people to forget and move on. After a year, the case was forgotten. A hundred other homicides had been committed by then, in the Bronx alone."

"And Ned knew that."

She nodded.

"Okay, that's good work, Dehan."

"Gee, boss, thanks."

"Wiseass. Let's go talk to Ned. I want some answers, and he is going to give them to me."

SIX

It was a five-minute drive to Ned's garage. When we pulled into his forecourt, he stepped out of the workshop with his hands in his pockets, staring at the Jag. He was tall, strongly built, of mixed race, with startling blue eyes. As we climbed out, he jerked his head at my car.

"That's a beautiful car. Jaguar Mark II. Midsixties?"

"1964."

He peered through the window and smiled. "Right-hand drive, walnut, spoke wheels. Man, she's a beauty." He glanced at me, still smiling. "You got the original British plates?"

"Yup, at home in the safe."

He made a face, looking at the car again. "I wouldn't want to work on her, man. You need a specialist. I ain't got that kind of skills."

I smiled and shook my head. "It's okay, I have a guy who looks after her. You Ned Brown?"

He looked at me more closely now, then at Dehan, then back at me. "Who's askin'?"

I pulled out my badge and showed it to him, and Dehan did the same. "I'm Detective John Stone, of the NYPD. This is my partner, Detective Dehan. We'd like to ask you some questions."

He looked genuinely confused. "What about?"

"Al Chester." I pointed at his right hand. The index and middle finger were crooked and slightly misshapen. "Did he do that to you?"

"Yeah, man. You know he did. What's this about? I thought that case was closed."

Dehan smiled. "Not closed. It just went cold, Ned. Now we're going to heat it up again."

He sighed. "Man . . . okay. Let's go inside."

He led us through the dark maw of the entrance into a dimly lit prefab. There were a couple of cars raised up on hydraulic lifts; a couple of others were standing with their hoods up. I saw a total of eight cars. Two of those were custom jobs. There were also a couple of guys in blue overalls who glanced up and watched us cross the workshop toward his small office. Ned was doing okay.

In the office, there was a desk, a kettle, a bunch of dirty mugs, a computer, two hard plastic chairs with wheels, and a couple of calendars with naked women on them. He sat against the desk and folded his arms. Dehan leaned against the doorjamb, and I sat on one of the hard plastic chairs.

I studied him a moment and he studied me back. I tried to visualize him stabbing a sixty-year-old schizophrenic. It wasn't impossible. I spread my hands.

"Convince me you didn't kill Al."

He frowned like he thought I was crazy. "Fuck you!"

I turned and smiled at Dehan. "This is the New Yorker's answer to everything he doesn't understand." I turned back to Ned. "You ever heard of the New York alphabet? Fuckin' A, fuckin' B, fuckin' C . . ."

He shook his head. "You're funny. So what else? You say I did it. Prove it. Meantime, let me get on with my job."

I gave a small shrug. "I'll tell you. Detective Dehan is convinced it's a slam dunk. You did it and she's going to prove it . . ."

"Yeah? Martinez thought the same thing."

"That's Detective Martinez to you, Ned. Me? I'm not convinced yet."

"Oh, you're not? Well, that's real big of you, man. The Great White Hope is gonna save my poor black ass."

"I didn't say that. If you killed Al, you'll take your punishment, and I don't give a damn what color your ass is. What I am telling you, and you'd be smart to listen, is that I am undecided whether I think you did it or not, and I would like to hear reasons why you're not. Talk to me."

He looked around at the walls and the ceiling, like he suddenly found his small office deeply unsatisfactory. "Man! I already been through this one time! How come I have to go through it again?" He gestured at the workshop with his open hand. "I got customers waitin' on their cars, and instead of doin' my job, I gotta be in here, talkin' to you!"

I nodded. "So stop wasting time, Ned. What happened that night? You tried to break into his house."

"Hey! You know what? I changed a lot since then!"

Dehan spoke for the first time. "Cut the bullshit, Ned. What happened? How did you break your fingers?"

"I *told* you guys already! Yeah, he broke my damn fingers and I went to the ER. The guys were with me."

I turned to Dehan. "He's right. There were about six guys involved in fabricating that piece of crap alibi. But thinking about it, at least two of those guys are doing time now. I think we should leave Mr. Brown to get on with his work, and go visit those alibis, start picking them apart. I think that will be quicker."

I went to stand, and he raised both hands. "Okay, okay . . . !" He sighed loudly. "That night, what happened?" He looked up at one of his nude calendars on the wall, over to his left. He didn't seem to see it, though. "Me and the guys was hangin', drinkin' some beers. It was cold, we didn't have nowhere to go, but we didn't wanna go home, know what I'm sayin'? It was early. So we was kind of prowlin' the hood. Then I saw that . . ." He shook his head. "Man, he was some kind of *freak*! Every time I saw him, he'd just do my fuckin' head in, man! He was *fat*, and *big*, with that crazy blond hair, and breathing like that, and *so fuckin' fat*, man! I mean, he must'a been three hundred pounds, at least! He shouldn't *be* that fat! And always breathin' through his fuckin' mouth, makin' that noise . . . Made me crazy." He shook his head. "I just hated that freak, man, more than I can say."

Dehan said, "Enough to kill him?"

"No. But every time I see him, I had to tell him. 'Yo, freak! You a fuckin' freak, man!' Like maybe if I made him realize what a fuckin' freak he was, it might help him to change. You feel me?"

Dehan snarled, "Yeah, you're a regular Fritz Perls."

I said, "You terrified him. He was a vulnerable, sick old man and you scared him half to death."

He avoided my eye, looking at the walls again, sucking his teeth. "Yeah, life's a bitch."

"So what happened that night?"

"I was talkin' to him, man, and he was just, like, ignorin' me, like I wasn't there. Like he was this big white dude and I'm the black dude and he don't need to talk to me, 'cause he's better'n me. You know what I'm sayin' to you? He disrespected me. So I went over and I talked into his fat, ugly face, and I pulled on his arm. And he goes crazy, makin' weird-ass noises, groaning and grunting like a fuckin' hog, and he runs. And I ran after him. All I wanted was to talk to him!"

Dehan snorted. "Why'd you try to get into his house?"

"I told you! I was tryin' to talk to him."

"What about?"

A sudden, incongruous smile split his face, and he emitted a high-pitched shriek of laughter. "I wanted to know why he was so fuckin' *weird*! I wanted to know why he was so fuckin' weird, man . . ." His laughter trailed away.

I nodded. "Yeah, you're a regular behavioral psychologist. A real genius. So what happened, you pushed through his gate. Was that all of you or just you?"

He didn't answer for a moment. His eyes flicked over my face.

"That was all of us. We was pushin' on the door. I got my fingers around it, then he slammed it shut, man. Broke two of my fingers. He did it twice."

Dehan snorted a laugh. "Must have hurt a lot. Witnesses said you were crying like a girl when you left the house."

His lips moved, his eyes narrowed, but he didn't say anything.

I said, "What happened next?"

"I went home, told my mom I got my fingers caught in a car door. She slapped me around 'cause she thought I'd been tryin' to steal cars, and I ain't never done that. But she could see it hurt real bad, so she took me to the ER. They give me some painkillers. Then the bros come to hang out with me at the hospital till they fixed me up."

Dehan said, "What time was that?"

"I don't know, 'bout nine. They give me some powerful drugs, man. I went home to sleep and the bros went home too. That's all that happened, man. You can check with the hospital."

Dehan shook her head. "Ned, you have just admitted to two police officers that the hospital released you an hour and a half before Ned was killed, and that the alibis you had previously provided were false."

His eyes went huge and round and brimmed with tears. "I told you the truth, man. You said if I told the truth, it would be okay. Well, I'm tellin' you the truth." He made a face that was both incredulous and outraged. His voice became shrill. "I weren't in no shape to go killin' nobody! You know how much my hand hurt? It hurt like a *bitch*! All I wanted to do was sleep! Besides, I ain't no killer!"

I pointed around me with my finger like a gun. "This..."

"What about it?"

"Where'd the money come from, Ned?"

He shook his head. "I don't know. They won't tell me."

"Who won't tell you?"

He shrugged and gave a small, helpless laugh. "*I don't know!*"

Dehan sighed. "Okay, you don't know. You're going to have to explain that."

"I don't know, man. I'm tellin' you. It was like ten, maybe eleven years ago. I was in a bad way, I couldn't see no future, I was even thinkin' about joining up, you know?"

"The military?"

He laughed. "No, man. A gang, the Cabras or somethin'."

I raised both hands to stop him. "Let me see if I got this straight. You were lost and had no direction in life, so joining the military was a laughable idea, but joining the Chupacabras made sense?"

"I told you I was in a bad way."

"Yeah, and the idea of getting up at six a.m. and doing a day's work scared the bejaysus out of you."

"Hey!" He became serious. "I ain't up at six, I'm up at five most days. And you know where you'll find me? You gonna find me in this shop, seven days a week. So you can shove your white Republican stereotype right where it ain't so white!"

Dehan snorted. "So you were lost. What happened?"

"We got a letter. It was from some attorney. It said I was the beneficiary in a will. Some relative of mine had deceased or some shit and he left me a packet in a trust. The condition of my gettin' that money was that I had to educate myself and get a trade. So that's what I did. I went to community college, learned about cars. I always fuckin' loved cars, man. So I learned all about them. I did my apprenticeship and then the money was released to me to buy these premises and get the equipment. First the bros used to bring me their rides, know what I'm sayin'? But I wanted to move on, distance myself. So I advertised and I always did a fine job, man. That was my *thing*! I did a *fine job*. I don't care if you black, white, Latino—I don't care *what* you are. I'm workin' on *your car*. You understand me? That's my philosophy, and word got around. Now I'm doin' good. I made a down payment on my house, and I am buyin' it. Only brush I ever had with the law was that whole Al thing. I was wrong to go after him, man, but he made me mad, ignorin' me like that. But I been straight these ten, eleven years."

I sighed. "You ever try to find out who this benefactor was?"

"Yeah, once. The attorney told me it was a condition of the . . . the *thing* . . . the grant, whatever, that I should never know where the money came from."

Dehan laughed and shook her head at the floor. "See, I think that's all bull. I think you took the money that Al had in his house. You heard the rumors, like everybody else, and you got to thinking, what if it was true? Half a million bucks, maybe more. And he was just a fat, ugly, weird freak, and he deserved to die anyway."

"No, man! I ain't like that!"

"So you killed him, you took his money to some crooked shyster and had him set up a trust for you. A perfect cover."

He stared at her for a moment. "You ain't as smart as you think, sister. If I was gonna do that, would I force myself to go through college and get a trade?"

She shook her head. "I don't know, Ned, maybe. I'll let you know when I make up my mind. I'm going to need the contact details for that attorney."

He pulled his cell from his overalls and started scrolling through it, looking for the number. While he did that, I asked him, "You knew about the money?"

He spoke to the screen. "Talk. I never believed it. He looked and talked like maybe he was once rich. But not anymore. He was poor as shit, man." He handed Dehan the phone and she copied the number. He continued talking. "The way he talked, he sounded kind of Ivy League. There were rumors that he was from some rich family, but they disowned him or some shit. They said he'd stashed money in his house. Some people said a quarter of a mill. Others said a million bucks."

"How much was it?"

It was worth a try, but he raised an eyebrow at me and said, "I don't know, cop. Probably nothing. I told you I never believed the story. He was too fat and too stupid to have that kind of dough in his house. It was bullshit."

Dehan handed him back his phone. "Big coincidence though, huh?"

"Yeah, big coincidence. Big coincidence that in New York City, with eight million people, somebody got an inheritance one year after the freak died. Big fuckin' coincidence." He held her eye a moment. "Tell me something, cop. If I was white, would you still think it was a coincidence?"

She nodded. "Yeah."

Hatred flickered in his eyes. "'Cause white people *have* rich relations who can leave them shit, right? But black people? Black people all poor as shit. They don't have rich relations. So if this black dude got a legacy, he must have *stole* that shit, and probably killed some white man while he was doin' it. Ain't that right?"

Dehan heard him out. Then she said, "No, dude, because you tried to break into his house the night he died. Wake up, asshole!"

I stood, suddenly bored with the conversation. "You're full of crap, Ned. You and half a dozen pals tried to break into a sick man's house, and I believe you did it with the intent to hurt him and rob him. That has nothing to do with him being white and you being black. It has everything to do with the fact that you were a scavenging punk and he was vulnerable. Maybe you grew up since then and now you're a decent human being. Maybe not. We'll talk to the attorney and see if we can find out who endowed you with that legacy. If I find out that you killed Al and stole his money, I promise you I will do everything in my power to put you away for the rest of your life." I paused and smiled. "You feel me, man?"

We stepped out onto the forecourt and I went and leaned on the roof of my car. Dehan looked at her watch. "My stomach says it's lunchtime. My watch agrees."

I nodded, only half listening to her. "What's your impression?"

She leaned on the roof opposite me and sighed. "My personal

impression, between you and me, is that he's an asshole who belongs in prison, and it makes me mad that a crook like him gets a second chance when people who work their butts off all their lives just get kicked in the face by the banks and the IRS."

"I'll vote for you. Now, again, but without the soapbox."

She stared at nothing in particular over my shoulder. "I didn't want to believe him, but it had the ring of truth. But, Stone, I am very far from convinced. My logic tells me that he and his pals went back after he was released from the ER unit. That is the most logical conclusion."

I nodded. "That is the most logical conclusion, and it's the one Martinez came to. How do we prove it?"

She shrugged. "We start picking his alibi apart, like you said."

I opened the car and climbed in. She got in the other side and we slammed the doors. I said, "Step one, we apply for a court order to find out who left Ned that money."

She made a face. "I'm not sure you'll get that order, Stone."

"Neither am I, but we have to try. Meantime, let's track down all of Ned's old buddies and see what they're doing these days. We pull them in and question them one by one. And we also go and talk to the Chester siblings. I haven't closed that door yet."

I shoved the key in the ignition and turned it, and the big old engine growled into life. "Right," I said. "A burger and a beer!"

SEVEN

We had chicken and rice and a couple of beers at El Sazon de Olga, talked in circles for half an hour, and made our way back to the 43rd not much clearer in our minds about what we thought had happened that night. At the station, we climbed the steps and knocked on the deputy inspector's door.

"Come, come!"

I pushed it open and stood back for Dehan to go in ahead. The DI was watering his bonsai orange tree on the windowsill and turned to smile at us as we went in.

"Ah," he said. "The Terrible Two." He laughed, and we smiled. "How are things? Margaret has been talking about having you both over for dinner. We must arrange that some day. What are you working on at the moment?"

Dehan looked confused and muttered noises about how that would be nice. I said, "The Al Chester case."

"Sit." He pointed at two chairs, frowned, and resumed his own seat. Then he shook his head and frowned harder. "No, doesn't ring any bells."

"Twelve years ago. Schizophrenic, sixty years old, white male, stabbed in the heart in his living room. Nothing obvious missing, but there were rumors that he had a stash of money in his house. None was ever found."

He nodded a few times. "The case went cold, obviously, or you wouldn't be looking into it."

"Yeah . . ." I sucked my teeth a moment. "It's complicated. There is a very obvious prime suspect. Martinez had the case, and he was convinced that this kid was the killer."

I filled him in on Ned Brown and how he'd had it out for Al and pursued him home that evening. When I had finished, Dehan took over.

"But here's what Martinez didn't know. Just after the case went cold, about a year after Al was killed, Ned Brown inherits a trust fund from an anonymous relative. The terms of the legacy were that he must get his life together, study a trade, and make something of himself. We went to see him today, and he's set up as a car mechanic with his own garage, servicing custom cars. He's bought the premises, and he is buying his own house."

The inspector flopped back in his chair. "So you think the rumors about the money were true, he killed Al and took the money."

Dehan said, "Yes."

I sighed. "The evidence certainly seems to suggest that, sir, but there are problems."

"Such as?"

"For a start, his hand. I don't believe he'd have been able to fire a gun or stab Al in the chest with two broken fingers. If he went back, he did not go alone. He went with at least one other person . . ."

"So look into his old associates, see how many of them also had rich, anonymous family members."

"Yes, sir, we plan to do that, but there is also the fact that it seems very unlikely that Ned would dream up an idea like setting up a trust fund for himself, especially one on terms like these, forcing himself to go to college and make something of himself."

He made a face. "You're right, it does seem a little unlikely. How do you want to tackle it?"

"The first thing I'd like to do, sir, is to get a court order compelling the attorneys who are acting as executors of the will to reveal the identity of Ned's benefactor."

He grunted and scratched his head. "That's a tall order. A person is entitled to anonymity, John, and the attorneys are compelled, as executors, to respect that anonymity. The courts, furthermore, are compelled to respect it unless you can produce very cogent reasons why they shouldn't."

I smiled. "Well, that money might be the proceeds from a burglary turned homicide. That's pretty cogent."

"Oh, certainly it is! But *is* it the proceeds of a burglary turned homicide? What reasons have you for such a belief, other than a coincidence which is not, in fact, that much of a coincidence? Are your *reasons* cogent, or are they purely circumstantial? I am afraid they're circumstantial and not very cogent. I'm afraid that all you have, at best, are suspicions. And we cannot have the general public victimized and harassed by the police simply on the strength of their suspicions. Imagine where that would end! Yes, it *is* a coincidence. But it is also possible that it is no more than that, a coincidence."

I sighed. "That's what I thought."

"Give me a report of what you have so far. I'll pass it on to the DA and ask her to talk to a sympathetic judge, see what we can do. But I have to be honest, I don't hold out much hope, especially as there are other avenues you can pursue."

I nodded. "There is another avenue I personally find more interesting."

"Oh, what's that?"

Dehan answered. "Well, sir, like he said, Stone is a little skeptical of the Ned Brown angle. But there is also Al's own family. They certainly had motive."

"Indeed?"

I watched his expression turn rigid as she filled him in on the

Chesters and on Al's background. When she had finished, he sat nodding for a while. "You two certainly have a genius for finding the cases that will cause the most embarrassment at the country club, don't you?"

Dehan didn't flinch. "That is our primary criterion, sir."

He smiled at her, then narrowed his eyes. "I wish I was sure you were joking. You realize that Max and Justinian Chester are close friends of the mayor's, don't you?" We didn't answer, and he sighed. "All right, do what you have to do, but please tread with care. I'll see if we can't find a judge to sign off on this will."

We thanked him and left. On the stairs going down to the detectives' room, Dehan glanced at me over her shoulder. "We're subtle. I think we're subtle, don't you?"

"I think we're pretty subtle, Dehan."

"Drop the Chesters as suspects in at the last minute. Fear of upsetting the Chesters, and their pal the mayor, equals pressure on the DA and the judge to sign off on the disclosure order. Nice."

"Immoral. It shouldn't be necessary."

"Preachin' to the choir, Mr. Stone. Preachin' to the choir."

We spent the rest of the afternoon looking into Ned's old pals, trying to find out what became of them and where they'd wound up. At six p.m., Dehan leaned back in her chair and rubbed her hands over her face.

"Julio Chavez and his brother Ernesto, fifteen and sixteen at the time of Al's death, both joined the Chupacabras in 2008. A year later, they were arrested, tried, and convicted of the murder of Geronimo Paez and his family. He was an informer for Vice, and it was a punishment killing. They went down in 2009 and are serving several consecutive life sentences upstate, with no chance of parole, because of the, and I quote, 'hideous nature of the killings.'"

She raised her boots and crossed her ankles on the corner of the desk. "I called Nick, he investigated Paez's murder. I asked him if he remembered the Chavez brothers. He said he'd never forget them. I asked him if he got the impression that they were sitting on a lot of money. I gave him the background to the Al Chester case. He said obviously he could not know, but he definitely did not have that impression." She shrugged her shoulder. "In any case, I think we should go talk to them."

I nodded. "Anything else?"

She grinned. "Yeah, Lenny 'Lucky' Marley, 2010 he mugged a Navy SEAL in one of the parking lots on Newbold Avenue, by the Circle. I say he mugged him. I should say he tried to mug him, at gunpoint. The SEAL broke his arm in three places and then ruptured his liver. Lucky Marley died in hospital. No action was taken against the SEAL."

"Who says the system doesn't work? That's what I call justice. Anything else?"

"No, what about you?"

"Nothing of any use. Delroy Evans, arrested in 2008 trying to hold up a liquor store on White Plains Road. He was high, and they found some meth in his car. They found more in his house, and now he's serving ten years at Attica. His cousin, Chicane Evans."

"Chicane? Seriously?"

"I guess Dad was a motor sports enthusiast. Anyway, Chicane died of a heroin overdose in 2015. He still lived with his parents on Thieriot. I called them and spoke to his mother. She laughed when I asked if around 2007 or 2008 Chicane seemed suddenly to have more money than usual. She said I must be crazy and told me his dying of an overdose was the best thing that ever happened to them."

"Nice."

"People are. Finally, last member of Ned's merry band, Simon 'el Loco' Ibanez. Stole a Corvette from a Sunoco gas station while the owner was paying for the gas. Nobody was chasing him, but still he hit a hundred and twenty down Castle Hill Avenue and ran straight into the back of a truck transporting quick-set liquid concrete to a construction site. The Corvette was a mess, but also the truck dumped part of its load into the car through the shattered windshield, and Ibanez drowned in concrete. Not a nice way to go."

She stared at me for a long time with no expression. Finally, she said, "That's true? It's not a joke?"

"No, Dehan. It's true. I wouldn't joke about something like that."

"No, sure. It's a terrible way to die. But hey, at least he achieved his ambition of becoming a hardened criminal, right?"

She slapped her thigh and laughed immoderately for a while. Even Mo at the next desk laughed while he typed. She made a high-pitched noise and shook her head.

"Hardened criminal . . ."

My phone rang, and as I answered it, I said to Dehan, "Arrange a visit to upstate for tomorrow afternoon or the following morning." To the phone, I said, "Yeah, Stone."

"Detective John Stone of the New York Police Department, Forty-Third Precinct?"

"Yeah, that one."

"I am Maximilian Chester's personal secretary. I am calling to inform you that Mr. Chester will receive you at his home in Manhattan at ten thirty precisely tomorrow morning. He will be free for half an hour, so he would be grateful if you could confine your questions to that time frame. Sixty-nine Leonard Street, the penthouse."

"We'll be there." I hung up. Dehan was still on the phone. When she hung up, I said, "Okay, we are meeting Maximilian Chester tomorrow at his Manhattan penthouse at ten thirty precisely. We are granted exactly half an hour in The Presence."

"Yeah, I gathered. Ernesto is in hospital with a broken jaw. We meet Julio tomorrow evening. It's a six-hour drive, so I figured if we leave around eleven or twelve, we'll be there about six. I said we'd confirm the precise time when we were en route."

"Good." I bounced a pencil a few times on its eraser. "The one thing that stands out to me, Dehan, is that there is no indication that any of Ned's friends suddenly came into money at the same time he did. In fact, within a year of Al's murder, the gang seemed to break up. The Chavez brothers joined the Chupacabras, and the others just kind of went their separate ways. None of them showed evidence of having come into a quarter of a million bucks overnight."

She pursed her lips, and her eyes became abstracted. She reached behind her head and tied her hair in a knot. "So his broken hand has put him in a real bad mood. This kid is not, by nature, a killer. But he doesn't like Al."

"Yeah, I got that impression," I said dryly.

"Shut up. He doesn't like him and he never has—but now Al has broken his hand, and that has made him real mad. So when he comes out of the ER, he tells his pals he's going home to sleep. He told us he was a little high from the painkillers, but he is also hyped up with rage and pain. So he takes a nine-millimeter and his mom's kitchen knife . . ."

I went to speak, but she raised a hand. "I know what you're going to say. He had a mean old knife in his pocket already. But I told you, Mr. Stone, that he is high on a dangerous mixture of painkillers, pain, and adrenaline—and maybe a little weed—and he wants a *real* knife. Something like his mom's big, bad kitchen knife, with a six-inch blade. He takes that and his nine-millimeter down to Al's and gets there about twenty-five past ten. He breaks in while Al is watching his thirty-first rerun of *Murder She Wrote*. Al hears him and panics. Al's panic makes Ned panic, and he fires his gun. The pain from his broken fingers—or the fact that he's using his left hand, take your pick—make the shots go wide. Al knocks the gun from his hand, and Ned plunges the kitchen knife, two-handed, into his heart. He then ransacks the place, searching for his money, and finds it."

I sighed, screwed up a small ball of paper, and threw it at her. She caught it left-handed and threw it back. I said, "He then uses his extensive knowledge of finance, trust funds, and equity management to set himself up as the beneficiary of an anonymous benefactor. You can't believe that, Dehan."

"I don't. I think it's exactly what I said to him back at the garage. He found himself sitting on a rucksack full of money, maybe half a million bucks, and took it to a high street shyster, told him, 'Okay, I got half a million bucks, what the hell can I do with it?' And the shyster came up with the idea of the trust fund." She gestured at me with both hands. "Who is going to believe that a petty crook like Ned would come up with an idea like that? Nobody. It's perfect. Besides..."

"What?"

"We got nothing else. You know as well as I do that neither the brothers nor the sister did it. They wouldn't know where to begin."

"How do you know that? It's too soon to reach that kind of conclusion. And anyway, they might know a man who does."

"So now we have a hit man to add into the equation?" She sighed and shook her head. "Jonathan, Jonathan, how many times do I have to tell you? *Entia non sunt multiplicanda, praeter necesitatem!*"

Mo looked over his shoulder at her. Then he looked at me resentfully. "This is your fault, Stone. Before, she was just a pain in the ass with an attitude. Now she's all that, plus she talks Latin. What kind of freaks are you?"

Dehan snarled, "Get back in your hole, Mo." To me, she said, "The simple explanation is there, Stone. You're looking for a complicated explanation when you don't need one."

"I know what Occam's razor states, Dehan."

"It's called Occam's razor."

"I know. I taught it to you..."

"It means don't complicate matters, Stone. The simplest answer is probably the right one."

"Did you book us somewhere to stay?"

"Same as before, Kilburn Manor, it's a restored old manor house, furnished with genuine antiques. Then I thought we could dine at the Riverside Steak House. It was very good last time, wasn't it, darling?"

She said it all with a very straight face while I tried not to laugh. Mo was staring at the ceiling, shaking his head. "Please, God, make me blind. Make me deaf. Better still, make them stay in Malone! Please!"

I stood and pulled on my jacket. "Come on, darling," I said to her, raising an eyebrow. "I don't think I like the atmosphere in this establishment. I find it distinctly *grossier*!"

Mo snarled over his shoulder, "Aaah, take a hike, willya!"

Dehan pulled on her jacket. "We'll be far too busy for that. We'll be working, you know. Not on holiday!" With that, she took my arm. "Shall we go, darling?"

"The Jaguar awaits, darling."

The last thing I heard before we made our way out to the car was Mo asking sweet Jesus to give him strength.

EIGHT

Max had his penthouse at the top of a handsome 1930s building at the corner of Leonard Street and Church Street. I parked at a meter out front, and we stepped into a lobby that looked more like a luxury hotel than an apartment block. He had his own elevator, and we had to buzz at an entry phone so his personal secretary could let us board it.

While we were riding up to the eleventh floor, Dehan gave me her expressionless look. "We had a Yale key and a dead bolt. Back door was a chub and a dead bolt. We had four floors and we had to climb the stairs."

I shrugged. "Your father should have been a doctor, like his mother told him."

She nodded several times, still with no expression. "Witty. Remind me why I married you."

"Because I'm witty."

"Pretty sure it wasn't that."

The doors hissed open, and we stepped into a spacious lobby about the size of my open-plan living room and kitchen. There was wall-to-wall deep burgundy carpeting and nasty Louis XV sofas and chairs in duck egg blue and gilt, with legs that seemed to have rickets. There was also a walnut escritoire inlaid with ivory, and a couple of coffee tables that might have been Chinese. All in all, the furnishings were probably worth as much as a small family home.

An invisible door opened, and a bunny girl in a business suit stepped through, cocked her hip, and smiled like she was sitting on the bonnet of a Mustang fastback.

"Dr. Chester will see you now. Please follow me."

We followed her through the door into a large, comfortable drawing room with gleaming parquet floors and lots of suede furniture set around a bronze firepit in the middle of the floor. The wall opposite was plate glass and offered a view of the Hudson across the rooftops of the Financial District. It was a good view.

Our bunny girl swung her hips with reckless disregard for the Ming vases, Picasso statuettes, and Phoenician pots that stood dotted here and there along our way, and led us through the drawing room and down a passage to a somber, mahogany door. Here she tapped lightly and pushed it open.

"Your ten thirty is here, Dr. Chester." Then she stood back, holding the door, cocked her hip, and gave Dehan a special "I hate you because you're beautiful" smile. "Please come in."

The study was everything that Maximilian Chester was not but wanted to be. For a start, it was big, while he, standing beside his desk and approaching us with extended hand, was not. He was probably five-two in his shoes.

The study reeked of old-world elegance: the walls were paneled in oak; there was a nineteenth-century sideboard with a silver tray of spirits in hand-cut Waterford crystal decanters. There were oak bookcases that, here and there, were scuffed and scratched from a couple of hundred years of good use. Queen Anne occasional tables sat discreetly, but elegantly, beside ancient Chesterfields around a marble fireplace. His desk, also oak, looked to my untrained eye as though it might be late Jacobean. There was a smell of furniture wax and pipe smoke that lingered reassuringly in the air.

He, on the other hand, was the only thing in the room that was out of place and jarring. His suit, in dark blue silk, was Italian and double-breasted, cut to hang like a roman toga. His shoes, slip-ons with a tassel, were also Italian and, like the suit, proclaimed their high price loudly and shinily. He, unlike his office and his pedigree, was vulgar.

He spoke as he shook our hands. "Dr. Maximilian Chester. Take a seat. Can I offer you a drink?"

We showed him our badges and I shook my head. "No, thank you, Dr. Chester. I'm Detective Stone and this is Detective Dehan, and we are on duty."

"I know who you are. So does the mayor. He speaks highly of you. He says you have a reputation for causing problems for people in high places." We all sat in the ancient Chesterfields and he leaned forward with his elbows on his knees. "Are you going to cause problems for me?"

I was about to answer, but Dehan spoke first. "We don't cause problems for people in high places, Dr. Chester. We cause problems for people who think they can get away with murder. Some of those people live in low buildings, others live in penthouses. But we don't go after them just because they are in high places. We go after them because they are criminals."

He regarded her without expression. "Do you think I am a criminal?"

She smiled sweetly. "That's what we are here to find out."

He turned to face me. "Are you as blunt as she is?"

"Yes."

"Good." He leaned back in his chair. "Then we can cut to the chase and speak plainly. You suspect that one of us was responsible for having Aloysius killed."

I was about to tell him we didn't suspect it, but it was a possibility we had to explore. Instead, Dehan said, "Did you?"

"No."

I crossed one leg over the other and studied his face. It was still completely expressionless. I said, "Great, well, now we've sorted that out, maybe you could answer some questions for us."

"Glad to."

"The house where Al lived . . ."

"His name was Aloysius. As far as I know, he was not working for the Italian Mafia."

"Aloysius, the house where he lived . . ."

"I believe it was in the Bronx, close to the practice of that Harvard quack friend of his."

"1932 Ellis Avenue."

"What of it?"

"When Aloysius died, that house passed to you . . ."

"I had no idea. I own well in excess of two hundred properties worldwide, Detective Stone."

"Why would he leave it to you?"

"He didn't. He had no capacity to make a will. When he died, there was the question of his shares in the family company. Our lawyers looked into it immediately because we didn't want some outsider muscling in on the family business. It was anybody's guess whom he might have left them to. Their instructions were to contest any will he might have made on the grounds, as I have said, that he was not fit to know what he wanted, or to make a rational decision. As it was, he had not left a will, so his possessions were shared out among his siblings. I didn't even know I owned it."

"Apparently it has been sitting vacant since he died."

"Oh."

"May we go and inspect it?"

He shrugged. "If you think it will do any good after twelve years, be my guests." He rose and went to his desk, flipped a switch, and spoke. "Penny, who has the keys to 1932 Ellis Avenue, in the Bronx?"

"The *Bronx*?"

"Yes, Penny, the Bronx."

"I guess Benny has them . . ."

"Get them. Have them sent to the Forty-Third Police Precinct in the Bronx, for the attention of Detectives Stone and Dehan. Have it done now."

"Yes, Dr. Chester."

He flipped the switch back and looked at his watch. "Was there anything else?"

I smiled. "Yes, Dr. Chester. I believe relations between you and your older brother were not good."

He returned to his chair. "Good? How could they be good? He set about deliberately humiliating and disgracing his family. Medicine, the Hippocratic oath, service to the public through medicine, all of these things have been sacred to our family for generations. He made a mockery of it all.

"Aloysius wrote an article in his student paper reviling the traditions of our family, accusing us of rampant hypocrisy and exploiting a corrupt, bankrupt system to line our pockets with gold. And that was just the beginning. Then he started smoking pot, taking acid and other hallucinogens, publicly displaying himself in scandalous orgies . . . It brought shame on all of us. We all vowed never to speak to him again and we disowned him."

I nodded like I understood. "It must have been very worrying that he owned twenty-five percent of the family company."

"Worrying?" He suppressed a bitter laugh. "Oh, yes, it was worrying. Especially as he was driving himself steadily out of his own mind. He went off to Mexico, with some Mexican girl. They lived in the desert, fornicating in some shack, drinking tequila and taking peyote and LSD. Who knew what the hell he was capable of doing in that state? He once told me he planned to *give* his twenty-five-percent share of the company to a commune! People's lives *depend* on the products our company makes! And this . . . this . . . *narcissistic*, self-indulgent *parasite* was going to put that company into the hands of a bunch of drug addicts who thought it was *cool* to destroy the neural pathways in their brains by taking acid!" He nodded several times. "So yes, it was, as you say, worrying."

I sighed. "I am not unsympathetic, Dr. Chester; I have little time for the drug culture myself, but I have to put it to you that what you and your siblings had was a very powerful motive for murder."

His reaction surprised me. His eyebrows shot up and he barked a loud laugh. "Do you think we didn't contemplate it? Do you think we didn't *discuss* it? Of course we did! But, and this may seem trite to you, accustomed as you are to hardened criminals and murderers, but my view—and we all agreed—was that we had all taken the Hippocratic oath, and we could not knowingly, intentionally, kill another human being. So instead, we set the company lawyers to tying Aloysius up in so much legal tape that he would never be able to do the company any harm.

"Of course, by the time he got back from his protracted tour of South and Central America, he had driven himself to the brink of total psychosis, and that offered us a far simpler, and entirely lawful, solution. We had him diagnosed as a paranoid schizophrenic and put him in the care of Dr. Epstein."

"Who had known him at Harvard."

"Apparently."

"Was that a deliberate choice? How did you come to choose him?"

He sighed heavily. His gaze was lost in the Persian rug on the floor. "That a member of our family should be brought to this . . ." He blinked and met my eye. "He was living rough in the Bronx, in the area of the Hugh J. Grant Circle, sleeping on benches and in doorways. There is apparently some absurd church in that vicinity that ministers to the poor and the homeless. There he met a woman who gave him some help. It emerged that she worked for a Harvard-trained psychiatrist who worked in the area, and also had this desire to minister to the poor and the homeless. We approached him and, for an annual retainer, he took care of Aloysius. They also assisted in the purchase of his house. He and Aloysius were of similar age and both from Harvard Med School, so it is not that odd that they should have known each other."

"Did you ever go and visit him at his home in the Bronx?"

"Certainly not."

"How about your brother and sister?"

"You'll have to ask them, but I very much doubt it." He glanced at his watch again. "Have you many more questions? I am going to have to ask you to leave soon, I am afraid. I have a very busy day ahead of me."

I considered him for a moment, then said, "Just one more question, Dr. Chester."

He sighed heavily. "Yes?"

"Do you know much about the setting up of trust funds, equity, trusts, wills..."

He shrugged. "I am no expert, but it is not a complicated business. Though usually my attorneys would take care of anything like that. That's what I pay them for. Why?"

I shook my head. "Nothing important. Thank you for your time. You have been very helpful."

He made a face. "I doubt it. Penny will see you out."

He returned to his desk, summoned the bunny girl, and she led us, in the wake of her swinging hips, back to the exclusive elevator, which took us back down to the mortal plane.

We had packed a couple of bags the night before, so we were ready to go, and as we stepped out into the sunshine, I threw her the keys. "Your turn."

She caught them, unlocked the driver's door, and we climbed into the Jag. Neither of us spoke as she pulled into Church Street and followed the Avenue of the Americas north toward the Holland Tunnel. She was silent, watching the road ahead, as we plunged beneath the vast, oppressive weight of the Hudson, following the stream of red lights toward Jersey. I also watched the road ahead, but my mind was elsewhere, thinking about Maximilian Chester and his family.

We emerged into the sunlight again on the I-78 in Jersey City. At St. Peter's Cemetery, we turned north and joined the steady flow toward the I-95. Then, finally, Dehan said, "I don't buy it."

I smiled at her. "I didn't think you would, but tell me why."

"Okay, don't jump down my throat, this is just for starters, but it just *feels* wrong, Stone. I mean, like he said, what would be their motive?"

"You're thinking of the three of them as a unit?"

She looked vaguely taken aback. "Well, no . . ."

"You say that as though you mean maybe, or yes."

"Well, I was kind of thinking of them as having a collective motive. I guess."

"Let's just focus on Max for now, until we've spoken to Justinian and Annunziata. They might have a completely different motivation."

"Okay . . ." She sighed. "What would *his* motive be?"

"Well, to begin with, by killing Al, he would immediately add eight point thirty-three percent of many millions of dollars to his personal net worth, because Al's twenty-five-percent share would be shared between the three of them. He would also remove a very big, potential problem from his life . . ."

"No, I don't get that. That's a fallacy. How could Al be a potential problem?"

I smiled. "Sure, as he was, but imagine if he recovered enough to be declared capable of taking his seat on the board."

She stared at me. "Is that possible?"

I shrugged. "He's not a chronic schizophrenic. His psychosis was induced by chemical abuse that caused damage to his brain. How neurons and glia work and whether they regenerate is something of a mystery, Dehan. And neurology—a field in which two of the siblings work as researchers, by the way—is advancing by leaps and bounds every year. Nobody would know that better than Justinian and Annunziata.

"That is just one way in which Al could cause them problems if he was alive. But basically, anything that challenged their legal control of his shares was a risk. And there is no shortage of lawyers who'd be happy to give that a go.

"And finally, there is not only the years of shame and embarrassment that he had already caused the family, but there was the ongoing shame of having him living in a small house in the Bronx, attending, as he put it, a Harvard quack's clinic. That was a shadow that must have hung over him every day."

She sighed. "Yeah, but he kind of covered that, Stone. He took the Hippocratic oath and, frankly, I thought he sounded sincere. He may be a cantankerous old fool, but I believed he was sincere. And then there was the point he made, why risk it? He didn't phrase it like that, but it was pretty much what he meant. They had him diagnosed as psychotic, in care and tied up in legal tape. By the time he was killed, there was nothing he could do to them anymore. So why wait till then to kill him? If they were going to have him iced, they would have done it a lot sooner. Why take the risk if it wasn't necessary?"

I looked at her. "Iced?"

"Yeah. You got a pwoblem wid de way I tawk? I'm from de Bwanx, see?"

"Captivating. Let's see how it plays out. Personally, I found Maximilian Chester a fraud, unconvincing, and a narcissistic egomaniac with no taste."

"With no taste? That bad, huh? Your Honor, I would ask for the reinstatement of capital punishment in view of the fact that the accused not only murdered his brother, but also had no taste."

"What can I say? I suspect the Chester siblings have a story to tell. We'll see what it is."

She wagged a finger at me. "This time you are going to be wrong, Stone, and I will be right. You *know* Ned is the guy. You're just trying to be smart. Occam's razor."

I shrugged. "You may be right. I think it is too soon to call."

"You know I'm right."

I didn't answer, and after ten minutes of silent driving, as we merged onto the New Jersey Turnpike and accelerated out of the city, she sniffed and said, "So, no taste, huh?" She gave her head a little twitch. "What was it exactly that was in bad taste . . . ?"

NINE

We arrived in Malone at six that evening, having stopped along the way for lunch. We didn't drop our stuff at the B&B but went straight to the correctional facility. I had called ahead from the car to give them our ETA, and they were expecting us when we arrived.

We showed our badges at the gate, and an officer came to greet us and show us to the interview room. As we made our way down the grim corridors, through vast, echoing steel gates, the officer looked at us curiously. "Chavez brothers, huh?"

I nodded. "Yeah."

"I guess they told you Ernesto is in hospital."

"They did. What happened?"

"Gangs. I don't know why they let gang members hang out together like that. Those brothers should have been separated. Instead, as a reward for good behavior, they get lodged together, in the same cell, and they hang with the Chupacabras, their old gang. You let that happen, it stands to reason pretty soon you gonna have gang warfare, right? So, a bunch of Angels got hold of Ernesto in the can, broke his leg, his arm, and his jaw before anybody noticed. It ain't right, but what can you do? It's the system."

I nodded, wondering if he was driving at something. "I guess so. The Angels have a problem with him?"

"Yeah, he weren't too smart. He called the head honcho a *maricon*. That's a queen in Spanish. So now the Angels are out for his blood. If we hadn't showed up on time, they would have killed him. Like I said, it's war." He shook his head. "All the system does is, it don't *eliminate* crime, it just moves it into the jails, where it's intensified. They keep right on killing, stealing, maiming, selling dope—they're just doing it behind walls."

I thought about what he was saying for a moment, then asked him, "Tell me something, the Chavez brothers, are they taken care of?"

He stopped, with his hand on a steel door. "By the Cabras?"

"Yeah."

He shrugged, made a face. "Not more than any other member inside. They look out for each other, senior members get cigarettes and care packets. But not Julio and Ernesto." He unlocked the door. "But if you're asking, will there be reprisals for what happened to Ernesto? For sure." He yanked the door open.

I nodded. "Thanks."

We went into a small room, about fifteen feet square. There was a table with one chair on one side and two facing it on the opposite side. A chain, bolted to the floor, rose through a hole in the middle of the table with a pair of manacles on the end. Dehan grabbed a chair, and I stood looking down at the manacles. I spoke absently, half to myself.

"One day, he was a cute baby, then he got spots and hormones and he was a troubled youth. When he was hanging with Ned, he could still have made it back, could still have found a path home. But then he made that decision, and in a second, it was too late. Sliding doors." I turned and looked down at Dehan. "You know what the officer was saying?"

"About keeping the crime inside walls?"

I nodded. "Do you sometimes wonder if there are invisible walls around some parts of the Bronx?"

She nodded. "In every country, in every city." She fixed me with her eye. "It's the big problem with modern society, Stone. Nobody knows what to do with the trash."

I laughed. "You saying we should recycle criminals? That's pretty Orwellian."

She shook her head. "It's been proved that recycling doesn't work. Modern incinerators are faster and cleaner."

I was saved from having to answer that remark by the door being pulled open with an iron echo, and Julio Chavez being brought in. He was dressed in an orange jumpsuit and had manacles around his ankles and his wrists. He wasn't big, but he was hard and wiry, and he had the dead eyes of a man who has learned to kill. The tattoos on his face said he was a Chupacabra, and that he'd burnt his bridges.

The officers brought him to the chair, sat him down, and manacled his wrists. The one with the keys said, "We'll be right outside, Detectives. He gives you any trouble, just shout."

We thanked them and they left, slamming the big steel door behind them.

Chavez looked at me, then took his time looking at Dehan, then he leaned to the side and took his time spitting on the floor.

I smiled and gave a small laugh, then leaned my back against the wall.

"Nothing left to lose, huh, Chavez?"

"Fock you."

I gave the floor my best lopsided smile. "Yeah, well, that's something you won't be doing for a while, right?"

Dehan looked at me and snorted. "He won't be giving, but hey, he might be takin'."

I studied his face for any reaction. There wasn't any. I cocked my head. "It's a funny thing, you know, about guys like you who live on the edge. Often, they will feel like they have nothing left to lose . . ."

A look of disgust distorted his features. "What is this? NYPD sending out inspirational fockin' gurus now?"

I ignored him and went on. "But it's then, when they feel they have nothing left to lose, that they realize what little they have left is what they most treasure, what they can least afford to let go of."

He turned to Dehan. "What the fock is he talkin' about?"

She leaned forward and looked into his face. "I think, *pendejo*, that he's talking about your brother."

Then I saw the reaction. His face flushed, and his eyes turned bright with anger. "What about my brother?"

I pushed off the wall and thrust my hands into my pockets, still looking down at the floor. "You know, I am willing to bet that, for all this hard man show you put on, underneath, what you are, basically, is a family guy. I'll bet that was all you ever really wanted, a family. Am I right?"

He didn't answer. He just watched me. I went on.

"But the big, bad world came along and they stole your family from you." I stepped over to the empty chair, looked into his angry face, and knew that I was reaching him. "What was it, Mom had a monkey? Turning tricks to pay for her habit? And Daddy? Well, he was probably just a gamblin' man, way down in New Orleans. And you and Ernesto got your education on the streets, right? It was all you knew. That's why you joined the Cabras, right? Because it was the nearest thing you believed you would ever find to a family. You and Ernesto, family, welcomed into the Chupacabras, your new family. Loyalty, devotion, protection . . ." I turned and looked at Dehan and repeated, "Protection?"

She shook her head. "Seems to me the Chupacabras family ain't doing much protecting here, Stone."

I watched her for a long moment, chewing my lip. "I was really disturbed," I said, and then turned to face him, "to learn of what had happened to your brother. How many bones did they break?" I didn't wait for an answer. "Who was it? The Puerto Ricans? The Jamaicans? Maybe the Angels . . . ? They all outnumber you in here, don't they?" I looked back at Dehan. "I think maybe, for his own protection, perhaps we should make a recommendation that Ernesto be moved, to a more secure prison, like Attica."

Dehan affected a frown and turned to Julio. "Do they have Angels in Attica? I'm pretty sure they do . . ."

"Don't do that." He shook his head. "If you send him to Attica on his own, they'll kill him. I need him here, where I can protect him."

I hooked the leg of the chair with my foot and pulled it out. I sat and frowned at the tabletop. "It sounds to me, Julio, as though you are asking me for a favor."

"What you want from me?"

"Not much. And while I am at it, let me make you aware of something. What I want, I can get from you or any of your pals from back in 2007. You are my easiest option, not my only option. Are we clear?"

"What do you want, cop?"

"I want to know who went with Ned Brown to kill Al Chester, on the night of the twenty-third of November, 2007."

He narrowed his eyes at me, glanced sidelong at Dehan. "That the crazy guy?"

Dehan answered, "Yeah, Julio, that's the crazy guy. How many people did Ned kill on the twenty-third of November, 2007?"

He shook his head. "He didn't kill nobody that night."

"Bullshit. That's bullshit and you know it."

"No, it ain't. That ain't what happened that night. Ned followed the guy to his house. We was havin' a laugh, scarin' the guy. Then Ned got crazy 'cause he said the old guy disrespected him. That gotta be punished, right? But when we was pushin' in the door, he slammed it closed on Ned's fingers, broke a couple. We had to take him to the ER, man."

We stared at him for a long moment, then I turned to Dehan and sighed. She shook her head.

"That's the story everyone knows, Julio. What we are asking about is what happened next."

"I told you what happened next. We took him to the hospital, to fix his fingers."

I nodded. "And they did. They fixed his fingers and dosed him with painkillers. You left the hospital, at about ten p.m., and then Ned and at least one other of your gang went back to Ned's house. You took a nine-millimeter pistol and a kitchen knife and you went to kill Al."

"You're crazy."

I turned to Dehan. "We're wasting our time here."

He shook his head. "No, man, listen. We lied to give him an alibi, that's true. That's what bros do. But what happened was, he was stoned on the painkillers and he wanted to smoke some weed on top of that to kind of take away the pain, 'cause his fingers were hurtin' bad. So he went back to his house, with Chevronne, and she was gonna give him a *hard* time. She thought he'd been stealing cars, man."

"Chevronne."

"His mom. She was real mad at him. We didn't want to get in the middle of that, so we just went home. That is all that happened that night, I'm tellin' you."

I thought for a moment, then stood. "Let's go. We'll talk to Evans . . ."

Chavez frowned. "Delroy?"

"Yeah, he was there that night, right?"

"Where's he at?"

"Attica."

"Shit . . . What's he in for, man?"

Dehan spread her hands and her jaw went slack. "Yeah, and say, how's your mom? How about a chocolate brownie? Cut the crap, Chavez! You got something for us or not? You want Ernesto here or you want us to send him to the Angels?"

"No, no." He shook his head again. "Don't do that. I'll tell you what happened. Just leave Ernesto here with me, okay?"

I sat.

Dehan said, "Talk already."

He slumped back, closed his eyes, and took a deep breath. When he released it, he started to talk.

"We went with Ned to the ER. We was waitin' a long time. We kept hasslin' the nurses and shit, but they didn't want to see us. In the end, they called security and these big mothers come and say, 'Hey, you want we should break the fingers on your other fockin' hand? So shut the fock up and sit down. They'll see you when they ready!' So we waited."

Dehan interrupted him. "You're breaking my heart, Julio. Nice boys can't catch a break no more! Just cut to the chase, will you?"

"I'm getting there, man. So finally they see him. They patch him up and the doctor, she gave him like a shitload of painkillers. I don't know what they was, but he was, like, high, you know?"

He stopped and swallowed. Looked at the door a moment and continued. "So, when we got out of the hospital, it was like real cold? And that was like, it woke him up, know what I'm sayin'? The cold woke him up and suddenly he was real mad at the crazy guy, because he was like sayin' all the time, 'That *pendejo* disrespected me, the son of a bitch. I'm gonna kill him.' An' you know, there was always this story about how the crazy guy had like a million bucks in his house, in a box or some shit. And so Ned starts to say, we should go get that fockin' money. Me? I never believed it was true. None of us believed that shit. But it was like Ned was high and kind of crazy. So I say, 'No, man, I don't wanna do that shit,' but Lucky, he says yeah, he's gonna go and get his Taurus from his house, and they gonna go an' teach that crazy motherfocker some respect. Know what I'm saying? An' tha's all I know. I went home to watch TV."

He looked at us both in turn. Then he shrugged and looked down at his manacles.

"Few days later, I heard that the crazy guy had been killed. So I says to Ned, 'You some badass motherfocker, man! You killed that old dude?' He says, 'Yeah, man. I stabbed that son of a bitch in the heart with a knife.' He weren't shot with no nine-millimeter. He was stabbed in the heart, way Ned likes to do it. That's what he told me."

"What about the money?"

"I don't know about that, man. He never told me nothin' about that. We all went our separate ways then. Me and Ernesto, we wanted to get more serious, you know. We had plans. We joined the Cabras. I don't know what happened to the other guys. I know Ned got his shit together, went to college. That's good. That's good for him. He was never..."

"What?" I waited. "He was never what?"

He looked up at me and shook his head. "He was never like us, man. His mom was different. She was on him, know what I'm sayin'? I mean, he was tough and badass. You need to be tough to kill somebody. It ain't as easy as it seems. And he could do that, you know. He had *cojones* to do that. But after that, he chose the right path."

Dehan grunted. "That's very moving. The reformed killer of vulnerable old men. Gee, I think I might cry."

"Yeah, well, that's the story. You gonna leave Ernesto with me? I'm all he's got, man."

I stood. "Desperado, nothing to lose but your family. I'm not going to take that away from you, Julio. But do you ever think? Do you ever ask yourself, what if instead of leading Ernesto to the Chupacabras, you had led him to the community college? What if, instead of killing Geronimo Paez together, you had gone to college together and built a future? What kind of family would Ernesto have then?"

"Fock you."

"Yeah, I kind of guessed you might say that. You know what, Julio? You can take your cheap, self-pitying lies about family loyalty and stick them where they belong, in the can. If Ernesto dies, that's on you and him, for the stupid, lazy, self-indulgent choices you made. Take it easy, Julio. Thanks for the information. I'll tell Lucky you said hi."

Dehan was by the door, hammering. Chavez snorted at me. "Lucky is dead, man. What kind of shit cop are you?"

I nodded and smiled. "A live one. Hang loose, dude."

The doors clanged open, and we stepped out. The echo of them slamming closed again behind us seemed to roll down the corridors and up the walls over our heads. We walked in silence, led by the prison officer, back through the long tunnel-corridors to the main gate, where more doors were opened among more iron echoes, and we finally exited into the vast floodlit parking lot, desolate under a black sky. Our feet crunched across the gravel, and as we reached the car, Dehan put her arms around my chest and squeezed. I held her a moment and kissed her. She smiled, but it was a sad smile. "Life sucks sometimes, Sensei."

I nodded. "It does." I kissed her again. "I prescribe buffalo steak, good wine, and Irish whiskey."

"See," she said, smiling foolishly, "*that* is why *I* married *you*."

TEN

We got a table near the open fire, where a couple of logs were burning in the grate, occasionally spitting small showers of sparks across the hearth, giving out an uneven heat and playing wavering orange light over Dehan's face. She was leaning back in her chair, holding a half-full glass of beer. Before her was half a bison steak, which she was working her way through with methodical enthusiasm. Right then, I was chewing, and she was watching me with narrowed eyes.

"As evidence, it's not worth much. It's hearsay, unless the judge admits it as a confession."

I did a passable imitation of Chavez. "'You some badass motherfocker, man! You killed that dude?' 'Yeah, man. I stabbed that son of a bitch with a *knife!*'"

She laughed.

I shrugged. "It might stand as a confession. But the rest of it is hearsay and relates exclusively to what Ned *said* he was going to do. We still have zero evidence to show that Ned or any of his pals were there that night after Al broke Ned's fingers."

She made a face, set down her glass, and attacked her steak. While she was chewing, she shrugged. "At least we now know what happened."

I raised an eyebrow, took a pull on my beer, and signaled the waitress for two more. "Do we?"

She shook her head in something like mild despair. "Don't we?"

I smiled and cut into the tender meat. "This is why you are not supposed to torture witnesses, Dehan. You can't be sure of what they tell you."

I stuck a chunk of meat in my mouth, leaned back, and chewed.

"On the way up here, I told myself, if we have to threaten him, he will implicate either Lucky, Chicane Evans, or Simon Ibanez, 'el Loco.'"

"Because they are all dead and they can't testify. That's why you made the crack about saying hi to Lucky."

"You heard his reply." I shrugged again and drained my glass. "Of course, Lucky was crazy enough to do exactly what Chavez said, but it is also true that we can't confirm it or deny it. Even if we got Delroy Evans to confirm Chavez's story, it does not prove, *beyond a reasonable doubt*, that Ned did it."

The waitress arrived with our beers, set them before us, and took her smile away with her.

I picked up my glass. "And there is another thing."

She nodded. "Ned's mother."

"Not only does she say he was with her, his pals all say she was there at the hospital, and they went home together..."

I waited, watching her. She watched me back. "You believe Chavez's original story."

I nodded. "I believe it more than the crock he gave us when he thought Ernesto was going to be transferred." I shook my head and laughed. "He was dosed up on diazepam and suddenly the cold November night woke him up? And out of the five guys who might have gone with him, Chavez names the one guy who was crazy enough to have done it, and was also conveniently dead. Besides..." I shook my head again. "You could see him making it up as he was talking."

She finished her steak and sighed. There was an edge of irritation to her voice when she asked, "So do you think Ned is off the hook?"

"No, I am not saying that. He may well have done it, and he is still our best suspect, but if he did, Chavez doesn't know about it."

"You know, sometimes you kind of complicate things."

"Just telling you what I see, shweetheart. Then you get mad if I don't tell you what I'm thinking."

"I'm a woman."

"I'm aware."

"You're a what?"

"Which leaves us, as a potential pool of suspects, his immediate family, who certainly had motive enough, in spite of what Max says, and the nightmare scenario."

"What is the nightmare scenario?"

"A passerby."

She puffed out her cheeks and blew. "Maybe from the hood, maybe saw the altercation earlier, has heard the rumors, goes and knocks, Al recognizes him from saying hello, opens the door, the guy steps inside..."

"It's a possibility we need to be aware of. Not so much framing Ned as exploiting the fact that Ned had framed himself."

She shook her head. "I'd rather look for a yellow needle in a haystack. That would be all but impossible..."

"Let's not get ahead of ourselves. It's just a possibility, and we have lots to look into yet. The house hasn't been touched since the crime. When Martinez examined the house, he was looking for evidence that Ned had killed Al. If Ned *didn't* do it—and I am not saying he didn't—but *if* he didn't, obviously Martinez wasn't going to find any."

"Okay, you're right. We have to look at the house again with a wider lens."

"And we also need to talk to Justinian and Annunziata. We

need to hear their side of the story." I smiled. "It's not disappointing, is it?"

She gave a small laugh. "No, Mr. Holmes, it is as insoluble as you promised it would be. By the way."

"Yes, my dear Dehan?"

"Where's that Bushmills you promised me?"

———

We got back to the station at midday. As it turned out, we didn't need to contact Justinian. He called us on the way back and said he wanted to come down to the station to make a statement. I told him twelve thirty, and we pulled into the small parking lot on Fteley Avenue at just after twelve. As we stepped through the door, Maria, the desk sergeant, gave me a shout.

"Hey, handsome!" Then she winked at Dehan. "You too, beautiful." She tossed me an envelope. When I caught it, I felt the keys inside. She said, "From Chester Cardio-Valves, delivered by messenger yesterday."

"Thanks, Maria." I showed them to Dehan. "The keys to Al's place."

She grunted. "You think they've been in to sanitize the place?"

"We'll soon know if they have."

We pushed through into the bustling detectives' room and made for our desks. She spoke over her shoulder as she walked. "If they haven't, that means either they didn't do it, or they are very confident."

I pulled off my coat and hung it up. "You keep talking about them as though they were one unit, instead of three distinct people. Max may be as pure and innocent as the driven snow. He may well have sent the keys over in good faith. Doesn't mean Justinian and Annunziata are innocent, or acting in good faith. You have to ask yourself, what has Justinian scurrying over here to talk to us? Could it be that we have these?"

I waved the keys at her.

"Okay, point taken. So why is he coming to see us?"

"What has prompted him to come and see us? Okay, baby steps: he is coming to see us because he has heard that we went to see his brother."

She nodded. "Which means that either A, he has something to add to what his brother has told us, or B . . ."

"He wants to know what his brother has told us. That—and it's a stretch—but it could mean that he fears his brother might have implicated him."

"That is a stretch, but whichever way you look at it, it's either a defensive move or an offensive one."

I thought about it and nodded. "Let's hope it's not just that he wants to gossip."

She laughed. "Yeah, it could be that too."

The internal phone buzzed, and Maria told me Justinian had been taken up to interview room two. We collected three paper cups of coffee-like liquid from the vending machine and went up. I went in ahead, and Dehan followed and placed the paper cups on the table.

Justinian stood when he saw Dehan. He was short, maybe five-five, slim and dapper. He was in his midsixties but looked fit and healthy. He had silver hair cut very short and moved with the exaggerated grace of a dancer. He watched Dehan with wide eyes and a smile, and when she'd set down the coffee, he held out his hand to her. "How do you do? Justinian Chester. You must be Detective Dehan."

She was taken aback, and I could see the laughter in her eyes. She took his hand. "How do you do, Dr. Chester?"

I pulled out a chair and sat. They sat too, and he reluctantly let go of her hand. "I am Detective John Stone; this is my partner, Detective Dehan. Have you got some information for us regarding your brother Aloysius' death, Dr. Chester?"

"Well, I'm not sure. I may have."

I gave him the dead eye for a second while he continued to

watch Dehan. I said, "What would it take for you to know, Dr. Chester?"

He wrenched his eyes away and looked at me, like he was trying to focus and failing badly. "Hmm? Yes, sorry!" He laughed. "Your partner is ravishing. Such skin! And the features! The bone structure! Sublime."

I sighed noisily, he sighed quietly, and Dehan gave a small cough. He repeated, "What would it take . . . ?"

"Your brother's murder, Dr. Chester. We are very busy and really haven't got time to waste."

"No! Quite! I see that. I mean, I'm not sure what Max told you. And have you spoken to Anne? Heaven knows what *she* will tell you . . ."

Dehan was blunt. "Dr. Chester. If you have come here on a fishing expedition to find out what we know, not only are you wasting your time, but that puts you in a very bad light."

Before he could answer, I asked him, "What do you think Maximilian and Annunziata might have told us, Dr. Chester? Why is that important to you?"

His eyes were wide. "Well! I mean! I only came in to help and you're practically accusing me of fratricide!"

I leaned forward. "Is that what it was? Fratricide?"

"Good Lord! Of course not! My interest, my questions, were in the interest of the family! We are very sensitive to scandal, you know. We have a reputation in this city."

Dehan spoke more softly. "Dr. Chester, what we know is what your brother told us. If you want to know what that is, then you had better ask him. The question is, did you come here just to try and pump us, or have you something to tell us?"

"No, no, I came to offer my assistance. I didn't realize it would be received with such hostility."

I let Dehan answer. She was being good cop. "We're just doing our job, Dr. Chester. Everyone is innocent until proven guilty." She smiled. "But everyone's a suspect until they're in the clear."

"Quite . . ."

"So what can you tell us about your brother's death?"

"Well, I mean to say, I don't know what Max and Anne have said to you . . ." He waited, glancing at us. We gave him the dead eye until he went on, wriggling slightly in his seat. "I just feel perhaps I should put things into context, a little."

I said, "That would be very helpful, if you could do that. What is it exactly you want to put into context?"

"Well, we were all so *worried*." He turned to Dehan. "*You* can understand."

She raised her eyebrows and nodded, like she could understand.

"And Dr. Epstein was so unhelpful. Professional privilege, my tush! Who is paying the bills here? Surely that gives *us* some kind of privilege!"

I grunted. "So you tried to get some information from Dr. Epstein that he was unwilling to share with you."

He winked at Dehan. "He catches on fast, doesn't he?"

She nodded. "He's pretty smart. What was it you were trying to learn from Dr. Epstein?"

He gave his head a quick shake, lowered his eyes, and shrugged all at the same time. "I mean, just stuff that related to poor Aloysius' future well-being. Some of us, you know, were not happy with the family having disowned him in that way. However foolish he may have been in his youth, he didn't deserve . . . *that*!"

I said, "What is *that*, precisely, Dr. Chester?"

"Well, that . . ." He grimaced. "That *house*, in that *neighborhood*, with that awful Jewish psychiatrist and his assistant . . ."

"Are you racist, Dr. Chester?"

"Not at all," he said frigidly. "Some of my favorite bankers are Jews. Is that relevant?"

Dehan answered. "I don't know yet, we'll have to wait and see. I'll run it by my rabbi, see what he thinks."

"Oh, Lord, I was only being flippant."

I nodded. "Can we get back on task? So you were thinking

about bringing Aloysius back into the fold? What did Maximilian and Annunziata think about that?"

He stared at me so long I was about to ask him if he was okay. But then, his eyes shifted to Dehan and back to me a few times. He drew breath and held it a moment before saying, "Well, that's the thing. I mean, people say things, don't they, in the heat of the moment?"

"Who said what, Dr. Chester?"

He spoke rapidly, staring at the wall, avoiding our eyes. "Well, all sorts of people said all sorts of things, but I mean to say, one does, but it doesn't *mean* anything!"

"Give me patience! What made you come here, Dr. Chester?"

He stared at me but didn't speak.

"If you have just come here to gossip and play the mysterious guy who knows something but won't talk, then I have a good mind to charge you with obstructing justice and wasting police time! Now cut the crap and tell us what you came here to tell us, or get the hell out of here!"

He went very white, then his cheeks flamed red. "We were afraid that Aloysius might do something stupid."

Dehan arched an eyebrow. "Commit suicide?"

"No, heavens! Far more stupid than that. That would have been quite sensible."

I slammed my hand down on the table. The noise made him jump. "I'm giving you ten seconds to tell me what this is about. After that, I will formally charge you and have the sergeant take you down to the cells! Am I getting through to you?"

He nodded. "We thought he was going to get married."

"*Married?*"

"Well, you can imagine the repercussions. It could have been catastrophic!"

"So what did Max propose doing about this?"

"Well, I mean to say! We didn't know *what* to do! I mean, his wife would acquire legal charge of him, the quarter share in the company would effectively be hers! She would have made decisions on his behalf at board meetings! She might have sold his shares!"

Dehan leaned across the table. When she spoke, her voice was like a particularly dangerous frost. "I am going to ask you one more time, Justin, what did Max intend to do about it?"

"Well, it wasn't just Max, it was Anne too. We had a meeting. They scared the living daylights out of me, I don't mind telling you! They said it couldn't happen. We couldn't allow Aloysius to become a problem again. Max said we couldn't go back to the dark old days. And they said, well, they *said*, that if he planned to marry, we should have him killed . . ."

ELEVEN

DEHAN HAD TURNED TO STARE AT ME. IF SHE'D BEEN the kind of girl who gaped, she would have gaped. Instead she just stared. I studied the tabletop for a moment, then held up a hand to stop him talking.

"Can we just go over that again? Are you telling me that Maximilian Chester and Annunziata Chester conspired together, in your presence, to kill your brother Aloysius Chester?"

He crossed one elegant leg over the other and looked away at the wall. "Oh, dear, this really is *not* what I had intended."

"Dr. Chester, will you please answer the question?"

He flashed a look at me. "Well, I mean! You phrase it like that and it sounds awful! 'Conspired to murder . . . !' Maxie and Anne wouldn't *conspire to murder* Ally! They just . . ." He looked pained, and his eyes drifted again.

Dehan said, "What? They just what?"

He made a noise like "B-b-b-b-b . . ." like his battery was flat and his mouth wouldn't start. Then he got going and said, "They just *talked*, in the abstract, about the possibility that it *might* be necessary, if he did in fact go ahead with the idea of marrying . . . But they didn't *mean* it! That's what I came here to tell you, whatever they said, or may say, they didn't *mean* that they intended to have him killed."

I nodded. "I understand. It was just abstract speculation."

He gestured at me like he was offering me a canapé. "There you have it. Abstract speculation. Exactly what I was trying to say."

I smiled, like I was pleased that he approved of my succinct phrasing, and went on. "And in this abstract speculation about a possible future situation..."

"Precisely, thank you."

"Who would have actually carried out the..."

I trailed off, waiting for him to finish the sentence for me.

"The-the-the . . ." He jerked his head a couple of times, as though he was gesturing at Al's dead body in his imagination. "The *execution*?"

"Yes, the execution. Thank you."

"Well, we never discussed that. At least they might have, amongst themselves, but I always assumed that Max would take care of that."

My eyebrows said I was surprised. "Max?"

He waved his hands at me in alarm. "Oh, no! No, lord no! I mean, he would know whom to talk to, in order to get it done. Probably his factotum would talk to an attorney who would know somebody who knew somebody, you know, down the line. Every link increases deniability, as I am sure you know."

"Yes, I see."

Dehan was making a note in her pad. She laid down her pen, drew breath, hesitated, and then asked, "So what made you think that he was planning to get married?"

It was his turn to look surprised, first at Dehan, then at me, and then back at Dehan again. "Well, he told us. I assumed you knew."

"You'd had contact with him?"

"Why, yes! He contacted us. He said he wanted to build bridges, make peace. He wanted a family reunion. He said he had wonderful news he wanted to share with us. Maximilian insisted we all meet at my house, where Aloysius would be less likely to be recognized. Annunziata was terrified that they might have found some way of treating his condition . . ."

Dehan scowled. "*Terrified?* Why the hell was she terrified about that?"

Justinian looked slightly terrified. I didn't blame him. "Well," he said, "most people in full possession of their senses are rational beings. But Aloysius in full possession of his senses was a very dangerous, chaotic man. To say he was a loose cannon would be a considerable understatement. The way he carried on, he could have brought the company to its knees in a year. So the prospect of his being given a clean bill of mental health, and fit to run his own affairs, would have been very scary news indeed, for all of us."

I said, "But it wasn't that."

"No, as it turned out, it was far worse. He said that he had met a woman, that he was in love with her, that he had proposed to her, and she was willing to marry him and look after him. Well, I needn't tell you that Max and Anne poured the most wicked scorn on him. But he stuck to his guns and said it was true, and that he wanted our blessing."

"Did he tell you who this woman was?"

"No, he said she was an angel and that he would introduce us to her. He was certain that once we met her, we would love her. Poor Aloysius. He was always so simplistic and naïve."

Dehan sighed and rubbed her face. "Dr. Chester, please think very carefully. This could be crucially important in finding out who murdered your brother. Did he give any indication at all, make any comment, about who this woman might be?"

He placed his palms on his lap and puffed out his cheeks. "He said she was an angel, that she was young and beautiful, since he had met her, she had turned his life around, and that he saw her every day. She came to visit him."

Dehan was watching him through squinting eyes. She chewed

her lip. "She visited him every day? How long had that been going on? Had he told Epstein about it?"

Justinian blinked a lot and seemed to shudder. "Which of those questions would you like me to answer first? He said every day. Frankly, I thought he was hallucinating this woman, if you must know. I didn't ask how long it had been going on, *not* being his mother! As for Dr. Epstein, you shall have to ask him about that."

He cast his eyes over me and said, "And now, if you will forgive me, I have suffered quite enough abuse and innuendo for one day. My intention was to assist the police. Had I known what I was exposing myself to, I should never have *dreamed* of coming!"

He turned to Dehan, sighed, and shook his head. "Such loveliness. You are *far* too lovely for this ugly job. You should be a model, or marry a millionaire."

"Thanks for the advice."

"I'm going. You won't tackle me on the way out and beat me up, will you?"

I shook my head. "Not this time, Dr. Chester."

He stood and stalked out, allowing the door to bang closed behind him.

Dehan got to her feet, thrust her hands in her back pockets, and did a full circuit of the room. Eventually, she stopped with her back to me, staring at the wall a couple of inches in front of her nose.

"You believe him?"

"Yes."

She turned to me. Her face said she was surprised and a little irritated. "You believe him . . ."

"Yes."

"You think Chavez is lying, but this guy is telling the truth."

"Yes, Detective Dehan, I do."

"You want to explain what it is that makes Dr. Justinian Chester, aka Maggie Smith, believable and Julio Chavez not?"

I nodded. "Sure. Chavez was lying to keep his brother in the same prison with him, and Max already told us they had discussed killing Aloysius and discarded the idea."

She went up on her toes a couple of times.

"Oh."

"What he didn't make clear was how serious they got before they remembered their Hippocratic oaths."

"Mm-hm..."

"The questions for us now are, how serious *did* they get? And also, *did* they in fact discard it? The notion that Max has a man who has a man, who has a man who takes care of things, is really not that hard for me to believe. And I can see that the scenarios that Justinian was describing, with Al married to some kind of evil manipulator, might well have scared them enough to take action. None of them wanted to go back to the dark days of the late sixties/early eighties. Maybe they decided to put an end to it before it even started."

Dehan sighed and nodded. "A professional hit would explain the lack of forensic evidence."

"It would. But the whole thing opens up a lot of issues."

She regarded me from under her brows and went up on her toes again. "Like?"

I thought for a moment and made a face. "For one, if it's true that he was considering marriage, as I believe it is, why didn't Maximilian mention it?"

"They would want to keep that quiet..."

"But more to the point, the question that really interests me is, why did *Epstein* not mention it? Surely that would have been a major issue for his guardian and his psychiatrist to be involved in. So why did he not mention that to us?"

She grunted, nodding. "Yeah, that is odd."

"It is more than odd. I'd say it's key." I held up my thumb. "One, if Justinian's story is true, why didn't Epstein tell us about Al's marriage plans?" I held up my index. "Two, if it is *not* true, then what is Justinian doing spreading this kind of story? What is his intention? What is he trying to achieve?" I held up my middle finger. "Three. If what Justinian is telling us is true, then *both* of the above apply."

She went up on her toes again, biting her lip. "Why didn't Epstein tell us about Al's plans to marry, and also, why *has* Justinian told us? His excuse was he didn't know what Max had told us, and he wanted to protect them from incriminating themselves. But that is pure, prime-grade BS. He had another motive, I agree."

I stood. "We need to go and look at the house."

She looked surprised. "Now?"

"Yeah."

"What about Anne—Annunziata? I kind of want to go and talk to her, don't you?" She was frowning, quizzical.

I smiled and pulled the door open. "Yeah, I kind of do, but I am even more curious to see how long it is before she comes to us."

She made a big O with her mouth. "Huh . . . okay."

She followed me out of the interrogation room, and we walked slowly down the stairs, side by side. Halfway down, she said, "What about Epstein? Aren't we going to ask him why he omitted to tell us about Al's marriage plans?"

I nodded and we went into the detectives' room, where I collected the case file from my desk. Then we stepped out into the afternoon sun and made for the Jag.

"Yes," I said, and I leaned on the sun-warmed roof of the car, tapping it gently with my keys. "But we don't know yet, do we, for a fact, that Al did intend to marry somebody." I studied the key a moment. "This has come right out of left field. I would like to be a little more sure of my facts before we tackle Dr. Epstein again." I shook my head. "Dr. Epstein is a very smart man."

I climbed in the car and slammed the door. She got in beside me. "What are you thinking?"

"I don't know." I fired up the big old engine and backed out of the lot, then turned onto Story Avenue. "I don't know," I said again. "But I have the feeling we need to pick over all these facts very carefully. There is something, right there in front of our noses, that we are not seeing. Something so obvious, it's invisible."

"And you think you are going to find that in his house. Where whatever trace evidence may be left is twelve years old?"

I nodded. "Maybe."

"Oh, okay..."

We turned onto White Plains and cruised steadily north without talking. We had the windows open, and I glanced a couple of times at Dehan, where she sat with her aviators and her hair whipping across her face. It was a thing I would never grow tired of looking at.

At Gleason we turned right, then left into Virginia Avenue, and right again into Ellis. There I parked and climbed out of the car. I stood, leaning on the open door and staring at the house. Dehan came and leaned on my shoulder. I pointed at the front door.

"They were there. Right there. Ned, Julio and Ernesto Chavez, Lucky, el Loco . . . all of them, right there, pushing on that door. And he was inside, panicking, terrified, haunted not just by these bastards, but by his own dark demons. He could feel some kind of darkness closing in on him. How did he describe it? A tsunami of darkness. Beings that had followed him from Mexico."

Dehan nodded. "He slammed the door twice, broke the little shit's fingers, and then managed to slam it closed. From there, he went and telephoned Dr. Epstein."

I jerked my head. "Let's go."

We crossed the road and pushed open the gate. The small, overgrown front yard lay in the dappled shade of a giant plane tree that overlooked the house. I trod the short path, climbed the five steps to the old, wooden front door, and slipped the key into the lock, trying to imagine what Al had felt that night, twelve years earlier, as he fumbled with these very keys, hearing Ned and his pals closing in on him from behind.

I pushed open the door, spreading a stack of mail across the dusty, beige carpet. Dehan stepped in behind me and closed the door. We were in a small entrance hall with a flight of steps rising to the upper floor on our left. On the right, after a small entrance porch, the space opened out into an open-plan living room and kitchen. The house was silent. The air was stale and musty.

We walked through into the living area. On the right, there was a couch against the near wall. In front of it, there was a coffee table, and beyond that, set on a kind of dresser, was a TV. The TV was connected by a cable to a DVD player beneath it, and stacked beside it were hundreds of DVDs, including the entire collection of *Murder She Wrote*.

Underneath the coffee table and, as far as I could see, under the sofa too, there was a large, dark stain on the beige carpeting. Dehan whispered half to herself, "They didn't even clean up his blood. That's what you call being disowned."

I hunkered down and checked the DVD player. It still had the disc in it. I shook my head. "They really haven't touched a thing. They just closed the door and walked away."

"That's pretty harsh. It takes a special kind of cold to do that."

"It does."

I pointed at the stain. "That's where his body was." I opened up the file and pulled the crime scene photos. "He was lying between the coffee table and the sofa. The knife had been removed, so he bled profusely till he died. He had his head toward the window and his feet toward the kitchen area, lying on his back."

She peered at the photograph, then took it from my fingers and positioned herself. "Which means the killer was standing about here, where I am, facing Al . . ." She frowned and scratched her head.

I nodded. "That's one of the problems I've been having too. How does that work? If he's facing him here, by the sofa, how do the shots wind up in the kitchen . . . ?"

Dehan shook her head. "No, whoever it is comes in, over there by the door. Either Al lets him in or he lets himself in. Doesn't matter right now. They meet, or stop, just over there, between the kitchen and the living area. The intruder pulls his gun. Al panics and they wrestle. The gun goes off, bang bang bang. Al knocks the gun from his hands. As they are wrestling, they turn around. The intruder pulls his knife and stabs Al in the heart."

I nodded several times. "You are right. That would seem to be the plausible, obvious explanation. There are just a couple of problems I have. One . . ."

I went and stood where she had indicated the shooter would have to be when the shots were fired, where Al and I would have struggled if I had been the intruder. I held out my arm as though it were a gun. "If I fired from here, I would hit the pillar by the side of the breakfast bar. In order to hit the kettle and the plates . . ." I walked to the center of the floor. "I would need to be standing over here, in the center of the floor, or right . . ." I crossed the room again. ". . . here, in the entrance to the kitchen area."

"Huh . . ."

"Also, my other problem is that when I look at Al lying on the floor in that picture, in that position, I just know: either he just got up from the sofa, or he was about to sit back down on it. That is *exactly* where he would be. And I, the killer, would be right where I would be if I had just come in and I was chatting with him."

"You're saying he knew his killer. But, sorry, Stone, you're basing that on pretty slim evidence."

"I know." I nodded. "I'm saying Al might have known, and trusted, his killer." I gazed into her eyes and smiled. "And I can tell you, sure as eggs is eggs, he knew Ned Brown, but he did not trust him."

TWELVE

The stuff in the kitchen had been left pretty much where the crime scene guys had left it twelve years earlier. There was a plastic kettle beside the sink. It had a neat, 9mm hole in one side, but the whole panel on the other side had shattered, leaving shards of beige plastic strewn across the work surface and in the sink. I repositioned what was left of the kettle, placing it where I would have it if I was Al. While I was doing that, I saw the hole in the wall where the slug had struck home, leaving a spider's web of cracks across a shattered tile.

There was a plastic shopping bag in the sink. It contained six medium-size plates. Two were whole, the other four were at various degrees of shattered. I took the debris from the bag, aware of Dehan leaning on the pillar at the end of the breakfast bar, which also formed a kind of entrance to the kitchen.

I held a whole plate in each hand and stepped back to scan the surface, looking for the obvious place to stack them.

"What are you doing, Stone?"

"I'm thinking. He was a big guy, almost four hundred pounds, tall, and sixty. Maybe he didn't like to bend all that much anymore. So these plates, the ones he used most often, he had up here on the work surface." I glanced at her. "That's how they got shot."

She was peering at me. "I'm afraid to be sarcastic, because I realize you are probably being brilliant."

"Not at all." I put the two plates in what looked to me like the obvious position and spoke absently. "Flagellate me with the whip of your tongue, scathe me with your scorn..."

I stacked the broken shards on top of the whole plates. Behind me, I heard her mutter, "Flagellate you with the whip of my *tongue*...?"

"We haven't got the radio. It's still in evidence. But it was one of those..." I made a rectangular shape with my hands. "Like a big cube of cream plastic with an LED display on the front, and a power cable coming out the back."

She nodded, still peering at me, though she was beginning to look curious. I fished through the crime scene photos and found a picture of the radio and placed it where the radio would have stood.

"Three shots," I said. "Where did they come from?"

She glanced at the kettle, the plates, and the radio, then glanced around the kitchen and living room. "Well, like you said, they had to be from here in the doorway, or over there in the middle of the floor."

I pulled my phone from my pocket and dialed the lab.

"Hey, Stone, do for you?"

"I'm at 1932 Ellis Avenue, here in the Bronx. It was a crime scene twelve years ago."

"If you're there, I'm guessing it was never solved and now you want me to solve it for you."

"See, Joe, that's why you got the top job, because you're smart. There were three shots fired, all apparently in, or into, the kitchen. At the time, the lead detective was pretty sure who the shooter was, and how it all went down, so he never bothered you boys with things like trajectory..."

He made a noise like somebody just put worms in his tequila.

"How much of the original crime scene is intact after twelve years, Stone . . . ?"

"It is exactly as it was when you guys closed and locked the door in 2007. And I have just placed the kettle and the crockery back as it was when it got shot. Can you do it with lasers? I need to know where the shooter was standing when he fired, and I need this to stick."

"Sure, we can do it with lasers for you, John. Would you like a cowgirl in a rhinestone bikini too?"

"Thanks, I've already got one."

He laughed noisily.

"I'll leave the keys at the station for you. How soon can you do it?"

"I'll send a team over this afternoon. Give you a call this evening."

"You're a pal. Thanks, Joe."

Dehan was still leaning on the pillar. "You going to tell me what's on your mind?"

"Sure." I shrugged. "I assumed you were wondering the same thing."

"Can it."

"What was he doing in the kitchen?"

She frowned. "Aren't we saying the shots went wide during a struggle?"

"That's what Martinez said. I'm seeing three closely grouped shots."

"Al was in the kitchen and the guy was shooting at him?"

I shrugged with my eyebrows. "However I try to explain to myself the movements and the positions of the people in this house on that night, it doesn't quite make sense."

"They struggled for the gun. Al was big and strong. He got the gun, and his killer took cover in the kitchen. Al fired at him and missed. Then the guy came out with a kitchen knife . . ."

I gestured back at the sofa. "Al retreats to the sofa, surrenders the gun without firing again, and gets stabbed cleanly in the heart."

She shook her head. "The only way it does make sense is if the shots came after Al was killed."

"Explain."

"There were two of them, like you said from the start. One with a gun, one with his mom's kitchen knife. They pick the lock while Al is engrossed in Jessica Fletcher. They surprise him. He lumbers to his feet, and the boy with the knife kills him. He drops there. Boy retrieves his knife, and Al bleeds out."

I nodded. "Okay."

"Now, meantime, Ned has found a box, a rucksack, whatever, full of cash. A row breaks out. Ned shoots at the boy, who takes cover in the kitchen and then escapes."

"That could work. What about Max and the gang?"

She spread her hands in a "what you want from me?" gesture. "It's either-or, Stone. Unless you want to argue that Max had his fixer pay Ned to do the job."

I smiled. "That would be neat."

"Too neat. Honestly, Stone, it is very easy to see Max talking a good fight and then going home and doing nothing."

I agreed. "It is. But it's also easy to see him picking up the phone and telling somebody to 'see to it.' I'm not sold on any theory so far, Dehan. What I am clear about is, to paraphrase Socrates..."

"Yes, I always like to paraphrase Socrates."

"... that I am not clear about anything. What happened in this room is not really explained by any of our theories. Even your two bad guys who turn against each other theory. How come bad guy number two never went after Ned? Ned gets a stash of money and tries to kill his pal. But the pal never seeks revenge or his share of the cash. Why did that never come to anything?"

She scratched her head. "So what do you hope to prove by fixing the position of the shooter? The shots may have come from more than one place while he was moving around."

I nodded and smiled. "*That* is exactly what I want to see. And *that* will tell me everything else."

"Oh . . ." She nodded. "So now you're going to be a smug pain in the ass and not tell me anything?"

I laughed and walked toward the door, speaking loudly over my shoulder. "You know my methods, Dehan! Apply them!"

We made our way back to the station. Neither of us spoke much. We both had the feeling that this might be the one that got away. It was, after all, why I had chosen it to write about. But the more involved we had got in the case, the more we had got to know Al, and the more we both had the feeling that we had to do the right thing by him and bring it home. I didn't need Dehan to tell me she felt that way. We both felt it, and we both knew it.

There wasn't much to do once we got back until the lab results came in. So Dehan started on some background searches on the Chesters, and I started digging up what information I could on Ned Brown.

At half past five, my phone rang.

"Yeah, Stone."

A woman's voice breathed in my ear. "Is that Detective John Stone, of the Forty-Third Precinct, NYPD?"

"The very same. Who am I speaking to?"

"I am the one Chester you haven't spoken to yet."

"Dr. Annunziata Chester?"

I glanced at Dehan. She was shaking her head and mouthing, *Son of a bitch.*

"Indeed, the very same."

"What can I do for you, Dr. Chester?"

"Please, call me Annunziata. Doctor sounds so, *recherché*! I am, after all, just a woman, like any other . . ."

"Good to know. So, what can I do for you, Annunziata?"

I was scanning a list of documents on my screen as I was talking to her. I wanted to know who Ned's father was. I knew his mother was Chevronne Brown, of Underhill Avenue, but I hadn't heard any mention of his dad.

Annunziata was saying, "I understand you have spoken to both my brothers, and Justinian is such a fool, he may have given you a completely distorted picture of the situation."

"You think maybe he said things he shouldn't have?"

"It is, sadly, Detective Stone, all too probable. Not only does Justinian often blab about things he should really stay quiet about, he will also ramble off on one of his blurb fests and give a body an entirely erroneous impression of the facts."

I had found a link to Ned's birth certificate, and I clicked it. Meanwhile, I asked Annunziata, "What facts exactly did you have in mind?"

She was quiet for a while. I sat forward, frowning. She said, "You are naughty. I mean, Justinian must have..."

I said, "Let's not talk on the phone. When can I come and see you?"

"Well, it's a little sudden..."

"You in New York or in San Francisco?"

"New York. I have a small apartment at 400 Riverside Drive."

"Tomorrow, one p.m."

She laughed. "My! You are assertive! Make it two, in time for postprandials. I shall look forward to it, Detective Stone."

"I'll be there."

I hung up and sat staring at my screen, typing at my keyboard. Dehan was watching me. "What was that? What's up?"

"We're invited for postprandials..." I said absently.

"What the hell are you looking at? What's wrong with you?"

"Well, I'll be damned!" I said, and flopped back in my chair. "Son of a gun."

"*What?*"

"Ned Brown."

"What about him, Stone?"

"He's adopted. And I am forbidden access to his birth certificate and his adoption records."

Her jaw sagged. "Son of a bitch. So the anonymous will..."

"Could have been either one of his biological parents."

"We need to see that will."

I nodded. "But this may well weaken our case. It makes the legitimacy of his fund more likely, and our grounds for wanting to see it weaker."

"So we should talk to his mother, his adoptive mother, Chevronne. See how much she will volunteer."

"Yeah . . ." I sighed. "But what she volunteers is going to be to protect her son. She's not going to volunteer anything that implicates him." I gave a small laugh. "I mean, the fact of his being adopted may well have prompted the idea of making a phony will . . . We need to see the will, but we also need to see his adoption papers. We need to know who his biological parents are—or were."

"Good luck with that."

I climbed the stairs to the deputy inspector's office. He was as polite and mannerly as ever. He told me to sit and listened with care to what I had to say.

"The problem is, John," he said, when I had finished, "it actually weakens your case. It makes the legitimacy of Ned's fund more likely, and your grounds for wanting to see the will consequently weaker."

"My words exactly, sir. On the other hand, the fact that he was adopted may well . . ."

He interrupted, nodding elaborately. ". . . have put the idea in his mother's head. Oh, yes, I see that. She and the son may well have colluded. No doubt. I see that very clearly. And it is very frustrating. But still, it is not a case the courts are likely to look on favorably. I have a meeting tomorrow with the DA and Judge Mathews. She's one of your hanging judges, you know. I'll put your arguments to her. You never know, she might be sympathetic. I'll let you know as soon as she's given me an answer."

I carried my frustration downstairs again. Dehan watched me lower myself into my chair and threw a small eraser at me that she'd picked out of the end of a pencil. "You've been erased," she said. Then she added, "We need to go talk to Epstein again. We need to know why he didn't tell us about Al's plans to get married, or if those plans were even real."

"I want to talk to Annunziata first." I flicked the eraser back at her. "You know, the English call these rubbers."

She threw her head back and laughed raucously. "Hey, little Sperm Guy, you have been erased by this rubber!" She did some more noisy laughing.

I looked at Mo and smiled. He ignored me but also shook his head and sighed.

When she was done, I said, "Anything on the Chesters?"

"Zip. But in any case, what we are looking for? We'd need another court order. If they paid for a hit on their brother, you can bet your ass that payment will be almost impossible to trace."

I grunted. "I know, and that, I fear, is one court order too far. We'll be lucky to get the ones we're after." I shook my head. "We need to come at this another way."

"Like what?"

My phone rang.

"Stone."

"John, it's Joe, from the lab."

"Hey, what have you got?"

There was a moment's silence. "I'm not sure what you were expecting, John. I had a quick look at the file. Martinez said he thought the shots were made while the killer and the victim struggled for the gun."

"That was his theory, yeah."

"Well, that isn't what happened."

"I had a feeling you might say that. What did happen? He stood in the kitchen doorway and let off three shots into that corner, right?"

"Yeah, that's exactly right. How did you know?"

"It just seemed to fit with all the facts I haven't got. Thanks, Joe. I owe you."

"Sure. We'll catch up."

I hung up. Dehan and I sat and stared at each other. Eventually, she said, "So, he stood in the kitchen doorway, Al must have gone in there to take cover when he saw the gun..."

"Somebody stood in the kitchen doorway..."

"To miss at that range..."

I drew breath, but she went on.

"But! He has two broken fingers, and if they are struggling, and Al is holding Ned's arm out, you know? Like a tango?" She demonstrated, holding her right arm out like she was dancing. "And because of the pain in his hand, with his broken fingers and Al squeezing his hand, he fires three shots almost simultaneously!"

"It's feasible. Let's go and talk to Ned's mother."

"I thought you didn't want to yet."

"I changed my mind. We're getting stuck, losing momentum. Let's go see what she knows. On the way, we can get some eggplant."

"Eggplant? What for?"

"You're making moussaka tonight."

As we pushed out of the detectives' room, I heard Mo muttering, "Ain't they just adorable? Ain't you glad they found each other?"

The rasp of his partner's nicotine-stained voice was just audible. "Yeah. I had an ingrown toenail once. I adored that more."

THIRTEEN

It was a short drive. Mrs. Brown had a pleasant, pale blue, two-story clapboard house on Underhill Avenue, near the corner with Watson Avenue. There was no front yard, but a flight of ten yellow brick steps led up to a small porch, which housed the front door. I parked out front and climbed out into the late-afternoon sun. I climbed the yellow steps and rang on the bell. Dehan stood behind me, looking uncomfortable.

The door opened to reveal a woman who, for a moment, looked oddly familiar. She had tightly curled black hair and large, serious brown eyes. She smiled, and it was a nice smile, but she held on to the door, and there was caution evident in her manner.

We showed her our badges. "I am Detective John Stone, and this is my partner, Detective Carmen Dehan. Are you Chevronne Brown?"

"Yes. What's this about?"

"I wonder if we could come in for a moment and talk to you about your son, Ned?"

The smile faded from her mouth, leaving only the caution in her face. "He ain't done nothing, has he?"

I shook my head and tried to look reassuring. "No, not that we are aware of. This is really just routine. We are investigating the death of Aloysius Chester, twelve years ago, and there are just a few, standard fact-checks that we need to make."

She sighed and stepped back. "You'd better come in, I guess."

We stepped into a bright, agreeable hallway, and she pointed toward the kitchen in back of the house, down a short passage where bright afternoon sunlight was lying in patches on the floor. Outside, I could hear birds singing. The smell of baking bread was on the air. It felt like home, and for a moment, I felt a rush of anger at Ned, for all he had thrown away. Chevronne Brown gestured again.

"I'm in the kitchen, if you don't mind. I'm afraid I am very busy."

Dehan smiled without a lot of feeling and said, "We'll be quick," and led the way to a large, bright room. There was bread baking in a large, blue AGA, the makings of an apple pie on the work surface, and the kitchen door stood open onto a large backyard with a well-tended lawn.

Chevronne went straight back to the cooker, where she started stirring some apples that were stewing in a pot. Dehan rested her ass against the sink, and I leaned on the doorjamb.

"Is Ned your only child, Mrs. Brown?"

She nodded as she stirred. "Yes."

"Do you mind telling us where his father is?"

"I wouldn't mind telling you. I wouldn't mind knowing either. He disappeared just after Ned was born."

Dehan was blunt. "Was he Ned's father?"

Chevronne stared at her. Her eyes were bright, but it was hard to tell if it was with anger or fear, or perhaps both.

"Of course he was! I just got through tellin' you he left *after* Ned was born. That means he was still here, so he was Ned's father. Is there something complicated about that that you don't understand, Detective Dehan?"

I sighed. "The reason my partner is asking that question, Mrs. Brown . . ." I paused, watching her face, and changed tack. "Mrs.

Brown, can you tell us who Ned's benefactor was? Who left him the money, on the condition he went to college . . . ?"

She returned to stirring her stewing apples. "Reason I can't tell you that is for the same reason why I can't tell you where his father is. I just don't know, see? We was notified by an attorney. We went along to his office on Metropolitan Avenue, we had to sign some papers . . ." She shook her head. "I couldn't believe what I was seeing and hearing, but however much I asked, 'Who done this?' they just kept on giving me the same answer. 'We can't tell you that. We are not allowed to tell you.'"

Dehan gave a small laugh. "Come on, Chevronne . . ."

"Oh, now I'm Chevronne? I'm not Mrs. Brown anymore? Do I get to call you Carmen and John? You tell me how this works, 'cause I'm just a stupid black woman who don't know nothing!"

"Mrs. Brown." I smiled at her. "We do not mean any disrespect at all. We just want to understand the facts about what happened that night. We have a few conflicting accounts . . ."

"Who from?"

I spread my hands. "Amongst others, Julio Chavez."

"That thieving bastard! You *know* him an' his no-good brother are with the Chupacabras!"

I ignored her and kept right on going. "He told us that Ned and Lucky left the hospital together . . ."

"And that's why you're here, asking about my son's father and his inheritance?"

I held her eye a moment. "Yes, Mrs. Brown. That is the reason."

"Why? Because a black boy can't inherit money? Is that a privilege preserved for the white folk?"

Every time she brought up the race issue, her accent changed. When she wasn't on the defensive, she had no definable accent, but when she got her claws out, it was recognizably Caribbean.

I shook my head. "No. The issue has nothing to do with race. In fact, if you can show us where that inheritance came from, then we can eliminate Ned as a suspect."

She froze. "He's still a suspect?"

I shrugged. "The case was never closed. Anyone who was a suspect back then is still a suspect now."

"You got any other suspects?"

Dehan nodded. "Yeah, but we can't discuss with you who they are, and you know that. But I can tell you they're white."

"Like hell!"

"You can believe it or not, Chevronne, but it's the truth. Now if we can say, conclusively, Ned's money did not come from a robbery at Al Chester's house, then we can also say we have no reason to believe Ned was there at all."

Her eyes were bright again, studying Dehan's face. "I was with him from when he got home with his f . . . with his loser friends. His hand was broken. I could see that with my own eyes. I took him to the hospital, I waited with him, and those no-good punks, and after they finished with him, I took him home and told his friends to clear off!"

"What time was that?"

She shook her head. "How the hell should I know? About ten o'clock? Something like that."

I pushed away from the doorframe and put my hands in my pockets. "Did Ned own a gun?"

Her eyes went wide. It looked like genuine shock. "*A gun?* No! Not in this house!"

"Mrs. Brown, can you swear to the fact that Ned stayed here the whole night after you got home from the hospital?"

"I just got through tellin' you that! I already told the *first* detective, and I ain't gonna change that!"

"Okay, that's fine. We're almost done and we'll leave you in peace. I just have one more question. Who did you adopt Ned from?"

It was as though I had slapped her in the face. Her skin, a deep brown, turned a pasty color. She laid down the wooden spoon she was holding and steadied herself on the work surface.

"He is my son."

"We're not disputing that, Mrs. Brown. We know he's your son, but we also know he's adopted. We just want to know where he was adopted from. More to the point, *who* he was adopted from. Was it the same person who left him the money? The inheritance?"

Her voice was almost a hiss. "I already told you I can't tell you that because I don't *know*!"

Dehan's voice was harsh. "You don't know where you adopted him from? Which orphanage?"

"I want you to leave now."

"What orphanage, Chevronne?"

"Why won't you tell us?"

"*Get out!*"

I gave Dehan the nod, and we made our way toward the front door. As I opened it, I turned to Chevronne Brown. "I want you to understand, Mrs. Brown. If we get this information, and it's aboveboard, your son automatically drops off the list of suspects . . ."

"Get out!"

"We *will* get a court order."

"*Get out! Now!*"

We stepped outside, and she slammed the door behind us.

The sun was still bright and warm, but the shadows were growing long in the afternoon. I went and leaned my back against the Jag and called the deputy inspector.

"John, hello! Some development?"

"Yes, sir. We went to see Mrs. Brown and asked her nicely who left her son the inheritance, and who she adopted him from."

"I see. Did you *actually* ask her nicely, or did Dehan try to put the fear of God into her?"

"No, nothing like that, sir. We were very polite, and we explained that if she could give us that information, we would in all probability drop her son from our list of suspects."

"How did she react to that?"

"She told us to get out."

"And you didn't threaten her."

"Not at all. Sir. We need that information, and I can promise you that she and Ned are hiding something."

"I can't take your hunches to the judge, John, you know that."

"I know, sir. I am just saying, we need this information."

"I hear you."

He hung up.

Dehan was leaning next to me, with her arms crossed on the car. She said, "What the hell do we do now?"

"You make a moussaka, and we wait till tomorrow. We'll see what Annunziata has to say. And who knows, we might get lucky with the inspector's hanging judge and the court orders."

I handed her the keys and we climbed into the car. As she fired it up, she said, "We could always go and see the attorneys ourselves."

"It would be a waste of time."

She pulled away, and I reached onto the back seat for the file. She drove slowly as I leafed through it and found Ned's attorney's address. "Hernandez and Heap, 1332 Metropolitan Avenue."

"Jeez! You ever get the feeling a case was almost incestuous? That is like *right* 'round the corner from Epstein."

"Same block."

She nodded. "Same block." She turned right onto Watson and then left onto Virginia. "I mean, right here." She pointed back over her shoulder. "Three hundred yards down there is Ned's house, and his garage. As I am saying that, we are coming up on the Church of the Sacred Apocalypse, we just left Chevronne's place, and just here, at this intersection, Gleason and Virginia..." She slowed and pointed left and right. "You've got Al's house a hundred yards up on your right, the church right here, fifty yards on my left, and Joy's house, two hundred yards past that, on Leland."

I was interested. "What's your point?"

"I don't know, but man! They are all right in each other's pockets."

She drove north to the circle, and even though it was slightly out of our way, she took us past the offices of Hernandez and Heap. They were on the ground floor, under a blue awning, less than thirty yards from Dr. Epstein's lobby.

I thought about it and sighed. "I guess it's in the nature of the case. It's all about people taking care of each other, and people rejecting each other."

She frowned at me. "What do you mean?"

"The Chesters were, are, a very tightly knit family, which is a kind of community, isn't it?"

"Yeah, sure."

"Al broke the rules of that community. The way he felt when he was twenty years old, he wanted to break every rule he could get his hands on, and then some. That's what it was all about for him right then, breaking the rules, breaking free! That was the sixties: peace, love, and above all, freedom. But when he broke the rules once too often, his community, his family, rejected him. He didn't care! He was twenty, good-looking, rich, and free. They couldn't touch him. So he continued to break the rules, every social rule he came across, he broke it. He abandoned his family, he abandoned Harvard, he abandoned the U.S.A., he abandoned civilization, until he ended up destroying himself in the process.

"Then, ironically, he sought the help of the communities he had rebelled against most violently: Harvard, the medical profession, welfare—society itself. Sadly, society has very little to offer a man like Al. So he kind of slipped through the safety net and wound up down and out in the Bronx."

"Where this community picked him up."

I nodded. "Babylon. On the one hand, he had people befriending him, helping him to find a place in their midst, helping him to belong and even, to some extent, to heal. On the other hand, he had people, living side by side with him, bent on hurting him, stealing from him, even killing him, simply because he was different." I sighed. "I digress. The point is that he was gathered up by a very different kind of close-knit society, who were willing to help him find a place and heal. Hence the very close proximity of the people to the church and to Dr. Epstein's practice."

She was very quiet. It wasn't till we had got to the Metropolitan Oval that she looked at me with narrowed eyes.

"You son of a..."

"Careful with that mouth, Eugene."

"What? Who is...? Never mind! You deliberately went off on that blurb about community and rejection and being gathered up, because you thought..." She stared at me and poked me as I started to laugh. "You *thought* that there was something significant in the proximity of all those places and you..." She started smacking me with her left hand. "You wanted to put me on the wrong scent! You *son of a*...!"

"Full marks, Little Grasshopper!"

"Bullshit! Who's Eugene?"

"It was a song, long before your time. Careful with that axe, Eugene. Mott the Hoople."

"Sometimes I wonder if we are speaking the same language."

"Mott-the-Hoople."

"Oh, okay. So it *is* significant that all those places are so close?"

"You know it is, Dehan. You don't need me to tell you that. Your reaction when you realized where the attorneys were, told you so. But what I said wasn't complete BS. This whole case hinges on that whole community thing. It *is* what brought Al together with his killer, and it is what caused the murder to be committed in the first place."

She glanced at me as we pulled up outside the El Paso deli. "You really think like that, don't you?"

I shrugged. "I guess I do. Everything *is* actually connected. It's not just a theory. That's how it works."

She nodded. "Minced beef, eggplants, wine. Go, fetch."

Late afternoon was turning to dusk, and lights were coming on in the street outside. I smiled and went to open the door. Her voice stopped me.

"You're deep, Stone. You're a pain in the ass, but you're deep with it." She smiled. "I can live with you being a pain in the ass, but I love that you're deep. That's kind of hot."

I grinned. "You're not so shallow yourself, Detective Dehan. Ply me with good moussaka and wine, and I might just tell you all about what I'm thinking."

She leaned close, breathed on my ear, and whispered, "*Show me, don't tell me.*"

FOURTEEN

Dehan got up first. She showered and went down to make breakfast. I would have made it, but she said that only somebody who'd been brought up as a Jewish Catholic could really understand the art of cooking bacon. It wasn't a point I was ready to argue—I figured she was probably right—so mornings when we had bacon, she got up first.

By nine o'clock, we were sitting outside Dr. Epstein's block, waiting for him to arrive. Joy showed first, at five past nine, looking like she was in a hurry. At twenty past, Epstein arrived, looking like his head was too heavy for his body. He went inside, and we climbed out of the Jaguar and followed.

His elevator had just left by the time we got there. We took the one next to it and caught up with him as he was going through his door into his office. He paused with his key in his hand, frowning at us as we stepped out of the elevator.

"Detectives Stone and Dehan. You are very early. I usually have a final cup of coffee at this time, before the onslaught begins . . ." There was a hint of reproach in his voice.

I smiled amiably. "Please don't let us stop you. We just have one question we want to ask you."

He sighed. "It couldn't have waited till lunch . . . Fine, come on in. Tell me, what is it?"

Joy emerged from his office with a can of spray-wax and a yellow cloth. She showed us a big smile. "We was up so late yesterday at the church, making parcels and preparing for them to be collected six o'clock this morning. I am *pooped*! Sorry, Dr. Epstein, I only just done your desk." She grinned at me and winked. "Carmen and John, you want a cup of coffee? It's real proper coffee, not that instant muck."

We told her that would be nice and followed Epstein into his room, where he dropped heavily into the chair behind his desk. From there, he gestured for us to sit opposite him.

"What is this question that must be answered at all costs first thing in the morning?"

Dehan arched an eyebrow at him. "*This* is first thing in the morning?" She turned to me. "Honey, we been getting it *all* wrong!"

I gave her a look that told her to shut up and turned my attention to Epstein. "Why didn't you tell us that Al was planning to get married?"

Nothing at all happened to his face. He stared at me so long it was almost embarrassing. Finally, he reached forward and flipped a switch on his desk. When he spoke, it was almost a roar. "Joy! Come in here, please!

"What," he snapped at me, "makes you think that Al was contemplating such an absurd course of action?"

I glanced at Dehan. Behind us, the door opened, and Joy hurried in with a tray. She placed it on the desk and scowled at Epstein, who scowled back.

"What's all this shouting?"

"I did not shout. I never shout. I growled. Sit!"

She pulled up a chair and sat.

He gestured at us with his open palm. "Detective Stone has just asked me why I did not inform him that Al was planning to get married . . ."

Her face and her body both seemed to sag slightly. The laughter drained from her expression, and she looked down at her hands in her lap.

After a moment, Epstein went on, "I am having to tell them that I did not inform them of this fact because I didn't know about it! Now, would you care to clarify things for *all* of us?"

She heaved a big sigh and gazed down at the floor, twisting her hands together and rubbing her fingers. "I never thought I was going to have to go over all this again. Poor Al." She glanced at Dehan. "He was awful lonely. He had a lot of people who would say 'Hi!' to him in the street." She raised her hand and waved and smiled to illustrate. "'Hey, Al, how's it going?' but nobody ever stopped by to have a cup of coffee, or a chat. I did when I could, but you know, the church has me so busy. And Dr. Epstein never give me no rest!" Her face creased and she laughed out loud.

"Joy, would you *kindly* confine yourself to the *relevant* facts!"

"So one day, long time before he went to the Lord, must have been midsummer, so about six month before he died, he come to get his medicine and he takes me aside, real excited and smiling, and he tells me he got a girlfriend. To be honest, I didn't believe him. I am thinking, some woman said hello, and now he's blown it all out of proportion in his head. 'Oh, fantastic!' I ask him, 'What's her name?' So he tells me, 'I can't tell you her name—or Dr. Epstein—she made me promise.'"

I leaned forward with my elbows on my knees. "His girlfriend told him to keep it a secret?"

"That's what he told me, but I didn't believe him."

Epstein cut in, "It was consistent with his condition that he would develop fantasies of this type."

"So I told him, 'You tell Dr. Epstein all about it. You have to tell him everything, you know that!' But he says to me, 'No, if I tell the doctor, she will stop coming to visit me. It has to be a secret. The doctor won't let me have her.'"

"You should have told me about that, Joy."

"Maybe I did and you just don't remember, old man!

Anyhow, I didn't think much about that. It was just one more of his crazy ideas. He told me later that she come to see him *every* night. But couple of times I passed by on the way to church or on the way back, I never saw nobody there. Lights out and him watching TV." She turned to look at Dr. Epstein. "He didn't have no girlfriend. Even if there was some woman crazy enough to get involved with him, he was too scared to get involved with any woman!"

"Even so, Joy. It was an important fantasy. I should have known about it."

I scratched my chin. "Apart from what he said, was there any indication at all—maybe something you missed at the time but in retrospect makes sense—that might have indicated there *was* somebody, a woman, in his life?"

Epstein raised his eyebrows. "Well, I began to observe, about six months before he died, that his general humor had changed for the better. He seemed more optimistic about the future, more cheerful . . . But it would never have occurred to me in a thousand years that it might be due to a woman!"

Joy shrugged and smiled at Dehan. "Love!" she said simply.

Epstein turned and frowned at me. "Where did this ludicrous notion come from?"

"Members of his family. He called a family reunion and told them all he was getting married."

"Good Lord! And they never thought to consult me, and see if it was true?"

I turned to Joy. "In retrospect, were there any other indications that he was seeing a woman? Any hint of who she might be?"

"No." She shook her head. "I mean, the doctor and I would often comment that he did seem more happy, but we thought it was just that he was . . . *integrating*. With the community, you know? Finding his place, making a few friends. By friends, I mean people who'd say hello on the street. Nobody ever visited him."

Dehan made a humorless smile. "Except his future wife."

Epstein shook his head. "I shouldn't give too much credence to that, Detective. There is a reek of tragedy about this. If his siblings heard from his own mouth that he planned to get married, and, typically for them, they believed him, instead of looking deeper, instead of checking with me . . . If they decided to act in some way on that information . . ." He let the words trail away and his face seemed to sag. "That would be too awful for words. Poor Al."

"Is it possible that some woman from the neighborhood, who had heard the rumors about him keeping a stash of money in his house, decided to move in on him? And when she discovered who he really was, thought maybe she could do better still by marrying him? Is that possible?"

Joy stared at Epstein with wide eyes. He expostulated. "Possible! Yes, of course it's possible! Everyone in the neighborhood had heard the stories about the stash of money he was supposed to keep in his house. So any woman unscrupulous enough . . ." He closed his eyes and heaved a deep sigh. "Forgive me, any woman who was in desperate enough need might be driven to do what you are suggesting. And he would undoubtedly have been receptive. The poor man was deeply deprived of love. But . . ."

Joy interjected. "We would have known. I would have known. You can just tell, right?" She appealed to Dehan. "Right?"

Epstein nodded and gestured at Joy. "As Joy is saying, we knew him so well. He would have . . ." He hesitated.

I said, "Told you?"

"We would have known. I am sure of it."

I watched him a moment, then asked, "So in your opinion, the chances are this woman didn't exist, except in his imagination."

He nodded. "That would be my guess."

I turned to Joy. "I'm asking you this, not as Dr. Epstein's assistant, but as a woman who is very active in the neighborhood. Do you think Al's woman was real, or a figment of his mind?"

She glanced at her employer.

Dehan smiled at her. "Never mind what he thinks. What do you think?"

She thought about it. Then her face became sad, and she shook her head. "The truth is, there was no woman in his life. If there had been a real woman, we would have known. He was alone."

We thanked them and left our coffee untouched on the tray. We didn't speak on our way down in the elevator. As we stepped into the lobby, we saw it was dark and shaded, and the glass doors at the far end were a brilliant glare of sunlight. Through it, a dark shadow warped and moved toward us. Dehan shaded her eyes. I frowned, and the shadow stopped a few paces from us. The voice that spoke was unexpectedly sweet.

"Detectives! Good morning! I didn't expect to see *you* here today!" She shifted around so the sun was no longer in our eyes.

I smiled. "Mary. I'm glad to see you. I was just thinking about you."

"Oh, really? I hope it was something nice." She put her hand to her mouth. "I hope that's not vanity and hubris! Do you think it is?"

I laughed. "No, not at all. We all want to be honestly appreciated, Mary. Listen, you remember Al, right?"

"Oh yes, he was killed. That was awful. They thought it was that awful Ned, but Mom says we should leave it to God to judge, while we should learn to forgive."

Dehan snorted. "Cops can't afford that luxury."

"Mary, how old were you when Al died?"

"Oh, well . . ." She brought her hands together, like she was secretly using them to count. "I'm not great with numbers, but I guess I was about ten?"

"How old are you now?"

"Twenty-two . . . ?" She smiled and hunched her shoulders.

I went on, "So you were about ten when he died. Did you see much of him?"

"Well, I guess we saw him as much as anyone else from the

refuge. Mom said he had extra special needs because he wasn't used to living down and out. He used to be a doctor, like Dr. Epstein, and he was real smart."

"Did you ever visit him alone?"

Her eyes went wide. "No! Only ever with my mom."

"He ever give you candy?"

"Only every time we visited!" She laughed. "He was real nice. We was real fond of him. I was sad when the Lord took him away."

"Did you ever see him and talk to him out in the street?"

She smiled and shook her head. It was hard to tell what, because she was still smiling sweetly, but something had changed in her expression, even in the attitude of her body.

"Well, I never went out alone. I only ever went out with my mom."

Dehan frowned. "What about school?"

"Well, they told us at the school that school weren't the best way for me. There were some special schools, but they were awful expensive. So Mom fixed it for me to have a teacher come in and teach me the basics. So most often I'd just stay at home, until Mom come in."

I murmured, "You don't want to be a girl alone on the streets of Babylon."

"That's what my mom says."

I nodded. "We'll let you get on, Mary. But before you go. Do you know whether Al had a girlfriend?"

Her face softened and she laughed prettily. "No, I don't think so. But who knows what goes on after dark in this city?" She skipped a couple of steps toward the elevators. "I have to go. Mom and Dr. Epstein depend on me being on time. So I am always a little early. I wouldn't dream of letting them down . . ."

She edged a step closer, and I laughed. "Go, hurry! Don't be late."

"Thank you!"

She climbed into the elevator we had vacated. She pressed the button and gave us a little wave, the doors slid closed, and we stepped outside into the morning sun.

Dehan spoke to the sky, as though she were addressing God. "This is turning into a nightmare. Everything contradicts everything else." She went and sat on the hood of the Jag. "As soon as it looks like an avenue has opened up, something else comes along and closes that avenue down again."

"I know." I went to the driver's side and unlocked the door. "We should get word about the court orders soon."

She didn't answer. She sat and sulked.

I said, "You want to ride to the station on the hood?"

She turned to face me, her brow twisted into a knot. "So what are we saying now, that Max had his brother killed because he *believed* Al's story that he was getting married, when all along it was just a fantasy?"

"A very long fantasy, that lasted six months."

"That is dark, and a bit depressing."

"Would you like to get in the car, please, Detective Dehan?"

She stood and opened the passenger door just as my phone rang. She slammed the door, and the deputy inspector's voice said, "John, it's John, I am here with the DA and Judge Mathews, discussing the dilemma of the court orders. Judge Mathews would like you to present yourself here and explain to her, and the DA, exactly why we feel we are entitled to a judicial order."

"Where is here, sir?"

"Excuse me?"

"Where are you, sir? Where do we need to go?"

"Oh, yes, I see, Hall of Justice, Stone. Chambers of Judge Mathews."

He said it like it was obvious.

"Half an hour, sir."

FIFTEEN

WE TOOK THE CROSS BRONX EXPRESSWAY AND followed it as far as the Alexander Hamilton Bridge. There we turned south, following the Harlem River as far as Macombs Dam Park and the Heritage Field. There I turned in and took River Avenue to East 161st and parked in the big lot opposite the Hall of Justice. Then we crossed the road to enter the vast, ugly, gray-green box where the criminal courts were held.

I had spoken to Judge Mathews before, and aside from her desire to bring back public birching, we were pretty much on the same page about most things. We took the elevator to the top floor and followed a blue-carpeted passage to her door. There, we knocked and were admitted by her secretary, who showed us through to the judge's chambers.

The carpet was the same deep, rich blue as it was in the corridors outside. The furnishings were modern and functional, but of good quality, and mainly wood. It was not a corner office, but the view from her large, double window was good.

Assistant District Attorney Bob Swindon and the deputy inspector stood as we came in. Judge Mathews smiled at me from where she sat behind a vast, oak desk. There was a bit of handshaking, but the judge spoke over it.

"Stone, Dehan, come in and sit down, and do me a favor, would you?"

Swindon and the inspector pulled up two chairs for Dehan. I figured she only needed one, so I sat in the other.

Mathews kept talking. "I have always had you down as that rarest of all things, a sensible cop."

"Thank you, Judge."

"But this, what you're asking for today . . ." She shook her head. "I'm here with Bob and John because it's you. I'm aware of your track record, and I'm aware of some of the garbage you've cleared out from the halls of power, so I'm here, listening, but I have to tell you, Stone, I am struggling to see exactly on what grounds you think you're entitled to these two judicial orders. So do me a favor, and explain that to me."

I drew breath to answer, but she plowed on, "And let me tell you something else, before you get started, an emergency injunction was granted this morning, by Judge Allende, preventing the NYPD from obtaining precisely the information you are trying to obtain with these two orders. Shoot. Convince me I should overturn Allende's order."

I smiled sweetly and held up three fingers. "Three."

"*Three* judicial orders?"

She looked at Bob and John with a "what the hell?" face. Bob and John looked at each other and then they all looked at me. I counted the orders off on my raised fingers.

"We need one to view the will by which Ned Brown was made a beneficiary of that trust. We need another so that we can have sight of Ned Brown's birth certificate and establish who his biological parents are, and we need a third one allowing us to view the financial records of the surviving Chester siblings."

ADA Bob Swindon half stood. He looked scandalized, probably because he played golf with two of the surviving Chester siblings. Meanwhile, Deputy Inspector John Newman, my chief, looked equally shocked, probably because he hoped one day to play golf with two of the surviving Chester siblings. He spluttered, "Now, John . . . !"

Judge Margaret Mathews did not look shocked or scandalized. She began to laugh, leaning first forward and then back in her large, black leather chair. She wiped her eyes and looked at Dehan.

"You married this guy, right?"

Dehan's eyes narrowed, and her jaw set like concrete.

"Yes, Judge."

Mathews shook her head. "The man has the balls of a bronco, the predatory instincts of a mountain lion, and what makes him most scary, he has the brains of a Sherlock Holmes." She turned back to me. "Okay, you got my attention. Explain to me how you are legally entitled to these orders."

I sighed, crossed one leg over the other, and smiled at her. "You set me a pretty high bar there, Judge. I'll see what I can do. Aloysius Chester was murdered. He was stabbed in the heart with a large kitchen knife, which was never recovered. That same night, we presume it was during the same incident in which he was murdered, three shots were fired in his kitchen, from a nine-millimeter pistol, which was never recovered either. A satisfactory motive for his murder has never been established. These are the bare, relevant facts which I want to highlight."

They were all watching me, frowning. Mathews was nodding, like she was going over the facts with me. I went on.

"We know that earlier that night, Aloysius had an altercation with Ned Brown, in which Ned and his friends tried to break into his house and assault Aloysius, but in which Aloysius, in fact, broke two of Ned's fingers. Ned and his friends left, and we now know that he went to the ER unit—with his friends and his mother. The story until now has been that Ned was given powerful painkillers and that he went home with his mother to sleep and recuperate."

Mathews was chewing her lip. She raised an eyebrow. "The story until now? How has the story changed?"

"Julio Chavez was one of the boys who were present that

night. He is now serving time upstate for the murder of Geronimo Paez. We spoke to him, and he told us a different story. He said that the painkillers and the marijuana Ned was smoking combined with the November cold and triggered some kind of craziness in Ned, and he and Lenny 'Lucky' Marley went down to Aloysius' place and killed him. Lucky, according to Chavez, provided the nine-millimeter. Chavez alleges that the next day, Ned did in fact confess to killing Aloysius."

ADA Bob Swindon muttered, "The word of a convicted murderer..."

I gave him the dead eye for a moment, then turned back to Judge Mathews. "I don't plan to take this to court yet, Judge, but it is a well-known fact, I can get you a dozen witnesses right now who will testify that there was a rumor in the neighborhood that Aloysius had anything from a quarter of a million dollars to a million dollars stashed away in his house, either in a box or a knapsack or a sports bag. It is not beyond the bounds of possibility that Ned, feeling both physically injured *and* that his pride and his reputation had been damaged, did in fact go, while under the influence of drugs, and kill Aloysius with the purpose of taking his money..."

She sighed. "John, I am being very patient here. I am still waiting to hear why I should make this order that allows you to look at a document the author of which expressly required it to be sealed! So far, you have simply added some detail to what Detective Martinez had originally speculated."

I raised a hand. "I am almost done. First, one or two witnesses to a confession to murder is more than a little detail. But here is the important point: Ned's trust fund, *assumed* to be a will, though nobody has actually laid eyes on it except the attorneys at Hernandez and Heap, was made available to him within a year of Aloysius' death. Clearly, there must be a suspicion that Aloysius did in fact have a great deal of cash in his house, that Ned found that money and took it to some local attorneys, and they advised him to set up an anonymous trust fund."

ADA Swindon sighed. "I believe you also discovered that Ned is in fact adopted. It is equally likely that the trust fund is an endowment from his biological parents."

"Of course, Judge, that is obvious. But it is equally possible that if Ned turned up at home with half a million bucks in a sports bag, his mother might well come up with the idea of the anonymous trust fund, recalling that he was, in fact, adopted."

He shook his head. "That is a hell of a reach, Stone."

"Is it? So far, it is the only theory that comes anywhere close to answering all the questions in the case. Besides . . ." I spread my hands. "There is one very simple way of putting these doubts to rest, and that is allowing us to have a look at the trust, find out who established it, when, and with what money." I turned back to the judge. "I put this very proposition to Chevronne Brown, Ned's mother, last night. I told her that if the trust fund was legit, it would clear her son from any suspicion of the murder of Al Chester, take him clean off our list of suspects. Her response was to throw us out."

The judge was nodding. "Assuming, for one moment, that your suspicions were founded, if Ned, conspiring with his mother and possibly even these attorneys, had in fact set up a fake trust fund, the documents clearly would not have Ned's name on them."

"Obviously, Judge, but if the trust was fraudulent and we got our fraud boys to look into it, it would very quickly come to light that the people who had established the fund were as phony as the fund itself. Which brings me to the second point. We need to know who Ned's biological parents are, because right now the *supposition* that the trust fund was set up by them is creating a possible smoke screen. If we find that his biological parents are John and Jane Doe, and John and Jane Doe have set up the trust fund with money they made sheep farming in Australia, well, that's fantastic. He is in the clear. But if we discover that the fund was set up by John Smith, and he is nothing to do with John and Jane Doe, well, then we have good reason to believe that the idea for the trust fund was borne of the fact that he was an orphan. We need to know who his biological parents are. He is our prime suspect in a murder investigation aggravated by the possible theft of hundreds of thousands of dollars, and he may be hiding behind that anonymous trust fund *and* his biological parents."

I stopped and waited. She stared at me for a long moment. Finally, she said, "You should have been an attorney. You make a compelling case. What about this nonsense about looking at the Chesters' financial records?"

I met her smile with a completely blank face. "If it were nonsense, Judge, I wouldn't waste your time with it. In our first interview with Maximilian Chester, he told us, quite blatantly, that they had discussed having Aloysius killed. But he said that his brother's descent into psychosis had obviated the need, because they were able to have him sectioned. Shortly after that, his brother, Justinian, called and said he wanted to talk to us. He told us, at some length, that Maximilian and Annunziata had conspired to have Aloysius killed, no longer because he was soiling the family name with his drugs and generally disreputable behavior, but because, shortly before his death, he had informed them that he planned to get married."

ADA Swindon sat forward, wide-eyed. "*What?*"

Judge Mathews narrowed her eyes. "Run that by me again?"

"Aloysius Chester contacted Maximilian, Justinian, and Annunziata and asked for a family get-together. At that get-together, he informed them that he was planning to get married. Clearly, that had serious implications for the family as a whole, for the three siblings personally, *and* for Chester Cardio-Valves, the family firm."

"Why didn't his psychiatrist know about this?"

"That's exactly where we've just come from, Judge. Aloysius had in fact mentioned it to his psychiatrist's assistant, but they had not taken it seriously. They thought it was a fantasy. Besides which, he claimed that his girlfriend didn't want Dr. Epstein to know about it, because he would disapprove. So it never really got discussed.

"Now, the point is, regardless of what Dr. Epstein did or did not know, Aloysius *did* go to his brothers and his sister and he *did* tell them that he planned to get married. It makes no difference whether it was true or mere fantasy, the *fact* is that he told them, and they believed him; and, according to Justinian, this prompted Maximilian and Annunziata to contemplate having him killed. So, on the strength of those facts, I think we are entitled to look at their bank records to see if around November or December 2007, any or all of them paid out a significant sum of money that cannot be readily explained: the fee for a hit."

She shook her head and flopped back in her chair. "This is insane. I have known the Chesters for years!"

I raised an eyebrow at her. "I fail to see the relevance of that, Judge, unless you see it as a reason to recuse yourself and call in another judge who has no personal association with the Chesters."

Her cheeks flushed and her eyes shone bright with anger. She turned to Dehan. "You see what I mean!"

"Yes, Judge."

I cut across the crap, feeling suddenly irritable and in need of lunch and a beer. "We need those orders, Judge Mathews. Somebody is getting away with murder—and a very substantial theft—and granting those orders can help us find out who. There is also the very pertinent fact that there is a young man trying to make something of his life, and he is going to have the suspicion of Aloysius' murder hanging over his head until the day he dies. If he is innocent, he deserves to have that known, even if it brings down the Chesters. If he is guilty, he is not entitled to the protection of the courts."

She sighed. "I am going to need some time to think about all this, Detective Stone. I don't mind telling you, you are a supreme pain in the ass, but you have made a very compelling argument. It is a credit to you and your eloquence that I didn't kick this whole request out from the start..."

"I hope it is also a credit to our diligent police work, Judge, not just my eloquence."

We gave each other the dead eye for ten seconds, then she said, "Get out of here. You'll have my decision within the next hour or two."

I nodded. "Thank you for seeing us, Judge."

We stood, and I opened the door for Dehan. As she was about to go through, the judge smiled at her. "How do you put up with him?"

Dehan stopped and gave me a lopsided smile. She spoke to me, not Mathews. "He's usually right, and he's all mine."

I shrugged with my eyebrows at the three watching faces and we stepped out.

We rode the elevator down and after a couple of minutes stepped out into the bustle and noise of the Bronx's downtown area. I looked at my watch. It was approaching twelve forty.

"We should grab some food and a beer and have a think."

"I can't think of any more ways to think, Stone. Think about what? Unless she gives us at least one green light, we are as screwed as..." She hesitated.

I said, "A two-dollar whore during shore leave?"

"Stone!"

"What? That's pretty screwed."

"Stop it! I can say things like that. You can't."

I took her elbow and we started walking east, pushing through the crowds toward the intersection with Morris Avenue. "Let's go to Aminas Café. I am in need of good Mexican food. And, to answer your question, what we are going to think about, Ritoo Glasshopper, is *strategy*. Strategy and tactics. We are not going to get our court orders..."

"You don't know that. How can you know that? We might. You were pretty convincing back there."

I shook my head. "Nah, she was much too complimentary.

Plus, there is no way she is going to upset the Chesters without a much bigger cause than what I gave her. No, she'll turn us down. She'll say she can't overturn another judge's ruling without much more solid facts. And to be honest, she'll be right. So we need to think, about how we proceed from here. Not a plan, we have a plan, but tactics and strategy."

We turned into Morris Avenue and crossed the road. As we did so, she asked me, "Plan? We have a plan? Seriously, Stone? It seems to me we are as lost today as we were the day we picked up this case. Maybe more so!"

I looked at her in surprise as I held the door open for her. "Really? It's very clear to me. All I need now is to find the proof."

She stopped dead in the doorway and turned to look at me as I squeezed past her.

"What? Are you telling me you *know* who killed Al Chester?"

"Don't you? I thought it was obvious. What do you want for lunch? I need a chicken taco, and a beer."

I sat at a table by the window, and Dehan sat opposite me, with a sour scowl on her face. "She was right," she said after a moment. "She had you pegged. You're a supreme pain in the ass!"

I gazed innocently, with raised eyebrows, at the menu.

SIXTEEN

I spoke around a mouthful of chicken and taco.

"Jush fink imfroo, Jeehang!"

She chewed and watched me through narrowed eyes. "Just think it through . . . seriously? You're telling me to think it through? I thought it through, up, down, across, and with every damn preposition in the English lexicon!"

"Wowm!" I said, refilling my mouth. "Dash pweddy goob."

"Stop talking with your mouth full. It makes me want to hit you."

I gave a small, derisive laugh. "Bwave werje."

"What?"

I swallowed and drained half my beer, sighed, and wiped my mouth. "Allow me to quote you, Carmen: *'Entia non sunt multiplicanda praeter necesitatem!'* Remember? Quite literally, things are not multiplied except where necessary, Occam's razor, the simplest answer is usually the correct one."

"I remember."

"Well, this case has been about all that: the individual against society, against the community, against the gang. Always too many people. Too many options and at the same time, too few."

"You going to keep BS-ing me or are you going to tell me?"

I chuckled annoyingly. "Okay, I'll give you a hand. Think of the shots. The shots are key. Think of that knife. Where is the knife? Whose knife was it? That is key too. And think, also, Little Grasshopper, about who would want that injunction so badly they would apply for an emergency hearing during the night?"

"I don't know, Stone! Tell me, please!"

My phone rang.

"Yeah, Stone."

"Detective Stone, this is Chevronne Brown. I need to talk to you. It's urgent."

"Sure. Where are you?"

"No, I'll come to you at the station."

I looked at my watch. "Be there for three thirty. We can't make it before then."

She was silent for a moment. "All right, I'll be there at three thirty. Please, don't be late."

"We'll be there."

She hung up, and I sat frowning at my phone. Dehan intruded upon my thoughts. "Something else you're not going to tell me about?"

"That was Ned's mother. Her tone had changed some."

"Really? What did she want?"

"She wanted to meet with us. She said it was urgent. She sounded worried and asked me not to be late..."

"Huh."

"Come on, Dehan. Let's go have Annunziata Chester talk at us. I am curious to see what's on her mind."

I left the car on West 112th and we walked the short distance to 400 Riverside Drive. As we rounded the corner, I was surprised to see Annunziata standing out on the sidewalk. She was dressed in a scarlet dress with a slash down one thigh, a small black pillbox on her head, and a string of pearls around her throat. She also had a large rat on a lead, which on closer inspection turned out to be a Chihuahua. I recognized her from her photographs and approached her.

"Dr. Annunziata Chester?"

"You must be the detectives. So good of you to come. Do you mind if we walk in the park while we talk? One never knows these days when one is being bugged. And what with all the warnings about Facebook and WhatsApp . . . one doesn't know whom to trust. Don't you agree, Detective?"

We identified ourselves, and all three of us crossed at the pedestrian crossing to walk in among the trees and gardens that border the Hudson along Riverside Drive. The bug-eyed rat trotted along beside her, looking permanently scared.

Dehan made a face that was skeptical and showed it to Annunziata. "You think somebody is bugging you?"

Annunziata eyed her a moment, like she was wondering who she was and what she was doing there.

"One never knows, does one?"

I began to fear that one was going to get stuck in the Land of the Vague if one wasn't careful and asked bluntly: "What did you want to see us about, Dr. Chester?"

She gazed up at me while we walked, chewing her lip without saying anything. I could feel Dehan getting antsy and started to feel a little irritated myself. I drew breath to ask her again, but she preempted me and said, "Justin."

Dehan growled, "What about him?"

"If you've spoken to him, you've no doubt noticed that he is . . . eccentric."

I sighed and didn't try to hide it. "That is not a crime, Dr. Chester."

"Do please call me Anne. I detest all this formality. It is so trying to be a Chester."

"You were telling us about Justinian."

"When I say eccentric, I mean that, though he is by no means psychotic, as poor Al was, he does have a tendency to fantasize a little . . ."

Dehan glanced at me. I read the look and gave her a small nod. She stopped in her tracks and faced Annunziata. "Dr. Chester, did you and your brother Maximilian conspire to murder your brother Al?"

Annunziata took a very deep breath, looked down at the path, and then up into my face, like she wanted me to rescue her.

"Yes," she said. "We did."

I had a strange sensation, like I had brain-ache. I screwed up my face and said, "Dr. Chester, Anne, are you aware that you just confessed to a very serious crime, that carries a very long prison sentence with it?"

She nodded and started walking again. "But when you hear all the circumstances, I think you'll understand. And once I have told you everything, you must . . ." She placed her hand on my forearm. ". . . do whatever it is you must do."

I met Dehan's eye again. Her eye was saying we should take this dame down to the station and charge her with conspiracy to commit murder. My eye told her eye to hold its horses.

"Come, Calypso." This was directed at the dog as she started to walk again. "We may not have many walks together after today."

"Tell us about this conspiracy, what was discussed, by whom, where, and when."

"It was in 1990. Al had returned from his stay in Latin America."

"How long was he there?" It was Dehan.

Annunziata studied her red satin shoes. They had little straps across her ankles. She answered glancing at me, as though I had asked the question, not Dehan. "In all, he was there almost ten years. Before that, he had been to Turkey, India, Indonesia . . . wherever he could find some kind of mind-altering drug in his constant search for true consciousness. He had read the Castaneda books when he first went to Harvard, and it became an obsession with him to become what he called a man of knowledge."

"So he spent ten years traveling in Latin America, and then he returned in 1990?"

"Yes."

We had come to the tennis courts. One of them was occupied by a young couple in whites playing a fast game. She walked up to the mesh and stood staring through. Her voice sounded strangely empty as she spoke.

"There was some stupid reunion; a group of alumni who had all dropped out around 1969 were going to have a reunion there, a long weekend where they were going to get stoned out of their minds. Al returned from Brazil especially for this reunion." She frowned. "He looked awful."

Dehan asked, "You saw him?"

"Of course. He flew into New York, and I went to meet him at the airport. I wanted to see what state he was in. He was frightful. Very slim and tanned, obviously. But his eyes were hollow, and there was a kind of manic look to them."

She turned away from the court and started walking again. "While he had been traveling, especially while he was in Latin America, he had not been a concern to us. He had given me his proxy vote on all board decisions, and all he wanted to do was travel and experiment with drugs. But when we talked that day . . ." She shook her head.

"What? What did you notice?"

"He was taunting me, saying he was tired of living in the jungle, he wanted to come back to civilization, write books about his experiences, take up his position on the board. The more he talked, the more manic he became. He wanted the family firm to move into hallucinogenic drugs and lead a campaign to legalize mind-altering substances. It was his destiny, he said, to bring about a new era in human evolution . . ." She sighed. "You can imagine how I felt."

Dehan replied, "Yeah. You felt like killing him."

Annunziata gave a small, private smile. "Not precisely, Detective Dehan. It took a little longer than that. He came to stay with me, and I urgently called Max and Justin to come and have dinner and see what they made of his condition. Conversation over dinner was much as it had been throughout the day, with Al ranting like a madman about his insane plans. He intended to herald in a new age of enlightenment, using everything he had learned over the previous twenty years about mind-altering substances.

"The next day, he traveled up to Boston for his reunion. Apparently, I learned later, he and his dropout friends had gone on what he called a 'raiding party,' picking up young students and inviting them to a party that night. The party was in fact an orgy of sex and drugs aimed at freeing the young students' minds and encouraging them to drop out."

Dehan asked, "How long did that go on?"

"For three days. We had to pull strings and call in a lot of favors to avoid it hitting the press. And that was when we had the first meeting. Max was the first to propose it. Justin was predictably against it. His reasoning was entirely sentimental. It went along the lines of, 'We can't just kill our own brother,' as though introducing the adjective 'own' made our brother somehow more difficult to kill."

She came to a bench and sat. Calypso sat beside her ankle and viewed the world through bulging, terrified eyes. Dehan stood facing Anne with her hands in her back pockets. I stood too, staring at the trees, thinking.

"Of course I didn't *want* to kill my brother, and obviously I would miss him. But those considerations, when weighed against the damage he was about to do to all of us, as a family, as individuals, to the company . . . It seemed to me that it was perfectly legitimate to consider that extreme alternative. I remember I asked Max who would carry out the execution. He was frightfully gruff and said, 'Nobody! I will drop a word in a certain ear, and it will be taken care of.'"

She sighed and went silent. After a moment, she took a small lace handkerchief and wiped her eyes. "We never quite got around to making the decision. We agreed to talk to him when he got back from Boston. When he did get back, it didn't take us long, especially Justin and myself, to realize that he had suffered serious damage as a result of all the drugs he had taken. At the time, we believed he was borderline psychotic, but within a matter of a very few weeks, we realized he was descending rapidly into full-blown paranoia and probably schizophrenia."

My voice was harsher than I had intended: "And that was when you decided to disown him."

She shrugged. "He was a loose cannon. He was actually dangerous. We put him in several clinics, we tried various therapies, but nothing worked. Eventually, at the turn of the millennium, we gave him an allowance that would, if managed sensibly, provide him with rent and food, but not drugs, and we cut him loose."

Dehan's voice was almost a rasp. "That is cold. That is ruthless."

Annunziata looked at Dehan full in the face for the first time. "I am really not interested in your judgment, Detective Dehan. We did what we did. Al gravitated to his natural level and wound up living homeless on the streets in the Bronx. However, Max thought we should have him sectioned, find a local psychiatrist, and pay him a retainer to keep an eye on him, and that was when we found Dr. Epstein."

I puffed out my cheeks and blew hard. "I very much doubt that any court would convict you on what you have told us, Anne. It is doubtful you ever actually formed the intention to kill. Certainly you never acted to put your discussions into effect. It sounds more as though you contemplated the possibility and rejected it."

She shook her head. "Not exactly, Detective Stone. We postponed it. It was never said openly, but we all knew it. We were kicking the can down the road."

I could feel myself getting mad. My patience was straining, and I wasn't precisely sure why. "What exactly do you mean by that, Anne?"

She reached in her purse and pulled out a gold cigarette case.

She extracted an unfiltered cigarette and lit it with a gold Cartier lighter. She took her time inhaling and then let out a long stream of smoke.

"You probably know that Dr. Epstein and his practice took Al to their bosom. He took his role as guardian very seriously and went to some pains to help Al. He put a great deal of pressure on us to buy him that grotesque little house he lived in. He also got him a cleaner to come in a couple of times a week, and apparently he encouraged him to drop in to his practice whenever he felt like it. And so it went on for years."

Dehan curled her lip. "And then he decided to get married."

Annunziata nodded. "We couldn't allow that to happen. The consequences were unthinkable. We had a meeting, and we decided that Max would employ a private detective to find out exactly who this woman was. What he discovered shattered us completely. Of all the things he had done over the years, none of them came close to this."

I sat on the edge of the bench, turned slightly to face her.

"What? What was it?"

"We learned that during his three-day orgy in Boston in 1990, Al had met a girl. She was an undergraduate, a psychology student from Harvard, his own alma mater. He had got her pregnant and then, in his inimitable style, he had simply abandoned her. She had eventually given birth to a boy." She paused, looking away from me. "It is very hard for me to talk about this. It . . ." She took a deep breath. "It emerged, from the private detective's investigation, that the child was of . . ." She closed her eyes, and I saw a tear on her cheek. When she spoke again, her voice was shrill. "The child, *my nephew*, was of *mixed race*! How dare he burden me with that! A Chester!"

Dehan's jaw had sagged. "No . . ."

Annunziata looked at her. "Yes. Ned Brown, that moronic *oaf*! Ned Brown is *my nephew*! If it ever came out! That a Chester . . . that a boy of mixed race . . ."

I barked a harsh laugh. "But he was going further than that, wasn't he? He was going to marry the woman he had abandoned seventeen, eighteen years earlier. He was going to marry Ned's mother."

She scowled at me. "You think that's funny?"

"If you hadn't killed Al, I'd think it was hilarious, but I don't find murder amusing, Annunziata. What happened?"

"We had dinner, Max, Justin, and myself. We discussed the detective's findings, and we all decided that he had gone too far. I don't think anybody actually *said* it, but it was understood. Aloysius had to die, before he brought the family down with him and destroyed us completely."

Dehan raised a hand. "Let me just see if I've got this straight. You decided to murder Al Chester because he was planning to marry a black woman."

Annunziata gave her a slow once-over, from head to toe and back again. "How could you possibly understand? Dehan, that's a Jewish name, isn't it? Like Dr. Epstein."

I said, "What happened, Annunziata? I need the facts."

"I don't know. It was always tacitly understood that Max would take care of it. But what he did, or how he did it, I have no idea."

"All right." I stood. "You're coming down to the station to make a statement. I haven't decided yet whether to charge you or not. On your feet. And leave the damned dog with your porter, will you?"

She got to her feet, and we made our way back to the car, and from there to the station.

SEVENTEEN

DEPUTY INSPECTOR JOHN NEWMAN REFUSED TO LOOK at us. Instead, he stared at his bonsai in the window. I sometimes wondered if he had grown attached to it, as some people grow attached to their cats or their cars, or if it was deeper than that, and he was seeking, by a process of total empathy, to become one with the bonsai. His face said that the prospect of prosecuting all the surviving members of the Chester family made him long to be a very small tree on a windowsill, rather than the deputy inspector of the 43rd Precinct.

"What I don't understand, John," he said at last, "is why on Earth she would do this. Why come forward and make this confession? She had absolutely no need to do it." He turned his chair to face me where I was standing, leaning against the door. "Has she given *any* explanation so far? Is she looking for immunity? What is it? Do you believe her?"

Before I could answer, he had turned to Dehan, who was sitting in a blue chair with her right ankle on her left knee. "Carmen, do you believe her?"

She sighed, shrugged her eyebrows and then her shoulders, like she was expressing three different levels of uncertainty. "I don't know, Chief. In some ways, it seems plausible. But it also raises a lot of questions."

He nodded vigorously. "Not least, why would she do this? This very action is guaranteed to bring down on her family the very shame and public humiliation they have been at such pains to avoid!"

"Sir."

He looked up at me.

"Both she and Justinian seemed to be very concerned about what the other siblings had said to us. Justin, in fact, came to us because he wanted to know what Maximilian had told us. Annunziata was worried about what Justinian might have told us. I think she's panicking and trying to cover her back."

"Has she asked for immunity?"

"Not yet."

"What's your plan?"

I looked at my watch. "Chevronne Brown is here waiting to talk to us in interview room three. She says it's urgent, and I am very curious to hear what she has to tell us. I think I'd like to let Annunziata sweat for a bit while we talk to Chevronne. Meanwhile, we need a DNA sample from Ned Brown. I'll see if we can get one from his mother."

He nodded and sighed heavily. "Fine, go ahead. And keep me posted. If it is still possible to avoid a scandal . . ." He trailed off and studied me a moment. "Your requests, by the way, the three court orders . . ."

"They were declined. I figured they would be, but we had to try."

"I suppose so."

We left his office, and I made my way to the coffee machine with Dehan beside me. She shook her head when I asked if she wanted a drink and leaned against the machine while I got coffee for me and for Chevronne.

"You really think you know who did it?"

"Maybe. I need to confirm a couple of things. Right now it's a hunch—a pretty good hunch, but just a hunch."

She stared at me a moment. "It's Max, isn't it? You knew from the beginning. The simplest answer, Occam's razor. He had the most to lose from Al staying alive, and the most to gain from his being dead. All that stuff about the box of money in his house, those kids knew it wasn't true. And there was no way Ned was going back with his system full of diazepam and two broken fingers. It had to be Max, all along."

I grunted. "It's looking that way. Listen, let's do something. You talk to Annunziata. See if you can get her to tell you *why* she dropped the dime on her brother."

A slow smile crept across her face. "Dropped the dime?"

"Yeah, I picked it up from one of those Mickey Spillane novels you read in the can."

She went away laughing, and I headed for interview room three.

Chevronne was sitting at the table and watched me sit, with resentful eyes. I slid a paper cup of coffee across to her with milk, sugar, and a plastic stirring stick. "It's almost like coffee," I said, but she didn't smile. "What did you want to talk to me about?"

"I told you almost two hours ago that it was urgent, and this is the first time I get to speak to you."

"I'm investigating a murder, Mrs. Brown. I can't always be where I want to be or do what I need to do when I need to do it. People don't make it easy for you, you know? You go to their house to ask them a simple question, and they kick you out and refuse to talk to you. Then they phone you up an hour later and demand to see you. I guess we just don't always get what we want. Now, are we going to waste time playing the blame game, or are you going to tell me why you're here?"

She rubbed her fingers across her brow and closed her eyes. "It's Ned."

"What about him?"

She opened her eyes to look at me. I picked up my coffee and sipped it.

She said, "He's gone."

I frowned at her and rubbed my own forehead. "You need to tell me what that means. Gone how?"

"He's not at his house. His wife don't know where he is. He's not at his workshop. The place is all locked up. He ain't left nobody a message. He's just gone. You pigs frightened him with your crazy investigation. Now he panicked and he's gone!"

I thought for a moment, stirred my coffee, and studied her a moment. She picked up her own paper cup and sipped.

I said, "Since when?"

She didn't answer.

I repeated the question. "Since when, Mrs. Brown?"

"He went out last night, about eleven. He never told his wife where he was goin'. He said he'd be back, but he never came back. This mornin' she call me, worried sick."

"Why didn't she call the cops?"

She sat up rigid, with wild, angry eyes. "Why do you think? Because you will take it as proof that he killed that stupid old man! Because you will hunt him down, like some kind of dog! But he didn't run because he was guilty! He run because he is *innocent*! And that's what you stupid cops cannot understand!"

I frowned, picked up my coffee, and stared into it, still frowning. I took a long pull, then put the cup down with a sigh.

"So, why are you here? You just told me you don't want the cops looking for your son. I'm a cop . . ." I spread my hands.

Something weird happened to her face: her eyes half closed, her brows knitted together, and her bottom lip curled up under her top one. Then she made a horrible, guttural noise and buried her face in her hands. She sobbed violently for a long while. When she finally stopped and raised her face from her palms, I handed her a clean, white handkerchief. She took it without saying anything, blew her nose, and wiped her eyes.

"He got a letter."

"A letter?"

"It was anonymous, letters cut out of a newspaper, pasted together. It said, 'We gonna kill you.'"

"Have you got it?"

She reached in her handbag, pulled out a creased envelope, and handed it to me. I pulled some latex gloves from my pocket, snapped them on, and pulled over the envelope. It was plain white, long, and creased down the middle where it had been folded in half.

I pulled out the note, opened it, and read it. It said simply: *We will kill you and your family, you black bastard.*

"When did this arrive?"

"This morning."

I examined the individual letters, but they didn't tell me much beyond the fact that the fonts were of a medium size favored by certain types of newspaper.

"Has he received any of these before?"

She gave her head three tight, rapid shakes. "No."

"Are you certain?"

"Yes."

"Chevronne, if you want me to help your son, you have to level with me. There is no point asking me for help and then giving me the runaround when I try to help you."

"I am not giving you the runaround. He never received one of them before."

"Have you any idea who might have sent it, any suspicion, however unlikely?"

Her face flushed with anger. "Probably some neighbor, got to hear about your damned investigation! Now he's thinking, 'Black men always killing white men! Now I'm gonna kill me a black man!' How many black men been killed by white men? How many black women been raped?"

"Please, Chevronne, let's stay on task. You want me to find your son, we haven't got much time. Where was this delivered?"

"To his house . . ." She started to cry. "Imagine if his children seen it!"

I sighed, pulled an evidence bag from my pocket, and dropped the letter into it. "We'll have this checked for prints."

I stood and opened the door, saw O'Connor, and called him over.

"Do me a favor, will you? Send this to the lab for me. And get me some paper handkerchiefs, will you? Sooner rather than later."

He gave a little frown. "Sure thing, Detective."

I called Joe at the lab.

"Stone, what can I do for you?"

"I'm sending you a package. It's urgent. It's a letter, a death threat, and the intended victim has disappeared. So a life could be in the balance. I'd appreciate if you could put a rush on them."

"Them? You said it's a single letter."

"You heard correct." There was a tap at the door. "Gotta go, but listen, the font is of interest."

O'Connor was there with a box of paper tissues. I took them and closed the door. I carried the tissues to the table, recovered my handkerchief, and sat.

"Are you prepared to discuss anything else with me? Are you prepared to answer my questions from last night?"

"I don't know nothing about that."

"You understand it might be connected with his disappearance?"

She wouldn't meet my eye but shook her head again.

"I don't know nothing."

"Have you any idea where he might go if he wanted to feel safe?"

"If I did, don't you think I'd be there now instead of wastin' my time with you?"

I sighed. "Will his wife be home now?"

"How should I know?"

I fought to control the hot anger that was welling up in my

belly. "I am trying to help you and your son, Mrs. Brown! Right now you are *not* helping Ned. So can the damned attitude!" I stood. "Go on, get the hell out of here. I'll call you when I know something."

Outrage tightened her face. "That's it?"

"What do you want? You want me to stay here and hold your hand while you insult me? Or you want me to go out and find Ned?" She didn't answer, so I pulled open the door. "I need your cell phone number and your son's. And what car he was driving."

She made a note, collected her things, shoved the piece of paper in my hands, and left.

I went to find O'Connor again, had a word with him, and gave him some errands, then went to find Dehan. She was still in interview room two, with Annunziata. They both looked up as I stepped in.

Dehan said, "Detective John Stone has entered the room," for the benefit of the recording.

I pulled out a chair and sat.

"When exactly, and I do mean exactly, did this meeting take place where you all understood Maximilian was going to have Aloysius killed?"

She had removed her pillbox hat and now ran her fingers through her black hair.

"I really wasn't expecting this. I thought you would be grateful."

I waited.

She shook her head. "I can't remember the exact day..."

"The week is good enough."

"I suppose it was toward the end of September 2007. I was over from San Francisco for Justin's birthday."

"Okay, good. Now, tell me something else, Anne. Why are you telling us all this? If the DA decides to prosecute you, you could be looking at twenty-five years in prison. So what has prompted you now, after twelve years, to come forward with this information?"

"Well, Justin called me and said that you had been to see him . . ."

"Justinian said that *we* had been to see *him*."

"Yes, and I asked him what he had told you, because he is so liable to exaggeration and, well, you know, he does fantasize, not like Al, but, you know, he does."

I spread my hands. "So?"

"Well, he said he had told you *everything*. And I thought, oh my God! Everything from Justinian could mean almost anything. Because, knowing him, he has included all *sorts* of nonsense that was never said or done, but he has *imagined* was said or done, when in fact it wasn't . . ."

Dehan let out a short laugh that wound up as an exhausted sigh.

"Let me see if I've got this straight. You have informed the police that you and your two brothers conspired to murder Aloysius, to avoid us taking Justin's story at face value, *in case it implicated you in Al's murder*? For crying out loud! You just implicated *yourself* in Al's murder!"

She didn't answer. She just sat and stared at Dehan.

Dehan made a helpless gesture, looked at me, and then looked back at Annunziata. "And you're a Harvard-educated neurologist?"

"Yes."

Dehan shook her head. "This is bull."

I said, "What is it you are hoping for, Anne? Detective Dehan is exactly right. In attempting to avoid being implicated by Justinian, you have implicated yourself. It doesn't make sense. Are you hoping that if we accept your version of the story, Max will go down and you and Justin will be in the clear? Is that the gamble you're taking? Or are you thinking that if you can get Max put away for the rest of his life, you and Justin can split the company between you, fifty-fifty?"

She shook her head. "I just want the truth to come out. Justin and I didn't really, *expressly* agree to it. It was a tacit understanding that Max would take care of things. He always has. If it had been discussed openly, perhaps things might have been different. But, one doesn't, you know, discuss such things openly, especially with Maximilian."

Dehan's eyebrows rose high on her forehead. She nodded several times before saying, "Murder."

Annunziata looked away, at the wall.

Dehan said, "Such things. One doesn't discuss such things openly. You're talking about murder, the murder of another human being—*your brother*, for Christ's sake! How is the murder of your brother 'such things'? I mean, what the hell are you lumping it together with?"

Anne spoke to the floor, as though the beige carpet had asked her the question.

"You know perfectly well what I mean. Subjects that are awkward or embarrassing..."

Dehan's jaw sagged, and she stared at me. I drew breath to cut the exchange short, but there was a tap at the door. I said, "Yeah," and O'Connor put his head in.

"Dr. Chester's attorney's here, Detectives."

I looked at her, gave a smile that was on the rueful side of bitter, and shook my head. "Thanks, O'Connor, show him in." The door closed. "What are you playing at? You called us, remember?"

"I didn't expect the kind of reaction I got from you. I thought you'd be more understanding. I sent him a text message while I was waiting for you."

Dehan exploded. "You confessed to conspiracy to murder! You're lucky you're not in the slammer!"

Annunziata looked at her and smiled. I realized it was only the second direct look she'd given her. "Oh, come, Detective Dehan," she said. "We both know that's not true. If you had grounds to arrest me, you would have done it by now."

I reached in my breast pocket and pulled out my pen and my

notebook. I wrote down the four symbols Led Zeppelin used on their fourth album, tore the sheet from the notepad, and handed it to her. "Do these symbols mean anything to you?"

She took the piece of paper and stared at it. Then shook her head.

I said, "Have a good look, Anne, it could be important."

The door opened, and a guy in a charcoal-gray suit with the kind of graying hair women find interesting stepped into the room. He was in his midfifties and smiled as though he'd been doing it all his life.

"Detective Dehan? How do you do? Paul Hirschfield, attorney at law." I watched him shake hands with her as a growing sense of unreality descended on me. Then he was smiling at me and actually making me feel warm and welcome in my own interrogation room. "Detective Stone. How do you do? Paul Hirschfield, Hirschfield, Roth and Cohen, attorneys at law." He shook my hand and smiled at Annunziata. "Anne, lovely to see you. Shame about the circumstances!" They both laughed. "What say we adjourn to someplace a little more cozy?" He turned to me with a small laugh. "I am assuming that you don't intend to arrest my client."

I shook my head. "Nope." I reached across the table and retrieved the paper with the four symbols.

"Super. Come, Anne, we have a loooong drive back to civilization!"

Dehan was watching them both through narrowed eyes. As Hirschfield opened the door, she said, "Yeah, mind you don't get your butts kicked out there in the Bronx Badlands."

The humor vanished from his face. His eyes were sharp and alert. "Is that a threat, Detective Dehan?"

Dehan smiled sweetly. "Not at all, Counselor, simply advice."

"Good day, Detectives."

They left, and the door closed behind them. She shook her head. "Do you mind telling me what the *hell* just happened,

Stone? And, Zofo? Seriously? Are you as crazy as they are or what?"

"I'll explain later." I thrust Ned's cell number into her hands and said, "Get me the location on that cell. Fast!"

And I went to look for O'Connor again.

EIGHTEEN

Ten minutes later, we were down at her desk and she was shaking her head.

"It's switched off. Or he's gone somewhere where there's no signal, maybe upstate . . ."

"Okay." I gave her Ned's license plate. "Get the GPS on the car. Find it."

While she did that, I called Bernie at the bureau.

"I'm not doing you any more favors till you buy me that drink you owe me, you miserable bastard."

"Bernie, not one, twenty. But listen, pal. This is urgent . . ."

"Oh, Stone, it's you! I thought it was my wife. What can I do for you?"

"I'm sending you a name and a photo, and a few other details. I need everything you can get me on this person in the next twenty minutes. Somebody's going to die, Bernie. It may already be too late."

"I'm on it, pal!"

I hung up and went back to Dehan. She was putting on her jacket. "Mamaroneck."

"Where?"

"North of La Rochelle, Mamaroneck, Mamaroneck Motel,

1015 Boston Post Road." She grabbed my jacket and shoved it at me. "And on the way you can tell me what the *hell* is going on!"

I followed her out, and as we clambered into the Jag, I said, "It's complicated."

"Complicated?"

She said it like I was four and trying to explain why I'd just painted big red stick men all over the garage door.

I reversed out of the lot and turned onto Story Avenue.

"Yes, Dehan, don't give me a hard time. It's complicated."

"So *explain it to me*!"

"Wait!"

I turned down Metcalf Avenue and then turned onto the Bruckner Expressway, headed east, and hit the gas. As we passed the Unionport Bridge, she said, "I'm waiting. You told me to wait. I'm waiting."

I sighed. "It is *really* complicated."

"What happened to Occam's razor?"

"You saw yourself, our simplest explanations did not cover all the facts." I hesitated. "It *is* simple . . ."

"Oh, *now* it's simple?"

"Yeah, it is. But it's damned complicated *to explain* when I am doing a hundred miles an hour down the expressway."

"Stay left on the 278."

"I know."

"Okay, don't get mad. Drive. I ask, you answer. Good?"

"Mm-hm."

We began to climb into the spaghetti junction. "Stay on the I-95."

"I know." I paused, then added, "So we're looking for Ned."

"Why?"

"That's not so easy to answer. He got an anonymous letter saying he was going to die."

"You got the note?"

"It's at the lab. Didn't tell me much. Standard printer paper. The letters had been cut from a newspaper. Probably the *Times*."

She laughed unpleasantly. "That's ridiculous. How could you know that?"

"I read the *Times*. I know the fonts they use for headlines."

"Oh. So he ran?"

"Disappeared last night."

She frowned. "When did he get the letter?"

"This morning."

"But that . . ."

"I know. I said it was complicated."

"So whatever reason he's run, it isn't the letter."

"No."

Her frown deepened. "So, he jumped in his car sometime between last night and early this morning and drove ten or fifteen miles to Mamaroneck and booked into a motel . . ."

"Yup."

"That doesn't make any sense."

"Unless he was meeting somebody."

"Huh, yeah." She nodded. "Who?" She snapped her fingers. "His adoptive parents!"

I smiled in spite of myself. "Grounds."

"What?"

"What are your grounds for that conclusion?"

"Well, who the hell would he be going to meet?"

"We'll soon find out, Dehan. I just hope we're not too late."

"Too late? I don't get why you think he's in danger."

"Okay, baby steps. We have established that we believe he did not flee, because as he hadn't received the note, he had no reason to yet. Also, he went no more than ten miles and stopped at a motel."

"Yes. That is not the behavior of a fleeing man."

"So from there, we reason that the most likely purpose for him to go to that motel in that way would be to meet somebody. There may be another explanation, but that is the most likely one."

I overtook a dark blue Audi that was only doing 90 miles per hour and was getting in my way.

"Yup."

"Okay, so the note. How does the note fit in to that? As I see it, we have a couple of options: one, it is totally unrelated; two, it is partly related; and three, it is directly related."

She nodded. "Baby steps, okay."

"Stay with me, this is important. Scenario one, it is totally unrelated; logically it will not affect what we are going to find at the motel."

"Okay, that makes sense. We still have to look into it, but it won't affect what we are about to find, because they are unrelated."

"Exactly." We were headed north now, and on our right, the city gave way to the open, green parkland around the Huntington Woods and the Victory Memorial. I saw the needle touch 110. "Now, scenario two: it is partly related. What does that mean? Maybe a white supremacist neighbor has heard that the cops are taking another look at the Al Chester case, maybe that has triggered old resentments, something of that sort. In which case, the timing of the letter's arrival is purely coincidental."

"Okay, I'm following you. In both scenario one and two, the timing of the arrival of the letter is a coincidence."

I nodded. "In my opinion, Dehan, it is one hell of a coincidence, in a case in which race just seems to keep cropping up in one guise or another."

"Okay..."

"However, be that as it may, in scenario three, they are intimately connected. So we need to ask ourselves the question, why was the note timed to arrive—it was, remember, delivered by hand—why was it timed to be delivered *after* he had left? Timing now becomes crucial."

She frowned hard. "Why would a note intended for him be delivered after he had left? The only explanation is that whoever sent it didn't know he'd left."

"Then we are in scenario two, not three."

I turned onto the exit for Orchard Beach. Dehan said, "The I-95 is faster. Your speed is limited on this road."

"The traffic's getting too heavy. No, in scenario three, the two events are intimately connected, Dehan. So, what are the implications of the note arriving *after* he has left? Whoever sent the note *knows* that he has gone. The two events are *intimately* connected, remember."

She shook her head, staring at me like I was crazy. "I don't know, Stone! What are you driving at?"

"It's clear! If the note was sent *after* he had left, it was not intended to be read by him. It was intended to be read by his wife, his mother, us. But not by him."

"Why . . . ?"

"No, not why? What? What would make a person arrange to meet another person at a motel out of town, and send a note that says: *We will kill you and your family, you black bastard*? What purpose is served by doing that?"

She screwed up her eyes. We sped through parkland and woodland onto the Pelham Bridge. Dehan stammered.

"It . . . it's a red herring! It makes us look for white supremacist, racist neighbors, it makes us assume he has fled . . ."

"Okay, good! Now focus on what you are saying, Dehan. Look for racist, white supremacist neighbors *for what*? What *has* happened if he has *not* fled?"

She stared at me. "He's dead."

"I hope not, but I fear he is."

"But *why*? Why would anyone want to kill Ned?"

I sighed and looked at her. "Because he's black . . ."

"*What?*" She turned to stare at me. "You are deliberately trying to drive me crazy. You just got through telling me that was a red herring from scenario two!"

"I told you it was complicated. You have to see it in the light of Ned's being Al's son."

"You mean all that crap Annunziata was talking about how a Chester could never be black or of mixed race?"

I shrugged with my eyebrows. "That's the context. It is the values, rules, and strictures of that family that triggered this whole affair from the get-go: Mexico, peyote, Brazil, ayahuasca, psychosis, and finally murder."

We had left Larchmont behind and were entering Mamaroneck. It was pretty, green, and clean, with a hint of sanity on the air wafting down from New England, just up the coast. We passed the Bank of America on our left, and then a grand old colonial building, and next thing, we were approaching the Mamaroneck Motel. Dehan had her cell out. She said, "We're real close. It's just up the road."

"You can see that on your phone?"

"Jeez, Stone. Did you bring your club? We may have to fight a brontosaurus. Oh, no, wait. This is the twenty-first century *AD*, not *BC*! The car's in the courtyard of the motel. Turn right here."

I turned in and saw Ned's cream Ford pickup parked across the lot. I parked next to it, and we climbed out and made our way across the courtyard to reception. A bell made an "Avon" sound as we went in, and a nice woman with a nice blue cardigan and a nice face framed by nice hair said, "Well, hello! How are *you* today?" like she didn't want us to think she was asking about somebody else.

I gave her a nice smile to go with her nice hair and showed her my badge.

"Just great. Detective Stone of the NYPD; this is my partner, Detective Dehan. Can you tell me who owns that Ford pickup outside?"

She looked past my shoulder to where I was pointing. "Oh, sure. That's Mr. Brown, he arrived last night. He's in room . . ."

"Has he left the room since he arrived?"

"Why, no! He left a message not to be disturbed."

"Has anyone been in to see him?"

"Not that I'm aware, but then people come and go. We don't keep tabs on them."

I nodded. "We have reason to believe the man in that room might be in trouble. We can go through all the red tape and contact the local PD . . ."

"They're just down the road . . ."

"Or you can give us permission to go in and have a look. While we are here talking, that man could be dying."

Her cheeks colored, she reached under the desk, formatted a key, and handed it to us. "I do hope he's all right . . ."

Dehan took the key, and we ran across the parking lot to his ground-floor room. She slipped in the card, the light turned green, and she pushed in. I stepped in past her.

The Venetian blinds were down on the front window and the one at the back, laying bars of dark light and shadow across the double bed. The bed was undisturbed apart from a small dent in the middle where somebody had sat on it. On the bedside table, rings where glasses had stood caught the light from the door. On the floor by the wardrobe, there was a black overnight bag. Apart from that, there was no indication the room had been occupied.

Two strides took me across the room to the en suite bathroom. I pushed open the door and stepped in. Dehan approached behind me and looked over my shoulder.

Ned was in the bath. He was bloated, and he had risen to the surface of the water, where he bobbed slightly. Time of death is notoriously difficult to establish, and almost impossible to establish from the temperature or condition of the body. Too many factors come into play, both environmental and relating to the person's own physical condition at the time of death. But one thing I could be sure of: if he had drowned, and been in the water long enough to generate enough gases to make him float, he had been dead a good while.

Dehan muttered, "He's still dressed, and he's floating."

I hunkered down at the end of the bath, pulled out my pen,

and used it to pull back his collar. "No bruising or scratching on his neck."

"He was drowned, fully clothed, and he didn't struggle."

I pointed at the floor. "There is some water, and wipe marks, like it's been rubbed or mopped."

"We should get out of this room." But as she said it, she pointed to the dirty linen basket. She took one long stride, opened it, and lifted up a wet towel. Then she dropped it again and closed the basket. "Let's get out, Stone, we're contaminating the scene."

We moved back into the bedroom and closed the bathroom door. I called the inspector.

"John, what news?"

"We found Ned . . ."

"Excellent! Good work!"

"Yeah, he's been murdered. We need the ME out here and a crime scene team. There's a Ford pickup too. They'll need to take a look at that. I also need you to square jurisdiction with the local PD."

"Local where?"

"Mamaroneck. The Mamaroneck Motel, 1015 West Boston Post Road. I'll contact the local PD; you better call the chief, sir, and square it."

"Yes, okay . . . John?"

"Sir?"

"Who killed him?"

"We need to examine the evidence, sir. See who was where and when. It's complicated."

"Yes, I see."

He hung up. I gave him five minutes, and Dehan called the local PD. They said they'd send a car over to close the area. While she waited for them, I went back to reception. The nice woman watched me come in. She looked worried. Like it was nothing personal, but she wished I wasn't there. I smiled in a way I hoped was reassuring.

"The local PD are on their way. Mr. Brown was murdered sometime between last night and this morning. I am hoping you have CCTV covering the parking lot..."

She had gone very pale. "Murdered? Here? In my motel?"

"I'm afraid so, and with every minute the trail gets colder. CCTV?"

"Well, we don't get much crime in Mamaroneck. We have a couple of cameras, one in here..." She pointed to it behind the desk, up on the wall, and the other at the entrance to the parking lot. "It gets most of the cars."

"I'll need the footage from last night, from the time Mr. Brown arrived until..." I glanced at my watch. It was four p.m. "Until an hour ago. What time did he arrive?"

She checked her computer. "Five minutes after midnight."

She went away and returned five minutes later with a DVD and handed it to me. "It's all on there. I hope it's okay."

I gave her a receipt. She looked at it like she really didn't want it. "Is it drugs? I hope we're not going to get a drug war here or something..."

"No, nothing like that."

When I stepped out again, there was a patrol car parked in front of Ned's car, and a couple of uniforms were putting tape up outside the room. As I approached, I showed them my badge and pointed at the Ford. "I want that sealed off too."

Dehan came to meet me.

"Nothing we can do here, Sensei. Let's grab a beer at the Boar's Head 'round the corner."

We fell into step, and she watched her boots a moment as we walked. "You know who did this?"

"Maybe."

"Don't tell me! Is it the same person who killed Al twelve years ago?"

"Definitely not."

"All right. I am going to tell you my theory, okay?"

"I can't wait."

"Don't mock me!"

"Mock you? I admire and adore you. You know that."

NINETEEN

We sat outside at the cute Italian Deli and Grill, which seemed also to be called the Boar's Head, and ordered a couple of beers while we waited for the ME and the crime scene team to show up. I waited in silence while Dehan sipped her beer, wiped her froth moustache from her upper lip, and stared at the lawn and the trees that fronted the large colonial building across the way.

"So," she said, apparently speaking to that elegant colonial building, "there is a way of putting all this together that does, actually, make sense."

I nodded and sipped my own beer.

"Don't talk!" She raised a finger, still staring at the building.

As I wasn't allowed to talk, I took another sip and watched the traffic. Finally, she turned to me with narrowed, all-seeing eyes.

"They are all insane!"

I burst out laughing.

"No, Stone! I'm serious! They all have a problem keeping a grip on reality. So Justinian and Annunziata live in this kind of ethereal half-light where nothing is quite real but everything is a bit real, but nobody ever really noticed because they played by the family rules of seemliness and were academically, and medically, brilliant."

"Sounds like a fair assessment to me."

"No, don't talk!"

I sipped.

She continued. "Maximilian is the most apparently normal, which kind of gives you the measure, but, like the other two, he is quite prepared to have somebody killed if it is necessary. So, twelve years ago, it went down just like Annunziata said. Al decided to get married, the detective discovered, somehow, that Ned's mother was the woman he had got pregnant eighteen years earlier. So they killed Al and silenced Ned and his mother with a payoff. In *classic* Chester style, they required the boy to, quote, 'make something of himself.' It wasn't enough they had killed his biological father, he had to earn the compensation."

"That is quite a theory. I like it."

"So the case goes cold, and twelve years later, just when everybody is happily getting on with their lives, along comes us and we start digging things up. If they had left it to Max, we might have wound up like Martinez, stumped..."

"I doubt it."

"But Justinian panicked and felt the need to come and bare his soul to us, while making sure that we knew that *he'd* had nothing to do with the conspiracy. Panic, as always, spreads, and when Annunziata realized that Justinian had panicked, she had to panic too and come and tell us *her* version of what happened. They are both as smart as Einstein, but they are both as crazy as a soup sandwich, and they made a hog's dinner out of Maximilian's best laid plans. So, what does he do? He arranges to meet Ned here at the motel and kills him. The letter was a lame attempt to direct our suspicions elsewhere. No doubt he had somebody else do it while he set himself up with perfect alibis."

"Alibis? In the plural?"

"Sure. Time of death is going to be within a frame of about twelve hours. He has to cover himself for that time. Take note, my dear Stone, that he will have an unshakable alibi for each one of those hours."

"Ah, yes, I see." I gave a little shrug. "I have a hunch Frank might be able to narrow down the time of death."

She frowned, then narrowed her eyes. "Why?"

"You and those open questions. What am I going to do with you?"

Her eyes went wide with ill-concealed impatience. "*What makes you think that?*"

"See? Much more focused. What can you tell me about the nine-millimeter used in Al's apartment?"

She looked at me blankly. "I don't know. We had said . . ." She trailed off.

"That was in the days when Ned was our prime suspect and he went along with Lucky to steal all that cash. Remember Chavez told us all about that? But now we are talking about a hit man employed by Maximilian. So who is our professional hit man shooting at in the kitchen? And what made him use a kitchen knife, of all things?"

"I don't know."

I smiled benignly at her. "In any case, I do believe . . ." I turned in my seat. "Yup, here comes the cavalry."

The ME, an ambulance, and a crime scene van filed into the courtyard, and we went over to talk to Frank and Joe. Joe and his team were climbing into white plastic suits while Frank's boys, dressed in blue plastic, were unloading a gurney from the back of the ambulance. Frank didn't say hello. He said, "There aren't enough bodies for you in the five boroughs. You need to come out here to find them?"

"He's homegrown, Frank. He just came out here to get killed. He seems to have been drowned in the bathtub, but he's fully dressed, and there are no scratches or bruises around his neck. So I'm wondering if he was drugged before he was drowned, or maybe he was killed some other way."

He nodded. "I'll let you know in good time."

He made off toward the room, and I turned to Joe. "There was water on the floor, but most of it had been mopped up with a towel. Maybe it spilled out of the bath when the body was put in, but that's unlikely. Moving a dead body is not easy."

He nodded and started to walk toward the room. We fell into step with him. "Besides, you put the body in first and then fill the bath."

Dehan nodded. "Right, and what's the point of making it look like a drowning? So I'm thinking the splashes were made during the drowning process. Maybe he sat on him, or knelt on him. The towel that was used to mop up afterwards is in the dirty linen basket."

We followed him into the room. The gurney was outside the bathroom door. Frank looked out.

"Joe, you boys want to inspect the floor before I take the body out? There's going to be a lot of water . . ."

We sat on the bed waiting while Joe's team inspected the floor. Eventually, they brought out the dirty linen basket sealed in a large plastic bag, with the wet towel sealed in another, and carried them out to the van. A moment later, we heard, "On three . . . one, two, *three*!"

There was a loud sloshing and the sound of men heaving. Then Frank's voice calling, "*Stone, Dehan!*"

His assistants stepped out and made room for us. Ned was lying on the gurney, with copious amounts of water draining out of his clothes onto the gurney and then onto the floor. Frank was making a cursory initial inspection of the body.

"There are no obvious puncture wounds, but I can't be conclusive about that until I get him back to the lab. There is water in his mouth and in his trachea, but that could have seeped in during the time he was submerged. Until I can look at his lungs, I cannot be sure he was drowned. Time of death I would put at ten minutes past two p.m., give or take a couple of minutes."

Dehan raised her eyebrows and looked at him as though he'd

just told her his best friend was a six-foot pink elephant called Toto. "Excuse me?"

He held up the dead man's left hand. The wrist was grotesquely inflamed around a watch with an expandable strap. "Water-resistant but not waterproof. It's analog. Stopped when the water got to the battery. Fifteen minutes past two. So I'd put time of death at shortly after two p.m."

I pulled an evidence bag from my pocket. "I'll take that with me."

With some difficulty, he maneuvered the watch over the swollen hand and dropped it in the bag.

I pointed at Ned's jeans. "Has he got his cell in his back pocket?"

"I haven't checked." Between them, they rolled him on his side, and Frank felt in his back pockets. "Yeah. Here. It's water-logged, but Joe might be able to do something with it."

Dehan pulled out another evidence bag, and Frank dropped it in.

"Anything else?"

I shook my head. "That about wraps it up."

"Good. Then let me do my job and I'll get the preliminaries to you as soon as possible."

"Thanks, Frank."

We stepped out into the parking lot. Dehan crossed to the Jag and sat on the hood. I took Ned's cell over to Joe, who was leaning against his van, waiting for Frank to vacate the premises. I gave him the phone.

"There is one thing I am interested in above all others on this phone." I told him what it was.

He nodded. "Okay, you got it. Depends how fast we can dry it out, but it shouldn't take long. I'll let you know. Oh." He snapped his fingers. "We found nothing on the envelope, nothing on the letter paper, but"—he gave a small laugh—"you were right, plenty of partials on the newspaper itself. Criminal masterminds just don't think."

I smiled. "Nothing on IAFIS, but..."

"No match on IAFIS. Not in the system. But like you thought, a score."

"Right. Listen, I need you to run a DNA profile on Ned, and make the comparison, will you?"

"Sure, no problem."

Frank came out with the body, and Joe and his team went in. A cool breeze found its way into the courtyard and made me shudder. I noticed the shadows were stretching and the sunlight had turned a burnished copper color.

I turned and made my way back to Dehan. She watched me approach with her arms crossed.

"How did you know?"

"How did I know what?"

"About time of death."

I shrugged. "It was a hunch. Come on, we need to go and give the bad news to Chevronne and Ned's wife."

I tossed her the keys and climbed in the passenger seat.

We drove slowly and in silence. I had no doubts anymore about what had happened. I just needed to prove it, and that was not going to be easy. It was going to require some very delicate timing.

We retraced our steps, taking the quieter Boston Post Road. At one point, Dehan spoke suddenly and said, "The nine-millimeter."

I looked at her a moment and nodded. "Yeah."

A little later, she sighed as we joined the Bruckner Expressway. Soon after that, we came off at exit 53 and turned into Chatterton Avenue. We parked outside Ned's house, climbed out, and crossed his long garden to climb the three steps to his front door. We rang, and it was eventually opened by a young woman in her late twenties. She was strawberry blond and blue-eyed, with rosy cheeks and a spray of freckles across the bridge of her nose.

I sensed rather than saw Dehan's surprise. I said, "Are you Ned Brown's wife?"

"Yes, Jane. Who are you?"

I showed her my badge. "Detective John Stone; this is Detective Carmen Dehan. May we come in?"

Her brow contracted. "Of course. Have you found Ned?"

We stepped into a broad hallway with a passage on the right that led to a kitchen at the back of the house. A distorted pattern of colored light lay on the floor and the wall, cast by the dying rays of the sun bleeding through a stained glass window. A movement down the corridor made me look, and I saw Chevronne approaching from the kitchen.

"Have you found Ned? Is he all right? Where is he?"

I saw the living room door ajar and pointed to it. "Can we go and sit down?"

Jane nodded and led the way. Chevronne grabbed my arm in two hands like talons, staring up into my face. "Tell me, please tell me! I'm his mother! Please tell me he's all right!"

I took hold of her and guided her through to a spacious, dark living room. A large bow window overlooked the front yard. A dark green sofa and dark green armchairs added to the somewhat gloomy feel of the room. I sat Chevronne on the sofa, and Jane sat beside her. They reached for each other's hands as they watched me sit. Dehan stood by the fireplace.

"Jane, Chevronne, Ned is dead. I am so sorry to have to give you this news."

Chevronne's face seemed to melt, like hot wax, into a silent scream. Both of Jane's hands went to her mouth. Her eyes seemed to glaze. She shook her head, denying what she was hearing. Chevronne made a sudden, shocking, visceral noise, as though something were being torn from her. Dehan sat next to her and put her arms around her. Jane's jaw trembled, tears spilling from her eyes.

"What am I going to do?" she asked, simply. "What am I going to do without him?" Her cheeks were shiny and wet. I handed her a handkerchief. She took it, and after a moment she said, "How?"

I avoided her eyes a moment, then met her frank, blue stare. "He was murdered."

She blinked, and her body rocked, as though she'd been hit. "Murdered? By who? Why? I don't understand. Why is this happening? Are you sure it's him? It's not a mistake?"

I shook my head. "No. It's not a mistake. I'm so sorry, Jane."

Chevronne pulled away from Dehan and pointed at me. Her face was ugly, like a clenched fist grasping on a thorn. Her voice was shrill. "I showed you the note! I showed you the note! You never did nothing! White people *always* pullin' together against the black man!"

"When did you get that note?"

Jane said, "This morning, about seven."

"When did you tell Chevronne?"

"Immediately." She turned to look at her mother-in-law. "I phoned straightaway, to ask if she'd had word from Ned. We were so worried. And I told her about the note . . ."

I turned to Chevronne, who had squeezed her eyes tight and collapsed against Dehan again.

"Why didn't you tell me then, Chevronne? Why didn't you call me?"

She screamed, hysterical, "*How do I know you ain't the one who killed him? White pigs always conspirin' against black men! How do I know you didn't kill him?*"

Jane stared at her mother-in-law, shaking her head. "Momma, stop it, please! Please stop . . ."

Dehan put her arm around her, and she collapsed into her lap, sobbing convulsively.

I turned to Jane. "Is there anyone we can call? Somebody who can be with you? Chevronne is going to need a sedative. You want us to call your family doctor?"

She nodded, then shook her head. "I'll call."

"Jane, I know how hard this is, but I need you to hold it together a little longer and answer me just one more question."

Her pupils were dilating, and she had gone very pale. I pulled

Ned's watch from my pocket and showed it to her. Dehan was frowning at me. I said, "Do you recognize this watch?"

She shook her head. "No."

"I need you to be absolutely sure about that, Jane. Do you want to have a closer look?"

"No. It's not his. Ned never uses—used—a watch. He said they got too dirty at work."

"Okay, thank you, Jane. You've been very helpful. Now, give me your family doctor's number and I'm going to call him. And a family friend."

After some talk, I called her doctor and she said she'd be right over. Meanwhile, Dehan went next door and asked Mrs. Santos to come and sit with Jane and Chevronne until Jane's sister arrived.

Finally, after half an hour, we were able to leave the house and make our way back to the car. Dehan threw me the keys. I opened up, climbed in, and she got in beside me.

"Okay," she said. "I think I am beginning to see now."

"Yeah?" I fired up the big old growler. "What?"

"The nine-millimeter . . . But I still don't see who."

I paused, hesitated, and turned to her. "It can only be one person, Dehan."

She shook her head.

"I don't get it." She growled and rubbed her face. "I'm tired. Where are we going now?"

"To visit Annunziata Chester."

She looked at me like I was crazy. "What for?"

"To talk about family loyalty, what else?"

TWENTY

But Annunziata was not at her Riverside Drive apartment. The doorman told us that her brother Justinian had sent a car for her, and he understood she had gone to stay with him for a few days at his Bayside residence. A little persuasive leaning elicited the address from him, and, as late afternoon started fading toward evening, we headed east, toward Queens.

In fact, according to the GPS on Dehan's phone, it was a half-hour drive if we went north back to the Bronx and followed the I-95 to drop into Queens over the Throgs Neck Bridge. I told her it made no sense to go backward in order to go forward, but she stared at me, and I drove north to go south.

Twenty minutes later, dusk slipped into evening as we sped high above the East River, and by the time we'd made landfall and turned onto 33rd Avenue, the sky had turned dark, and the lights of elegant suburbia were winking on beyond lawns, behind drapes, and in some cases beyond hedges and walled gardens, while nineteenth-century iron streetlamps cast mottled shadows across the sidewalks and the blacktop from behind plane trees and chestnuts.

Justinian Chester's house was both large and grotesque. A double-ended drive fronted the house like a closed bracket. From that drive, and the lawn that had been set between the entrance and the exit, four powerful lamps floodlit the facade with warm light.

Seven semicircular marble steps rose, like the tiers on a wedding cake, to a set of vast iron and glass doors that appeared to have been borrowed from the set of *The Matrix*. Above this flight of steps and its vast doors, there was a white, tubular balcony oddly reminiscent of the *Titanic*, and beyond that rose a Byzantine dome complete with oxblood tiles.

On either side of that strangely unsettling combination of styles stood two wings that did not echo or complement each other in any way, except that the windows on the lower floor were shaded by eaves which were reminiscent of Japanese pagodas. The house was hideous, and if the architect was dead, I felt quite sure he was in hell.

We parked, climbed the seven steps, and rang the bell. I saw the drape flick over on my right, and a moment later, there were raised voices echoing in the hall. Then the door was wrenched open by Maximilian, who stood glaring at us with a face of outrage.

I smiled at him. "Good evening, Dr. Chester. We are here to see Annunziata."

His face flushed a deep red and he roared, "*What the devil do you think you're doing?*"

I wasn't sure what to answer. Dehan frowned. "Um . . . we're here to see Annunziata?"

"*You can't just show up, take people off the street, hold them for questioning . . . ! I'll sue the city! You think I won't? I'll have words with the mayor!*"

"Dr. Chester . . ." I smiled. "Dr. Chester . . . ?"

"*What?*"

"We need to see Annunziata. Now, you can let us in and we talk to her quietly inside, or I can come back with a SWAT team and a battering ram, and a few news anchors. I suggest you make the smart choice."

"This is blackmail!"

Dehan pulled her cell from her pocket. "I'll call for backup."

"Wait!" His body seemed to quiver for a moment. Then he took a step back and barked, "*Goddamn it!*"

The entrance hall was like a small, Greek cathedral. It had a high, domed ceiling and two white marble staircases that climbed, from either side of the hall, to a galleried landing above. The floor was white marble, and at the center, there was a fountain displaying a cherub with a serious bladder problem.

Over on the right, a set of tall, white doors with shiny brass plates stood open, and leaning against the frame, in a pose that Lauren Bacall would have done justice to, was Justinian.

I nodded to him. "Dr. Chester."

"I knew you'd come," he said. "Sooner or later."

"Oh, do shut *up*, Justin! You and your damned sister! You're both out of your *minds*!"

I raised my eyebrows at Dehan. "Sounds like we made it just in time." To Maximilian, I said, "Where is she?"

He jerked his head toward the open doors. "In the drawing room."

As we stepped in, Justinian narrowed his eyes at his brother. "How you could! To say such a thing, at this time! Sometimes I think you have no soul, Max!"

"*Shut up!*"

The room was grotesque in a way that defied description. It was as though he had selected the worst of three centuries of excess and brought them all together in one fantastic orgy of tastelessness. The floor was strewn with lion skins, tiger skins, and zebra skins. The chairs and sofas were white rococo with gilt highlights. There was a huge, white marble fireplace, and the drapes had drapes with frills that had frills, and were tied back with tasseled gold ropes.

On one of those white sofas flanking the fireplace was Annunziata. She was encased in turquoise Chinese silk and wore a diamond choker around her throat. Her black hair was, with exquisite recklessness, high on her head. She watched us with sultry eyes and sucked on a Balkan Sobranie.

"Hello, Anne."

"Shouldn't you be talking to my attorney?"

I crossed the room and sat in one of the chairs beside the sofa, leaning forward with my elbows on my knees, staring hard into her face. "Don't you think we ought to take this one step at a time, Anne? Or would you rather dive right in the deep end?"

"What do you mean?"

I was aware of Dehan taking a chair on my right, and Max and Justin standing behind her, watching Annunziata, frowning.

"Ned Brown, your mixed-race nephew . . ." I turned and examined Max's and Justin's faces. They were frowning, but there was no surprise there. I turned back to Annunziata. "He's dead."

Her face drained of blood. When she sucked on the cigarette, her hand was shaking. "When?"

"When what?"

"When was he . . . When did he . . ." She tapped ash and winced. "What happened?"

"Well, that's what I wanted to ask you, Anne. What happened?"

"How would I know?"

Max erupted, "I'm calling Paul!"

I sat back and spoke loudly, still keeping my eyes on Annunziata. "That's probably a good idea, Max. But you might want to ask your brother first how he feels about having his driveway full of patrol cars, and the media watching his sister being taken out of here in cuffs."

He took a couple of steps toward me. "What the hell are you *talking* about?"

"You want to tell him, Anne?"

She shook her head. "I don't know what you're talking about either. I think you're insane."

"Your nephew . . ." I pointed at her and then at Max and Justin. "Your nephew, Ned Brown, was murdered."

Annunziata said again, "When?"

"Two p.m."

She burst out laughing, her cheeks flushed with relief. "Well, honestly, Detective Stone, I don't know why you're talking to me! I was *with you* at two p.m.! You and your . . ." She gestured at Dehan with her open palm. ". . . your assistant!"

I gave a laugh that was both short and humorless. "Of course, we arranged to meet at two. Well, you arranged to meet at two. Was that why you chose that time, because you knew you were going to kill Ned?"

"Now hang on!" Max was roaring again. "You had better have facts to back that up, Detective! Or I swear I'll have your job!"

I snorted and pulled Ned's watch from my pocket. "Facts like this watch, worn by the deceased, showing the time the water reached the battery as two fifteen, and on this helpful dial here, fourteen hundred hours and fifteen minutes."

Everybody, including and especially Dehan, looked at me as though I had just contradicted myself, argued myself into a corner, and shot myself in the foot. They were all frowning.

I smiled with a little more feeling. "Did you know he had his cell in his back pocket?"

She didn't react.

"He had it in his back pocket, and obviously after all those hours in the water, it was completely waterlogged. And . . ." I turned to Dehan and waved a finger at her. "This was one of the things that completely foxed me. You all, as doctors, know that it is almost impossible to set time of death simply by the condition of the body. But if he'd died at two p.m., he had barely been in the water more than three hours, and yet already he was floating, puffed up with gases from decay. I guess it could happen, but it struck me as odd. So I gave Ned's cell phone to the boys at the lab. They'll dry it out and they'll be able to establish at what time the phone got waterlogged. Then we'll see if it coincides with the watch. What do you think, Annunziata? You think the two times will match?"

She shrugged. "How should I know? If the water was warm, it might have accelerated the decay and the release of gases."

"But what if the phone says he died, say, last night, at two a.m., instead of p.m.? What happens to your alibi?"

She sat up suddenly, savagely stubbing out her cigarette. "Do I *need* an alibi? So far, all you seem to have against me is the fact that I *may* not have an alibi for the time of his death. I and eight million other New Yorkers. Maybe I have no alibi, but neither have I motive, means, or opportunity. And what *you* have is not a shred of evidence against me! All this is is some kind of envy-fueled vendetta against me because your Third-World partner has some kind of chip on her shoulder!" She narrowed her eyes savagely at Dehan and snarled, "*Put ketchup on it and eat it up, sister!*"

The room went very silent. Annunziata fished her cigarettes from her purse and lit up a second, blowing smoke in Dehan's general direction.

"Motive." I smiled.

She looked at me. "Well?"

"You certainly had motive. And more than one. As soon as you discovered that Ned was Aloysius' illegitimate son, you had motive to kill him. You all did. For a start, the moment he discovered he was Al's son, and who Al really was, you would each stand to lose eight point three percent of the company shares which you own, to make up his twenty-five-percent share. And then there would be the claim for his rightful inheritance, going back to Al's death in 2007, plus interest accrued. We are talking about many millions of dollars."

Max waved a wild finger at me. "Aloysius' death! A death which *he* caused! I know enough law to know that a criminal may not prosper from his crimes!"

Dehan laughed. "Yeah, that's cute. Go explain it to your pissing cherub. The rider to that legal principle is, '*if they get caught!*'"

I added, "Ned was never convicted, and he is no more likely to have killed your brother than you are." I turned back to Annunziata. "But your real motive, stronger by far than the possible loss of money, was that he would not only become a member of the board of directors at Chester Cardio-Valves, he would become part of the Chester *family*, and he was black. The humiliation for your family would be beyond what you could endure. He had to die."

Max erupted again. "This is calumny and slander! What evidence have you got to back this nonsense up?" He stared at Annunziata. "Anne? Tell him!"

She sighed and looked at her brother. Not for the first time, I noticed an unfathomable arrogance in her eyes. "Of course it's lies, Max. Where is his evidence? It's surmise, not even guesswork. It's fantasy."

I ignored her and went on. "Getting Ned to meet you at the Mamaroneck Motel was not difficult. Any number of lures would have got him there, but—and this *is* a guess—I think you enjoyed telling him you were going to reveal secrets about his father, tell him the truth about his origins, his bloodline. Was that how it went? What I didn't fully understand, for a while, was why you sent that rather childish anonymous note, threatening to kill him and his family."

Her eyes shifted to meet mine. The implied insult had stung her. I smiled. Then it dawned on me. "How was it phrased? *We will kill you and your family, you black bastard.* 'We,' not 'I' but 'we.' You couldn't have pointed the finger at yourself more firmly. With your dumb broad act, foolishly implicating yourself in a conspiracy that could never be proved, while pointing the finger at Maximilian, the patriarch who would 'take care of business' by making a phone call, you stood out like . . ." I shook my head, momentarily lost for words.

Dehan growled out a few for me. "Like a neon dildo at a vestal virgin convention."

I nodded. "About as much as that. The purpose of the anonymous note was to point suspicion at your brother, without ever proving anything, and subtly distancing yourself from the conspiracy. It was subtle, I will grant you that."

She sighed and sucked on her cigarette, squinting through the smoke as she released it. "I hear you talking, Detective, but I don't see you saying anything. It's all yammer yammer, but no substance. No . . . *facts*!"

I eyed Max's face for a moment. He looked like an outraged pomegranate. "Annunziata . . . ?"

"Not now, Max! *Pas devant les étrangers!*"

I laughed out loud. "Yes, Max, not in front of outsiders!" I scratched my brow. "You know, people make mistaken assumptions about all sorts of things. You assumed Detective Dehan was from the Third World, when she is an American and a New Yorker, just as much as you are. You assumed we didn't speak French, when in fact I do, and, most important of all, for you, Annunziata, you assumed that paper doesn't hold fingerprints, when in fact it is one of the best possible surfaces for printing."

She froze. I smiled because I knew there were questions she desperately needed to ask, but she couldn't ask them without admitting she'd put together the note. She watched me a moment, and I watched her back.

"You're thinking that you used latex gloves on the note and on the envelope, so where the hell did you leave your prints? You are also thinking that you are not in the IAFIS database, so what the hell would I match them with, even if I got some prints?"

"I'm thinking no such thing." But she said it without conviction.

"You gave me a fine set of prints for comparison, Anne, when I asked you if you could identify those symbols."

Her jaw sagged a little.

I waited a moment, then smiled and shook my head. "The newspaper, Annunziata. The *New York Times*. You handled it when you read it. No prints on the note or the envelope, but they were all over the newspaper cuttings."

Her pupils dilated wide; her face went ashen. She tried to

stand, but her legs buckled under her and she fell to the floor, sprawled across a dead, skinned lion. Max and Justinian rushed forward and lifted her back onto the sofa. Justin went to get her a brandy, and Dehan pulled her cuffs from her belt.

"Annunziata Chester, it is this Third-World Jewish-Mexican's pleasure to inform you that you are under arrest for the murder of Ned Brown. You have the right to silence, you do not have to say anything, but anything you do say can and will be used against you in a court of law. You have the right to an attorney; if you cannot afford one, one will be appointed for you. Do you understand the rights I have just explained to you?"

Annunziata screwed up her face and spat the words at her, "Screw you!" Then she turned to Max. "If you had just *done* something! If you had had the balls to *do* something! But all you ever did—you pussy!—was to talk and talk and talk, while that piece of *shit* brought our family down!"

Max's eyes were wide. "Annunziata! You *killed* a man? You're a *doctor*! For God's sake, woman! What have you done?"

Her voice was shrill and wild. "*Killed him! For us! And what did you do, you pansy? Daddy would be ashamed of you! Ashamed!*"

Dehan snapped the cuffs on her prisoner and smiled at me. "You heard me Mirandize her, right?"

"I did."

"Sound like a confession to you, partner? Sounded like one to me."

"Sounded like one to me too, partner."

TWENTY-ONE

Later that night, at shortly before ten, Dehan and I sat at our desks, drinking coffee-like liquid from paper cups. The detectives' room was almost empty, most of the lights were off, and Annunziata, having spoken at length with her attorney, was now in the cells, awaiting a bail hearing in the morning. Dehan's boots were on the corner of her desk, crossed at the ankles.

"So," she said, "here are a couple of things I *still* don't understand. And number one is, did Annunziata Chester kill her brother Aloysius? Because that, to me, is the million-dollar question. Do we know yet who killed Aloysius Chester? Because I gotta tell you, Stone, this case . . . What was it Annunziata called me? Your assistant? Well . . ." She pointed her finger at me like a gun. "There have been times during this case when that is exactly what I felt like."

"Was there a question in there? Somewhere?"

A voice echoed from the door. "Ah! You two are still here?"

Dehan removed her ankles from the desk, and the deputy inspector approached us with uncertain, faltering chicken steps. "Carmen, John, congratulations are in order. A most difficult case. I am still not entirely sure myself . . . um . . . what happened." He grinned. "Golf with the mayor on Sunday! No doubt he'll be asking me . . ."

I smiled and pulled him over a chair with my foot. "Still an open investigation, sir."

"Naturally . . ." He nodded a few times. "It is?" He looked at Dehan, and they both burst out laughing.

I laughed too, and when they had settled a little, I said, "In 1990, or thereabouts—I hope we will get those court orders now, sir?"

"By the morning, John."

"Thank you, sir. So, in 1990, Aloysius Chester, now in his early forties, returned from South America to attend a dropouts reunion at Harvard. While he was there, he met a young black woman, a student at the university from which he had dropped out twenty years earlier. They spent a few days together, and she got pregnant. He returned to New York and forgot all about her. She had the baby, dropped out of university, and, a few years later, moved to New York.

"Whether it was intentional, fate, or a mixture of the two, Aloysius, his son, Ned, and Ned's mother all wound up living in the same neighborhood. By this time, Al had descended into deep psychosis and didn't recognize his ex-four-night stand. I am guessing she only just recognized him, but recognize him she did, and eventually, she approached him and told him that she wanted to marry him.

"He did not want to tell Dr. Epstein because he knew that he would disapprove, but he contacted Max, Justin, and Anne and told them what he planned to do. Now, here is where it gets complicated. Annunziata raised with her brothers, not for the first time, the idea of having Al permanently removed. They responded as they always had, telling her it was not an option. But this time, as so much was at stake, she decided to take matters into her own hands and employed a private detective to look into the woman Al was proposing to marry. Remember, at this stage, nobody knew that Ned was Al's son.

"But the detective began to unearth facts: that the girl in question had been at Harvard, that she had dropped out after she hooked up with Al, that nine months later she had a baby; piece by piece the full extent of the problem became evident..."

"So now, Annunziata is faced with far more than simple embarrassment for the family. If Ned finds out who his father is, they are looking at having him inherit his father's share of the company, which at that time was under the control of the siblings, *and* becoming a legitimate Chester. As long as he never finds out, they have no problem. But if he does find out..."

The deputy inspector leaned forward. "So she killed her brother! But what about the nine-millimeter, and the shots in the kitchen?"

Dehan nodded.

I said, "Let me cycle back to that. When Al died, initially everything was fine. The case went cold, and Ned had no idea who his father was."

Now Dehan leaned forward. "But why didn't his mother just tell him?"

"I'll be able to explain that in a while. What concerns us right now is that, once we decided to investigate, our interview with Max rippled through the Chesters like a seismic wave. Max was largely oblivious to everything that had happened. He was just relieved that Al was no longer a problem. Justin, on the other hand, had a hunch somebody had done something, and was keen to distance himself from the whole affair, in particular the discussions they had had about icing Aloysius.

"But Annunziata, that was a different story. On the one hand, she was aware that Justin could get her and Max in trouble because of his loose tongue and his febrile imagination, but more than that—much more than that—she was terrified that our investigation would unearth what her private investigator had unearthed, that Ned was Al's son."

"So she killed him."

"She arranged a meeting with him, telling him she had

information about Aloysius and his private benefactor. They met in the motel, and she gave him a drink." I turned to Dehan. "Remember the rings on the bedside table? I wondered then where the glasses and the bottle were. She fed him a dose of anesthetic and, while he was docile and pliant, she led him to the bathroom and dumped him in the bath. Lab results should confirm that in the next day or two. The water on the floor, and the wet towel, that was where she knelt on him till he drowned."

"Holy cow . . ." It was Dehan.

I nodded at her. "Annunziata was a hard, ruthless, and subtle woman. She played the dappy, dumb broad who didn't really know what she was doing or saying, but you don't become a doctor of neurology at Harvard by being stupid. She played a very subtle game indeed, whereby she scattered suspicion, without ever giving enough to convict. And she almost got away with it. She just overplayed her hand with the note."

Dehan was shaking her head, and the deputy inspector was watching her and nodding. "But," she said, "*who killed Aloysius?*"

I sat biting my lip for a long moment. Finally, I shook my head. "I can't say just yet. But I am pretty sure I'll have the confirmation I need by tomorrow."

Dehan sagged back in her chair, and the inspector, for just a moment, looked like a kid who's been told he can't have a bike for Christmas. "Well," he said, "keep me informed. Good work so far."

"Thank you, sir, we'll walk you out. We're on our way home anyway."

In the parking lot, he made for his Focus, waving good night to us, and we crossed the blacktop under the streetlamps toward where the Jag was waiting. My phone pinged a couple of times, and I thumbed the screen. It was an email from Bernie at the bureau, with several attachments. I had a quick glance, then climbed in behind the wheel. Dehan was sitting, waiting in the passenger seat.

I fired up the engine and drove slowly down Story toward White Plains. Dehan frowned. "We taking the scenic route?"

I nodded. "I just need to think a bit."

At White Plains, I turned north, over the Bruckner Expressway, and kept cruising slowly toward the Church of the Sacred Apocalypse. I glanced at Dehan. "We were going up here, remember? You were pointing out how close everybody was to each other. You paused right here, by the church, and you pointed right to Al's house, the church behind, Epstein's practice up the road..."

She was staring at me. "I remember..."

Instead of continuing on up toward Morris Park Avenue, the way we would go to get home, I turned left for a block along Gleason and then right into Leland Avenue. There I stopped outside a pleasant, two-story redbrick house with a gabled roof and a porch over a garage.

Dehan sighed. "This couldn't wait till tomorrow?"

"Come on, we're passing."

We climbed out, crossed the street, and climbed the steps to the front porch. There I rang the bell. It was opened almost immediately by Joy, still in her coat. She started when she saw us and laughed.

"Oh, my goodness! I only just walked in. Another late night at the church! What can I do for you, please come in! Mary's in the kitchen. Can I offer you anything?"

"We won't keep you. We just came to give you some news."

"News?" She removed her coat and hung it up. "Please, come through to the living room and sit. What news?"

We followed her through. It was comfortably and tastefully furnished. There were low bookcases well stocked with well-thumbed books. Persian-style rugs partly covered oiled, wooden floors. There was no coffee table to bang your shins on, but there were attractive incidental tables scattered here and there. Lighting was from handsome lamps, which were placed strategically around the room.

A flat-screen TV stood to one side, where it was unobtrusive. It was attached to a DVD player, and I saw on the shelves, besides the books, an extensive collection of movies.

She sat in a white calico chair, and we sat opposite her on the sofa. She waited attentively, and I held her eye. "Has Chevronne Brown been in touch with you?"

She sat up straight, and her eyes widened. "Chevronne...?"

I waited.

"No..."

I nodded. "I imagined she wouldn't. She's in a pretty bad way at the moment."

"I don't understand. What..."

"Joy, your son, Ned, he's dead."

Her hands went slowly to her mouth. Her eyes welled with tears that spilled when she blinked and soaked her cheeks. She tried to hold it back but couldn't and began to sob. I pulled my handkerchief from my pocket and handed it to her. She blew her nose, then dabbed at her eyes. I was aware of Dehan staring at me.

A shadow moved across the room, and I looked up to see Mary standing in the doorway. I turned to Joy.

"Does your daughter know?"

She shook her head.

Mary said, "What's happened?"

I looked up at her. "Could you get your mom some tissues, please, Mary?"

She nodded and went away.

I said, "Annunziata killed him."

She sighed, wiping her eyes. "He was doomed, like his father. It was never going to come out right. That family, they were dark, crazy people. Especially her. He was trying to escape, but look what he did. Drove himself crazy." She smiled briefly, staring down at the carpet. "He was a beautiful man. He had a beautiful soul in many ways, you know? But he was out of control, like a supernova!" She laughed. "Beautiful to see, but stay out of its path. It will destroy everything that comes before it."

Mary came back with a box of tissues. I took them, handed them to Joy, and retrieved my handkerchief. As I took it, a lopsided smile creased her face. "You're a clever son of a gun. Now you got my DNA, and I can't deny it. Don't worry, I ain't going to deny it."

I smiled, but it wasn't a happy smile. "I know Chevronne is close family to Ned, but I also know he's adopted. So what is she to you? You have no sisters, so she is your cousin?"

"How you know I got no sisters?"

"I had a friend at the bureau check you out, Joy. You got a scholarship to Harvard to study psychology, and you gave it all up for four days with Aloysius Chester."

"He was the craziest, most fascinating man I ever met."

"Why'd you have your cousin adopt him?"

"When I had to drop out from my degree, because of the pregnancy, and then, on top of that, Al just left me and disappeared without a word, I went into a bad depression. Chevronne can't have kids, so she said she could adopt him till I got back on my feet. By the time I did get back on my feet . . ." She shook her head. "It would have been pure wickedness to separate them. He thought she was his mother, she loved him like a son. So I stepped back, let them be happy. I married, had Mary. Bill, my husband, died when she was young."

Mary went and sat on the arm of her mother's chair. "Mom, is everything okay? Are you okay?"

"Yes, sweetheart, everything's going to be okay." She held my eye, challenging me.

I sighed. "Why did you kill him?"

"I didn't want to. But I felt justice should be done. I had borne his son, and lost him, because of Al's arrogance and egotism." She paused, biting her lip and dabbing at her eyes with a tissue. "I felt I was entitled to something. He never recognized me, you know that? He grew to love me, because I was always there taking care of him. And I still loved him, in some crazy way; even in his psychosis, there was such a deep, restless soul there." She laughed. "So I told him, hey! Let's get married! I will look after you. I'm already your nurse! So I can nurse you all day, take care of you, and look out for your interests. Our interests, after all, will be the same. So I was going to demand from that family, for both of us, what he had stolen from me."

Dehan nodded. "Yeah, Al told his brothers and his sister he was going to marry a woman. That was you."

"That was me. And we were both happy. I knew Dr. Epstein would kick up a fuss, but I was pretty sure I could handle him. How you going to prove to a court that it would be bad for that man to have me as his wife?"

She laughed out loud, then her lip curled in and she started crying again. "Poor Al. He was so scared of his sister. I used to go and visit him *every night* for maybe ten minutes or half an hour. He was always watching his TV show, *Murder She Wrote*, and we would spend a little while together, I would make sure he was okay, and then I would go home." She paused. "But then he started to tell me, he was scared. That Annunziata was getting real mad, that she was going to cause problems. And then he told me, he did not want to marry me. His family had been giving him a hard time, you know? And he was going to tell them the marriage was off." She sat staring at the floor.

I said, "So you decided to kill him."

"I was not going to get what I deserved. I was not going to get what they had stolen from me. My son was not going to be acknowledged as his heir. I was just going to get chucked back on the scrap heap, one more time, picked up and thrown away, one more time. That was not going to happen again, not to me."

"Where did you get the gun from?"

"That used to belong to Bill. He lived in the southwest for a while, bought a gun, and liked to have it around, for protection."

"So you picked a movie that would be on at ten thirty on the night of the twenty-third, and started building Mary up, looking forward to seeing it. You mentioned it to a few friends too, you needed to be away from the church by ten so you could see the movie. You planted that fact firmly in everyone's mind.

"But you popped in to see Al long before that, at six or six thirty, on your way to the church from work. Maybe he let you in, but I am figuring that by then, you had a key and let yourself in. He was watching his show and got up as you entered the living room, and as he stood, you stuck him in the heart with your own kitchen knife. Then, I am guessing you put the knife in a plastic bag and took it away with you. Once home, you washed and bleached both the knife and the bag."

"Yes."

Dehan said, "But what about the nine-millimeter rounds? What about the overturned furniture, and the shots in the kitchen?"

I nodded. "It was clever." I turned back to Joy. "You were very cool. After you'd killed him, you went to the church, did all your duties, with the bloody knife still in your bag. And you diligently reminded everyone that you needed to be back for ten thirty, to see the movie. You left at ten or shortly after and you went back to Al's house. Now you turned over the living room, though you couldn't bring yourself to break anything, and you went to the kitchen, where you changed the time on the clock to ten thirty, and after that, you stood at the doorway and emptied three rounds into the corner of the kitchen, as though they had been random shots fired during a struggle. But you made sure that one of those shots hit the clock. You knew the boys in the lab would be able to establish at what time it stopped working, and so get the time of death set at ten thirty."

"You pieced all that together? That was smart."

"And finally, you took his money. Because there was money, wasn't there?"

She smiled and nodded. "One million dollars, kept for years in a sports bag up in the attic. He told me about it maybe a year before. He called it his safety net, if he ever decided to escape back to Mexico. And that was what started me thinking about marriage. I would never have killed him if he had married me."

"So then you hurried home. You had already set up the DVD of the movie you wanted to watch, and your daughter . . ." I stared at Mary and searched for a diplomatic way to say it. "Who doesn't question you . . ."

"She's simple, Detective, just say it. She knows it. She don't care, do you, sweetness?"

Mary smiled and shrugged.

I went on. "She unwittingly helped establish your alibi. You were home in time for the film, at precisely the same time Aloysius was being shot at and stabbed in his house. Did you realize at the time that by doing that, you were putting Ned in the frame for his murder?"

"Of course not. When Al phoned me and told me what had happened with Ned, I had no idea how serious it had been. But in any case, they had no evidence against him."

"You waited a year for the dust to settle, and then you went 'round the corner to Hernandez and Heap, the attorneys in Dr. Epstein's block, and set up your trust fund. I'm guessing they were not too fussy about the legal proprieties."

"They didn't care where it came from, so long as they got their fee and their percentage."

We sat in silence for a while.

Finally, she said, "How did you know it was me?"

I shrugged. "It couldn't be anybody else. When the injunction was taken out to prevent us from seeking an order to disclose the adoption papers and the trust, it dawned on me. I had to reason backward. So I asked myself, 'Okay, of the people who had the opportunity to kill Al that night, who would have an interest in taking out that injunction?'"

She and Dehan both frowned. Mary played with the hem of her skirt.

I went on: "Ned had never been a serious suspect for me. The broken fingers precluded him from firing a nine-millimeter, and also from stabbing him with such accuracy. Besides, at that time, he was knocked out with diazepam and weed.

"A random passerby or a neighbor were absurd, because they would have no interest in taking out an injunction to stop us prying into Ned's past. That left Ned's mother. But I had half a dozen witnesses that put his mother with him that night, tending to his broken fingers. And in any case, she was his *adoptive* mother—now, two got you twenty that it was one or both of the biological parents who had taken out the injunction, so I asked myself, of the people who'd had an opportunity to kill Al, which of them might be Ned's biological parent?

"That narrowed it down to one person, who walked past Al's house most nights at about the time that Al died. And the more I thought about it, the more I saw your face in Ned's and Ned's in yours. Of course, he was paler and had those blue eyes, but that was because of his father. And then there was the fact that both you and Chevronne had Barbadian accents.

"So I had my friend at the bureau look into you, and there it was. You had been at Harvard, studying psychology, in 1990. We've got Ned's DNA, and Chevronne's and yours . . . And we will have the court orders tomorrow to see the trust fund and the adoption papers. It is over, Joy."

She stroked her daughter's hair, where she sat on the arm of her chair. A tear ran down her cheek. "Who's going to look after my little girl now?"

Mary frowned at her. "Are you going to leave me, Mom?"

"For a while, baby. Dr. Epstein will take care of you."

I sighed and pulled my cell from my pocket.

EPILOGUE

About two months later, I was sitting on the balcony of the Madison Beach Hotel, barefoot and bare-chested, enjoying the sunny, salty wind on my face. I had a dry Martini sitting in front of me and my laptop, with the Word application open. I had written one word: One.

I tried out Chapter One but decided against it. One felt more terse.

Dehan kissed the top of my head, which was distracting, and then sat next to me in a bikini, which was more distracting.

"Maybe I'll start after lunch," I said.

She examined my face for a while. "You don't *have* to do it, you know."

"No, I want to. It would be good to tell their stories. Especially Aloysius. He had a story to tell. He had something to say. But bad luck, chaos . . ."

"A few pretty bad choices."

"That too."

"Okay, we'll have some lunch, a glass of wine or two, then a walk on the beach, and give it another try then."

"By then, I'll want a lie down."

"Well, okay, maybe a lie down will inspire you."

I nodded. "I think it might," I said.

And not for the first or the last time, I marveled at my own good fortune.

Don't miss DEATH IN DEXTER The riveting sequel in the Dead Cold Mystery series.

Scan the QR code below to purchase DEATH IN DEXTER.

Or go to: righthouse.com/death-in-dexter

NOTE: flip to the very end to read an exclusive sneak peak...

DON'T MISS ANYTHING!

If you want to stay up to date on all new releases in this series, with this author, or with any of our new deals, you can do so by joining our newsletters below.

In addition, you will immediately gain access to our entire *Right House VIP Library,* which includes many riveting Mystery and Thriller novels for your enjoyment!

righthouse.com/email

(Easy to unsubscribe. No spam. Ever.)

ALSO BY BLAKE BANNER

Up to date books can be found at:
www.righthouse.com/blake-banner

ROGUE THRILLERS
Gates of Hell (Book 1)
Hell's Fury (Book 2)

ALEX MASON THRILLERS
Odin (Book 1)
Ice Cold Spy (Book 2)
Mason's Law (Book 3)
Assets and Liabilities (Book 4)
Russian Roulette (Book 5)
Executive Order (Book 6)
Dead Man Talking (Book 7)
All The King's Men (Book 8)
Flashpoint (Book 9)
Brotherhood of the Goat (Book 10)
Dead Hot (Book 11)
Blood on Megiddo (Book 12)
Son of Hell (Book 13)

HARRY BAUER THRILLER SERIES
Dead of Night (Book 1)
Dying Breath (Book 2)
The Einstaat Brief (Book 3)
Quantum Kill (Book 4)
Immortal Hate (Book 5)
The Silent Blade (Book 6)
LA: Wild Justice (Book 7)

Breath of Hell (Book 8)
Invisible Evil (Book 9)
The Shadow of Ukupacha (Book 10)
Sweet Razor Cut (Book 11)
Blood of the Innocent (Book 12)
Blood on Balthazar (Book 13)
Simple Kill (Book 14)
Riding The Devil (Book 15)
The Unavenged (Book 16)
The Devil's Vengeance (Book 17)
Bloody Retribution (Book 18)
Rogue Kill (Book 19)
Blood for Blood (Book 20)

DEAD COLD MYSTERY SERIES
An Ace and a Pair (Book 1)
Two Bare Arms (Book 2)
Garden of the Damned (Book 3)
Let Us Prey (Book 4)
The Sins of the Father (Book 5)
Strange and Sinister Path (Book 6)
The Heart to Kill (Book 7)
Unnatural Murder (Book 8)
Fire from Heaven (Book 9)
To Kill Upon A Kiss (Book 10)
Murder Most Scottish (Book 11)
The Butcher of Whitechapel (Book 12)
Little Dead Riding Hood (Book 13)
Trick or Treat (Book 14)
Blood Into Wine (Book 15)
Jack In The Box (Book 16)
The Fall Moon (Book 17)
Blood In Babylon (Book 18)
Death In Dexter (Book 19)
Mustang Sally (Book 20)

A Christmas Killing (Book 21)
Mommy's Little Killer (Book 22)
Bleed Out (Book 23)
Dead and Buried (Book 24)
In Hot Blood (Book 25)
Fallen Angels (Book 26)
Knife Edge (Book 27)
Along Came A Spider (Book 28)
Cold Blood (Book 29)
Curtain Call (Book 30)

THE OMEGA SERIES
Dawn of the Hunter (Book 1)
Double Edged Blade (Book 2)
The Storm (Book 3)
The Hand of War (Book 4)
A Harvest of Blood (Book 5)
To Rule in Hell (Book 6)
Kill: One (Book 7)
Powder Burn (Book 8)
Kill: Two (Book 9)
Unleashed (Book 10)
The Omicron Kill (Book 11)
9mm Justice (Book 12)
Kill: Four (Book 13)
Death In Freedom (Book 14)
Endgame (Book 15)

ABOUT US

Right House is an independent publisher created by authors for readers. We specialize in Action, Thriller, Mystery, and Crime novels.

If you enjoyed this novel, then there is a good chance you will like what else we have to offer! Please stay up to date by using any of the links below.

Join our mailing lists to stay up to date -->
righthouse.com/email
Visit our website --> righthouse.com
Contact us --> contact@righthouse.com

 facebook.com/righthousebooks
 x.com/righthousebooks
instagram.com/righthousebooks

EXCLUSIVE SNEAK PEAK OF...

DEATH IN DEXTER

CHAPTER 1

The September sun was rising behind us, turning the sky to bronze and stretching the shadows of the firs and the pines long across the black water of the St. Regis Pond, just south of Dexter. The pond was at its widest point here, maybe two hundred yards across, lapping lazily at the banks in wet ripples, deep enough for small boats, fed by the narrower, deeper St. Regis River, which moved densely and quickly under the Dexter Bridge before slowing and pooling here.

It wasn't really a pond; it was a slowing, a widening and shallowing of the river for two and a half miles, before the banks closed in again under the Santa Clara bridge and the river continued on its course north toward the St. Lawrence.

We were standing in a clearing in the forest, where the Alder Brook oozes through multiple muddy channels into the larger waterway. There was a light mist rising in strands off the water. The ground was muddy, though a protracted Indian summer had baked much of the mud into dry, crumbling clay. There was sporadic birdsong, which I couldn't identify; it echoed in the woods, as though it belonged to another, darker, secret world. Other than that, there were few sounds: the lapping of the river, the sighing of the air in the pines, and Tex Goodwin, the Franklin County sheriff, talking to Dehan.

"This is where she was found." He was pointing at the shoreline. "Right there beside the water. Breaks your heart, that kind of thing. Just seventeen, month before. Nobody could understand it. Still can't."

I stepped over to the spot and stood sideways on it, trying to imitate the position with my own body. "She was on her side, right? With her back to the water..." I looked at him. "You saw it yourself, didn't you?"

He nodded. "Deputy Corfe called me straightaway, says, 'You ain't gonna believe this, Sheriff. There's been a murder, here, in Dexter!'" He shook his head. "Why, they ain't had s'much as burglary here since 1865." He studied my face for a moment, then Dehan's. "That ain't a joke. Debbie's murder was traumatic for this town. There's maybe two hundred people in Dexter and its environs. They all know it was one of their own who done it. That's a hard thing to swallow. It shook 'em hard."

Dehan was looking through the file and handed me a large photograph, six by ten, of a young girl lying on her left side. Her legs were bent into right angles, not quite a fetal position. Her arms were stretched out in front of her, slightly bent at the elbow. Her hands were open.

Her hair was shoulder length, but it was matted and filthy, and it concealed her face. She had one Converse sneaker on; her other foot was bare. She had on a pair of denim shorts that were very short and an open blouse. No bra and no panties. There were signs of bruising on her upper arms.

Dehan was looking over my shoulder. "Her hair is wet."

Sheriff Goodwin nodded once. "Yup. We noticed that. Her face was wet too. But her clothes weren't, and she didn't die of drowning."

Dehan was leafing through pages and said, "Cause of death was strangulation, though she was stabbed perimortem..."

The sheriff finished for her: "In the heart, single stab wound with a large hunting knife."

Dehan glanced at him. "We only received the report yesterday, Sheriff, and we set out immediately. We haven't had time to digest it."

He seemed not to hear her. He was staring at the spot where the body had been lying. "We weren't sure what to make of it. Most of the crime we get up here is in Malone, and it's rarely serious. She was so young . . ."

"Just turned seventeen," I said. "The month before. Eighteenth of August, 2012."

"That's right."

"She had just reached the age of consent."

He frowned at me and pointed at where the body had lain. "Well, she never consented to that! She was beaten bad, slapped, punched on the jaw, and her arms were gripped so hard she had bruising from her wrists right up to her shoulders."

"Ligatures?"

"Uh-uh, no. Just finger marks."

I looked downriver toward the Santa Clara bridge. "Semen was deteriorated. That's quick in less than twenty-four hours."

"Yeah, it was deteriorated, but above all, it was contaminated." He shrugged and hesitated.

I said, "As though she had been raped by more than one man, or had sex with more than one man."

"Yeah."

"Any idea how the body got here?"

He looked surprised. "I figured she was raped and killed here. Probably her head was in the water, that's how it came to be all wet an' muddy."

I looked at Dehan. She was already pulling out the photos and showing them to the sheriff. "Of course, the photo isn't the same as being there, Sheriff, but it looks to me as though there are no footprints. It had rained recently, and you can see the ground is muddy. There are at least three different sources of DNA inside her, which means she was probably raped by at least three men. You would expect to see at least some sign of prints, and struggle. But there's nothing. And I believe there were no tire tracks in the forest."

He sighed. "It was hard to tell. By the time they found her, the ground had been driven over by several trucks. But Bart, who found her, said he never saw no tire marks."

Dehan listened, watching him as he spoke, then said, "So there is a question mark over how she got here. There should be at least three sets of footprints, and signs of struggle, but there didn't seem to be. Was that your impression at the time, Sheriff?"

There was a hint of resentment in his voice when he said, "Yeah, that was my impression at the time."

I scratched my chin. "Now, I am interested in this, Sheriff. Talk me through it. Bart, the man who found her, was her stepfather, and also the man who was eventually prosecuted . . ."

He shrugged, then crossed his arms. "Bart Campbell. His family have been in this area a good four hundred years. Scottish, and always tended to marry Scottish, Presbyterian . . ." He nodded a few times. "Good people. He was a bit wild when he was young. Had a few run-ins with the deputy, nothin' serious, a few brawls, bit rowdy when he was drunk. What you'd expect of a twenty-year-old Scot."

He grinned and laughed, I smiled, and Dehan frowned. He went on.

"Anyhow, Dianne, that's Debbie's mother . . ."

Dehan turned a leaf. "Smith. Dianne Smith . . ."

"Uh-huh, her husband had died back in two thousand, when Debbie was just five. Dianne did her mournin', but she met Bart and they were crazy about each other. They were real good for each other too. He settled down, stopped drinkin' so much, she started dressin' pretty, even little Debbie looked happier. It was nice to see."

"That was back at the turn of the millennium?"

"Yup. Old man Campbell had died not long before and left the boys, Bart and Danny, some land and some money. Bart weren't scared of a bit of hard work, so pretty soon him and Dianne bought a house and moved in together."

He stared out at the dark water awhile, then across at the far bank, and pointed. "Just right up there, on Dexter Road. He loved the kid like she was his own, and she loved him like he was her daddy. They were a happy family."

Dehan smiled. "The way you're telling it, sounds like that changed."

He studied her face while he nodded. "It surely did. Somethin' happens to kids when they hit fourteen, fifteen, sixteen . . . I don't know what it is, and I'm pretty sure it didn't happen when I was a kid, but that little angel started to change. She went wild. When she hit puberty and started showin' signs of becoming a woman, if you know what I mean. She started . . ." His hands tried to say it for him but got embarrassed too. "Well! She was developin' a pretty body, is what I'm trying to say. And she knew it. Started answering back to her parents, being impertinent. That caused a lot of stress between Dianne and Bart, because when he went to discipline the child, Dianne felt she should stick up for her daughter."

I arched an eyebrow at him. "How severe was this discipline?"

"Nobody ever saw her bruised, if that's what you mean. An' she never went out with long sleeves in summer neither. Dianne would not have stood for that kind of thing, nor would her neighbors. This is a tight community, Detective Stone. We look out for one another. He was just a good dad, and sometimes a good father has to be strict."

Dehan was going up and down on her toes, listening to him. "So what happened?"

"It became ever more difficult for them to control her. By the time she was sixteen, she was goin' out and comin' home late. There was a few rows at home. The deputy had to be called a few times. She was hangin' out with a bunch of kids who like to think of themselves as a biker gang. They'd've pissed their pants if they'd ever met a real Hells Angel, but they liked to look tough and wear leather. One of 'em, James, had an old, secondhand Harley; the other two, Zak and Gunny, they had a couple of Japanese bikes, and then there was a bunch of hangers-on. They'd usually hang out at Jake's Grill, but after Bart came and dragged her home a couple of times, they started going to towns nearby, comin' back at two in the mornin'. Made Bart mad as hell."

I had an idea where he was going and asked, "You think he was jealous? You think he was getting a thing for Debbie?"

He sighed. "You ain't read the file . . ."

"As Detective Dehan told you, we received the file yesterday and came straightaway. We've scanned it and digested what we could."

The sun peered over the tops of the trees and momentarily blinded me. I stepped into the shadows as he started to speak again.

"On the fourteenth of September, just a month after her birthday, they had a huge bust-up in the house. I don't think anybody in Dexter realized just how bad things had got. But Dianne said she couldn't take any more and she got in her car and she went to her mother in Plattsburgh, leaving Debbie and Bart alone in the house. To my mind, Dianne was half hoping that if she left him alone with Debbie, he might whip some sense into her. But that's just my thinking.

"Anyhow, on the twenty-first, one week after her mother went to her mom's, Debbie says she's going out with her boyfriend, James."

Dehan said, "The guy with the Harley."

"Uh-huh. There was a ruckus, and he may have slapped her and grabbed her arms. His prints were found on her face and arms. She went out and she never came back. There was a search at first light, and it was Bart who found her. They called me in from Malone, and I have to say, my first instinct was that Bart might have done it. So as part of the investigation, we checked her underwear, from home, for traces of semen to see if she was having a sexual affair with anyone. We only found one trace of semen, on one pair of her panties, and that was his."

Dehan sighed. "That's depressing."

"Yeah, so naturally he became our prime suspect."

"What about the party?"

"It looks like she was at the party, briefly, but then left. We never found out where she went or what happened to her. She just showed up here next morning, dead. But what was clear was that Bart had hit her and gripped her real hard, and he had previously had sex with her. It kind of pointed to a crime of passion, murder with jealousy as a motive. I think the jury would have convicted . . ."

Dehan was frowning at the file, leafing through it. "But he had an alibi . . ."

"He sure did. Pretty good one too. He was with Harry Corfe, the deputy, all that night. Alibis don't come much better than that. They was friends from when they were kids, though Harry was a few years older, and I think the jury might have been swayed the other way if it hadn't been for Bart's lawyer. He got himself a fancy lawyer from the city . . ."

"Bernard Shaw."

"That's the one. He got Bart to confess that he and Debbie had had consensual sex just once, the week before, that he was deeply ashamed as soon as it was over. He also got Bart to testify that he had had a row with Debbie that night, telling her she could not go out with James and his gang. She had basically blackmailed him and said if he stood in her way, she'd tell everybody that he had raped her. I figure that's why she kept the panties. She was real manipulative like that."

"If it's true," Dehan said, looking at the trees all around us, and the water, now turning a deep blue under the rising sun.

The sheriff nodded. "Well, that's why I requested your help. I heard the Forty-Third had a crack cold-cases team, and this case has been playin' on my mind for the last seven years. She was wild, she was maybe even a bit stupid, but she didn't deserve to die like that. And Bart . . ." Again, he shook his head. "I've known Bart all his life . . . I tell you, I followed the evidence where I thought it was leading me, but I never really believed, in my heart, that Bart could do somethin' like that—not to anyone, but especially not to Debbie. Broke my heart what happened to that family. And poor Dianne, I swear it nearly killed that woman, after losing her husband an' all."

Dehan stared at him a moment while he stared down at the muddy bank where Debbie had lain seven years earlier, with her muddy hair covering her face. She blinked and half smiled. "We'll do the best we can, Sheriff."

Something in the tone of her voice made him look at her, almost as though he were startled. Then he returned the smile and started to walk back across the clearing, toward the tree line and the Ford pickup he'd left parked on the Santa Clara Road, a quarter of a mile away.

"I'm a God-fearin' man, like most people 'round here, but I ain't superstitious. However . . ." He took a deep breath as he walked over the tufted, uneven grass. "With Debbie, I just have this feeling that she can't rest till this is sorted, till her killer is brought to justice, one way or another."

We walked on in silence through the forest until we broke out onto the highway, shaded on either side by the tall firs and pines. The lights flashed, and he pulled open the driver's door, then stopped. "All kids, when they hit their teens, go a bit crazy. All them hormones and changes goin' on. Hell, that'd drive anybody crazy. And I guess rebellion, disobedience, wanting to explore new experiences, that's all part of it. I don't think Debbie was any worse than any other kid. She just needed the kind of guidance that, in the end, Bart and Dianne didn't know how to give her.

Maybe you can bring some peace to her soul, and to Bart and Dianne."

He shrugged and clambered into the truck. "Come on, I'll introduce you to the deputy. He'll give you any help you need."

We climbed in after him and headed into the town of Dexter, to meet Deputy Kent Oaster.

CHAPTER 2

The local sheriff's office was on a short street with no name that ran between Back Street and Center Street. It was the only building on that stretch of road and looked more like a cozy cottage than a law enforcement office. Deputy Kent Oaster came out as we were swinging down from the Ford. He gave us the slow, expressionless look of a man who'd like to know when you're leaving, and then shook hands with the sheriff.

"Kent, these are the detectives from New York. Like I told you, they specialize in cold cases, and they're going to have a look at the Debbie Smith case."

Kent gave a single nod, upward, and sucked his teeth. He followed that up by examining Dehan head to toe, like he was planning to buy her and send her to a stud farm. Meanwhile, the sheriff was saying, "I want you to give them any help they need, Kent, and maybe we can close this case and give Debbie some peace."

Kent gave me a look that said I wasn't going to the stud farm and turned his gaze on the sheriff as he told us he'd leave us to it, climbed in his truck, and headed off back to Malone.

Kent took a moment to examine his boots then said, "Offer you guys some coffee?"

Dehan answered. "Yup. And some information too."

He turned and went inside. We followed him into a room that was on the darker side of comfortable, with a couple of distorted patches of sunlight lying crookedly on a wooden floor. There was a wooden desk and behind it a leather swivel chair. An old, threadbare couch and a couple of chairs that were secondhand in the '70s sat about a round coffee table with a few magazines strewn on it. Over in a corner, there was a coffee machine, where he was gathering three cups.

"How'd'ya take it?"

I said, "Black, for both of us."

He handed us a cup each, and as we sat at the low table, he propped himself against the desk. He hadn't made any coffee for himself.

"What you wanna know?"

I watched his face as I sipped and waited for Dehan to answer him. She didn't take long. She leaned forward and put her cup on the table while she sucked her teeth and seemed to measure the floor with her eyes.

"We were handed this file yesterday at lunchtime. We were working on another case, but the chief told us he had received a request from the Franklin Sheriff's Office and, as a courtesy, he wanted us to put our case on the back burner and drive out to Dexter to give you guys a hand. So we made the arrangements and set out at one a.m., to be here in time to have morning coffee with you. Now, you ask, what do we want? Well, we want to help you solve the Debbie Smith murder, that's why we're here, and for that, we need all the information and cooperation that you can give us." She turned to look at me. "Am I talking out of my ass, Stone, or does that make sense to you?"

I sighed. "It makes sense to me, Detective." I looked over at the deputy. His face was flushed, and his eyes were bright. "I think what my partner is saying, Deputy, is that we would like to know, in your own words, what happened that night, and your take on it."

He stared at the wooden floor a moment then shook his head. "Nobody knows what happened that night. Debbie had turned seventeen just the month before. She was the prettiest girl in town, and in most of the towns 'round about. All the boys liked her. And the way she behaved, you thought at first that she was givin' out."

I frowned, thinking that at the time, he couldn't have been much older than Debbie himself. I said, "What do you mean by that?"

"She was always teasin' the boys, making like she was into you and maybe you had a chance, and then she'd drop you and go off with some other boy."

Dehan asked, "Some other boy?"

He thought about it. "I guess she'd kind of do the rounds, play with all the boys, get them hoppin' mad, and then go with James."

"The badass with the Harley."

He nodded. "He wasn't so badass, but he always hung out with Gunny and Zak, and a bunch of other kids who wanted to be cool like him, so if there was ever any trouble, they had his back."

I reached for my coffee. "And was there ever any trouble?"

"Nah . . ." He shook his head. "Few scuffles, nobody ever got hurt. It ain't like that up here. Anytime things got out of hand, Jake would get hold of his old peacemaker . . ." He started to laugh.

I said, "The Colt revolver? He has a Peacemaker?"

He shook his head, still laughing. "No, not a revolver. It's a big old knobby stick he keeps under the bar. He boasts he knows exactly where to hit a man so it don't kill him but he wishes it had."

Dehan laughed, and Kent seemed to soften a bit.

"Jake has the grill on Back Street, just down the road. He could handle most any situation, but if ever he felt he couldn't, he'd call Harry Corfe . . ."

"Your predecessor."

"Right. Everybody respected Harry. Even the kids. He never lost his cool, but you knew you never crossed the line with him or he'd whip your ass."

He went quiet.

After a moment, I said, "You're talking in the past tense. What happened?"

"After the trial . . ." He took a deep breath and started again. "At the trial, Bart got himself a smart city lawyer. He specialized in winning unwinnable cases. Most people 'round here believed Bart had killed Debbie. It was Harry's testimony, that he had been with Bart all that night, that got Bart off. That, and the way that lawyer tore into the defense and made the jury see that it might just as easily have been James or one of his boys—or anybody else, for that matter. He got Bart to go on the stand and confess that he'd had sex with Debbie a few days before she was killed, and he somehow twisted that into proof that Bart never killed her." He paused again and drew breath. "Like, he admitted he was with her, but that night he was with Harry, talking, havin' a few beers.

"The jury acquitted him 'cause they felt they had to, but the town never forgave Bart, and I guess by association, they never really forgave Harry either. I figure most people still believe he killed her."

Dehan rested the ankle of one long leg on her knee. "They thought Deputy Corfe lied to protect Bart?"

He made a face, like he was reluctant to answer that.

Dehan pressed him. "What do you think?"

He drew a deep breath. "I don't know what to think, Detective. Bart's DNA was on Debbie's panties. His fingerprints were on her arms and on her face, where he'd grabbed her and slapped her . . ."

"What about her throat? She was strangled, right?"

She asked it, but she already knew the answer. "There were no prints on her throat. The ME said the killer had probably used gloves. Like I said, I don't know what to think. Bart and Harry are good people. I've known 'em both all my life. I can't imagine either one of them doing something like that..."

I interrupted him. "If he gripped her and slapped her in a fit of rage, and then went and put on a pair of gloves to strangle her with, and a knife to stab her in the heart with, that is a lot of premeditation."

He scratched his head and looked around the office before nodding and saying, "Yeah. You put it like that and it's hard to imagine Bart doing that, and even harder to think of Harry backing him up. But like I told you, Debbie could drive you out of your wits in a matter of a couple of minutes. She'd had sex with him, and she'd driven her own mother out of the house. She was going to destroy that family—she *did* destroy that family. That kind of thing can drive a good man to do bad stuff. So my answer is the same as it was. I don't know what to think."

I drained my cup and sat forward. "He resign, or was he sacked?"

"Neither. He got a transfer to Albany, where his wife's mother lived. It was bad weather, and his car came off the road. Him and his wife was killed."

Dehan's eyebrows shot up. "He died the day he left town?"

The deputy scratched the side of his nose. "Detective Dehan, forgive me if I seem impertinent, but this ain't the Bronx. Debbie's is the only murder we've had in this town since the Civil War. We don't get complicated conspiracies here where people kill folk to silence them. But we do get inclement weather, where it's dangerous to drive on the roads. It was November, it had been raining, and then the water froze on the roads. Harry went over the side."

Dehan stuck out her lower lip and nodded. "Just a coincidence."

"Not even that. It happens around here."

I cut in. "Where can we find Bart? Is he still around?"

"You'll find him up South River Road, they're harvesting trees there. It's early, we usually wait till the cold sets in and the ground is nice and hard. But winters are gettin' shorter, so they're doing what they can before the rain sets in."

I stood. Dehan remained sitting, staring at her boot and running her tongue over her teeth. I said, "What?"

She glanced at me and then at Oaster. "There's just something I don't get. Okay, Dianne goes to stay with her mother because she's had enough of Debbie and Bart fighting with each other. For whatever reason, Debbie comes on to Bart while they're alone and one thing leads to another. Maybe she wants leverage over him, maybe she's got a crush on him, maybe she's just crazy. We'll never know. Either way, that night, the twenty-first, she says she's going out with James. He says, 'Think again,' she goes wildcat on him, and he grabs her, trying to shake some sense into her. She starts screaming and struggling and he slaps her." She spread her hands. "From that point on, it can only go one of two ways. She throws herself on the bed and sobs herself to sleep, and we know that's not going to happen, or she storms out and there is damn all he can do about it. What isn't going to happen is that she waits patiently while he gets a pair of gloves and a hunting knife.

"So she storms out and he does what guys always do in that kind of situation. He calls a friend, and they have a beer or two. Meanwhile, she goes to this party with her biker pals. You already told us she's a prick tease, so some guy gets sick of being teased. It's September. If he drives a bike, he already has his gloves. And if he's a badass biker, he has a knife. When she goes home, he goes after her. Punches her to make her compliant, rapes her, and kills her with the help of a couple of pals. That is not a hard scenario to imagine, and for me, it has the ring of truth. How come you guys never explored that angle?"

He took a moment to scratch his ear. "It was before my time, so you'd have to ask the sheriff that question. But as I understood it, the only people who fit that description were James, Zak, and Gunny. They all alibied each other, and there was a bunch of other people who alibied them too. They were all at a party that night. So that was a dead end."

"They were brought in for questioning?"

"I don't know."

She nodded for a while, then stood. "Thanks for the coffee and the information, Deputy Oaster."

He didn't look at her when he answered, "Sure, anything you need, just let me know."

We stepped out into the morning sunshine on the road with no name and started walking slowly down Adirondack Park Road toward the highway. Our B&B was down the Old Route 72 there, near the banks of the river. As we walked, Dehan shoved her hands in her pockets and looked up at the fresh blue sky.

"What's your take, Stone?"

"You know me, Dehan, no take till I see something I can grab a hold of."

"Okay, so if you had a take, what would it be?"

I laughed. "Turning my own tricks and ploys against me, huh?" I sighed. "It's tricky. A toxic family can turn nice people into homicidal maniacs. So I am not ready to dismiss Bart as a suspect, even if he is protected by the double jeopardy rule. We can still nail him for rape if we need to. But in my opinion, the alternative scenario you painted is the obvious one."

"Thanks."

I smiled sidelong. "And, may I say, compellingly presented."

"Asshole."

"But it suffers from a total lack of evidence."

"Because they didn't bother to go out and get any. As a working theory, it beats the hell out of a sworn deputy that the whole town trusts perjuring himself to get his pal off a murder charge."

"As a working theory, it's fine, if we can find some evidence to support it. There is a third possibility."

"What?"

"That it was none of the above. It was somebody completely different."

She frowned at me. "Well, what evidence have you got for that?"

"As much as you have for your theory. Zilch. But at this early stage, Little Grasshopper, instead of coming up with theories, we need to keep an open mind and start finding actual evidence."

"Yes, Sensei."

"I want to meet Bart and hear what he has to say before I start forming an opinion about him. I also want to talk to Dianne. I'd like to know what *they* think of their daughter. So far, nobody has said it, but it's there under the surface, even from the sheriff."

"What is?"

"The judgment: she had it coming. You notice Deputy Corfe had to leave town because they thought he'd lied to them. But Bart is still here and well thought of. Because what he did, well, she had it coming."

We'd reached the Cherry Orchard B&B and stepped into the gravel driveway of the eighteenth-century cottage, where the old Mark II was lurking, waiting for us. Dehan went around to the passenger side and leaned on the sun-warmed roof, watching me through narrowed eyes.

I unlocked the door and said, "What?"

"You. You're a good man, Stone. You have a noble heart."

She opened the door and climbed in. I climbed in after her and slammed the door. "Why does that sound strange?"

"Maybe . . ." She shrugged and patted my shoulder as I turned the key in the ignition. The big engine growled. I waited. She shrugged again. "Maybe I don't say it often enough."

I smiled, a little surprised. "You okay, partner?"

She smiled a surprising, simple, affectionate smile.

"Yeah." We crunched over the gravel toward the blacktop and she went on, "Also, I just happen to believe all cock teasers should be shot and dumped in the East River for fish food."

I laughed. "See? That's why I married you."

She looked pleased.

CHAPTER 3

We followed the South River Road through forest that was thick enough to be a jungle. The trees were mainly cedar, pine, fir, and maple, intense shades of green, just beginning to turn autumn copper at the edges. The road was broad, made of beaten earth, and after half a mile, it forked, with the left branch curling away toward St. Regis Falls and the right branch plunging deeper into the forest. Seventy yards down that track, we could see large trucks, stacks of timber, and a wide expanse dotted with tree stumps, where men were at work. A temporary barrier had been set up across the road, and as we pulled up and climbed out of the Jag, a guy in a red-and-blue shirt with a blue helmet on his head roared up on a quad bike, climbed off, and made his way toward us. He spoke over the whine of the saws.

"You can't come down here, pal. We're harvesting timber and it ain't safe."

I showed him my badge. "Detective Stone, this is Detective Dehan. We need to talk to Bart Campbell."

He sighed. "What's he done?"

"Nothing that we're aware of. We just need to talk to him. Sooner rather than later."

He sighed again, turned on his heel, and marched away

toward where a tall tree was keeling over and crashing down into the expanding clearing. The tree hit the ground in an oddly soft motion, almost like a feather, though the noise was deafening. The guy got back on his quad and roared off toward where men with chain saws were setting about cutting off the branches of the felled tree.

We waited five minutes, sitting on the hood of the Jag, then heard the roar of a second quad approaching up the path. It pulled up, and a guy I figured was Bart climbed off. He was tall, a good six foot two. He was well built, with broad shoulders and an upright posture, and I wondered if he'd been in the military. He pulled off his helmet; his dark hair was cut short, and his eyes were hard and wary. He approached, looking at each of us in turn. I showed him my badge, and Dehan did the same.

She said, "I am Detective Dehan, and this is my partner, Detective Stone. Are you Bart Campbell?"

"Isn't that who you asked to see?"

I said, "Just answer the question."

"Yeah, I'm Bart Campbell. Why?"

"We need to talk to you about the murder of your stepdaughter, Debbie."

His face screwed up like a fist. "You *what*? I was already tried for that and found not guilty! You can't come at me again about that!"

Dehan's voice was even and calm. "Nobody's coming at you with anything, Mr. Campbell. The case was never closed, and the sheriff has asked us to look at it. You want to find out who killed her, don't you?"

He stared hard into her eyes. "I don't give a solitary goddamn if you find who killed her or not. That child was the spawn of Satan, and her mother stood by and watched while I was crucified and did *nothin'* to help me. She knew. She knew what that child was like. Why d'you think . . ." He pointed with his right hand across his body to the east. "Why d'you think she went to her mother's, leavin' me with the damned child? She couldn't take no more—of her own daughter! So you're askin' me . . ." He stopped dead, staring at Dehan, then at me, and took a step toward us, poking the air. "You're askin' me if I want to find her killer?" He shook his head. "No, I don't give a *damn*!"

I scratched my chin. I needed a shave. I kept my voice quiet. "You ought to give it some thought, Mr. Campbell."

He caught the hint of a threat, and his eyes were quick to rise to the challenge.

I met his gaze and kept talking. "We're from the Bronx, Mr. Campbell. I head up the cold-cases department there. Sheriff Goodwin has asked me to look at this case and see if we can't finally close it. And that is what we intend to do."

"So do it. I still don't give a damn."

"Stay with me, Mr. Campbell. To do my job properly, I need as much information as I can get. If I don't get all the information I need, then it becomes more likely that I will arrive at a mistaken conclusion." I paused for him to assimilate what I was saying. "Now, you are protected by the double jeopardy rule from being prosecuted again for Debbie's murder. But you were never prosecuted for her rape."

His face flushed red, and he grabbed hold of the barrier with powerful hands that I knew could easily kill a man. He vaulted the barrier, snarling, "Why, you son of a bitch . . . !" and he stopped dead, looking down the barrel of Dehan's Glock. I smiled without much humor.

"That's quite a temper you have there, Mr. Campbell. I'd have thought you might have learned to control it a bit by now. Let me be clear. You take a swing at me with those fists, I'll break your arm, put you in prison, and then sue you for damages. That's if my partner doesn't shoot you first. Do we understand each other?"

He didn't say anything.

"I'm going to tell you for the second time, Mr. Campbell, to answer the question. Do we understand each other?"

"Yeah," he snarled, "we understand each other, Detective Stone."

Dehan holstered her piece.

I shrugged. "I'm not asking you to give blood, Mr. Campbell. I'm just asking you to talk us through what happened that week, and especially that night."

His shoulders sagged, but after a moment, he gritted his teeth and pointed at me with his fist palm up. "But I did *not* rape that girl! *Never!*"

I nodded. "I believe you. But courts of law are about fact, not truth. And a fact is something you can prove to a judge and jury. Something like DNA. So let's start talking instead of threatening each other."

He scowled and pulled a radio from his belt. It crackled, and a voice snapped, "*What?*"

"I'm taking an early lunch. I have to talk to these cops."

The reply was something you wouldn't want to publish. I opened the back door of the Jag, and he climbed in.

We drove back to town in silence, kicking up big billows of dust behind us. We made the intersection, still enclosed and enveloped by the ever present trees, crossed into the town, and parked beside the long, rambling wooden shack that was Jake's Grill.

It had a long porch with chairs, but no tables outside. We pushed through the tall, glass-paned doors into a broad, bright wooden room with a bar along the back and tables set out for dining along the left. What looked like an original '50s jukebox stood beside a fruit machine against one wall, and at the back, in a nook, I could see a couple of pool tables. Behind the bar, there was a man who was big enough to be two men. He had a bald pate to his head, a ponytail that reached his ass, and a scraggy beard down to his large belly. He watched us approach the bar and nodded to Bart.

"Coffee and a burger, please, Jake."

I glanced at Dehan. She shrugged and nodded. I said, "Make that three."

We went and sat in the dining section. Bart hunched with his elbows on the table, looking down between his fists at the wood. Jake brought over our coffee, gave me and Dehan a look that would have curdled milk, and made his way back to the bar.

"Okay, Mr. Campbell, I've heard it from the sheriff, and I've heard it from the deputy, and about nine-tenths of it was opinion. Now I want to hear it from you, and I'm hoping that what I'm going to get is facts."

He slumped back in his chair, with his big hands cupped on either side of his coffee. "Where d'you want me to begin?"

"Where do you think it starts?"

His eyes flicked up, like he was surprised by the question.

"Where does it begin?" He thought for a long time, staring at the table. Finally, he began to talk. "It starts when Debbie turned fifteen. She didn't develop early, like other girls. When she was twelve and thirteen, she looked like a child. At fourteen, she started to develop. She was always a pretty kid. Her face was angelic. She wasn't 'specially tall, but as she hit fourteen and fifteen, she started to get a real pretty figure. Her mom and me were proud of her. We used to buy her pretty clothes and stuff. Only, her personality started to change."

Dehan asked him, "Change how?"

"At first, it was kind of cute. Like she was being sassy, answering back, giving her mother lip, but always with a cute smile and a laugh. And if we got serious with her, she'd back down and apologize. But when she turned fifteen, it changed again. There was all the sass, but none of the cute smiles and laughter. She became surly, moody, impertinent, downright rude. We punished her, but it's hard to punish a fifteen-year-old girl. You can't hit her, not these days. We did things like take her cell phone away for a day or two days, eventually it was a whole week. But she bought herself a burner we never knew about. We started grounding her, but how do you enforce that?" He pointed over at the door, as though Debbie was about to walk out through it. "If she says she's going out, you can't stop her. If you physically restrain her, you're looking at assault, physical abuse, child abuse."

I sipped my coffee. Dehan frowned and asked, "So what did you do?"

"It got pretty crazy. We started locking ourselves in so *she* couldn't get out. Then she'd scream and holler and smash things. If she went up against you, whatever you did, she'd do ten percent more. She would always go the extra mile to break you down. It got worse and worse with every weekend we didn't let her out."

I drummed my fingers on the table. "What was the main reason you wouldn't let her out?"

"At first, we'd ground her for answering back to her mother, for being rude, that kind of thing. But later on, it was more because of the crowd she wanted to hang around with."

"James, Zak, and Gunny."

"Yeah, those boys. I should of took them apart from the start. Maybe this would never have happened. She said James was her boyfriend." He shook his head. "I tried to explain to her about boys like that. I'd been a boy like that, till Harry Corfe beat some sense into me. But she wouldn't listen. She said she didn't care; used language you wouldn't believe in a kid her age." Dehan drew breath to ask him a question, but he sighed and shook his head and said, "But that wasn't the worst of it."

I said, "What was the worst?"

"When she turned sixteen. That was when we lost her completely. I swear she turned evil. I didn't recognize the little girl I'd helped rear. I'd come to think of her as my own child, but this person, this screaming, crazy, evil person, was not anybody I knew. And the worst thing was when she started to come on to me, right there in front of her mother."

Dehan arched an eyebrow. "Come on to you how?"

He puffed out his cheeks and balled his fists. "Every way you can imagine. First time she really came out, overt like, we was in the kitchen. I'd come in from work and I was tired, just sitting down having a beer before takin' a shower. Dianne was cooking supper, and we were talking about the day. All of a sudden, Debbie walks in, in her panties and bra. Both were kind of lacy and transparent. She was sixteen and already had a woman's body. She says to me, 'Bart, do you like me in this? Do you think they're too transparent?'

"Well, I went crazy. Thank the Good Lord her mother was there and gave her all sorts of hell, or I would have taken my belt to that child. And thinkin' back, I often wonder if I shouldn't have. It just got worse after that. One time, she came into the living room where we were watching TV. She was real contrite and serious. I remember she was wearing real small denim shorts and a silk blouse. She says to me, 'Bart, you've always been like a daddy to me, and sometimes I ain't nice to you the way I should be. I give you and Mommy lip, and I am disobedient, and I just wish things could go back to how they was before.'

"It was real moving, and her mom started to cry. She gave her a big hug, and Debbie says to me, 'You remember how you used to sit me on your knee and tell me stories and sing me songs.' I laughed." He nodded several times. "I laughed with relief and joy in my heart, thinking I had my little girl back. I even thanked the Lord. Then she jumps on my lap and flings her arms around my neck, and as I hugged her back, I realized she had no bra on. That worried me, but the next minute, she's whispering in my ear to go to her room that night when her mom's asleep. And as I pushed her away, she opens her blouse for me and she winks."

Dehan winced. "What did you do?"

"I pushed her away from me and I called her everything under the sun that a father should never call his daughter. She screamed right back at me. Things she said were pure evil."

"Like what?"

"Did I think she hadn't noticed the way I looked at her. She knew I watched her getting dressed and undressed. She said I watched her when she was in the shower. That I was bored and tired of Dianne because she was old and her breasts sagged. It went on like that. Dianne became hysterical. They both screamed at each other, and I do believe that if Dianne had formed a united front with me, Debbie would have backed down. But instead, they both screamed at me and at each other, and the whole house went to pieces. Dianne packed a bag and stormed out, accusing us both of conspiring against her. I wept, I begged her to stay. But she'd made up her mind, and she went to her mother's house." He sighed. It was a deep, tragic sound.

I said, "What happened then?"

He didn't answer for a moment, like speaking it was painful. "That was when things turned real dark. Real dark."

"How?"

He turned his head to look at me. His eyes were hard, like eyes that had seen things nobody should ever see. "That was when she decided to make peace with me. And that was the beginning of the end."

Scan the QR code below to purchase DEATH IN DEXTER.
Or go to: righthouse.com/death-in-dexter

Printed in Dunstable, United Kingdom